MAGIC UNDYING

Dragon's Gift: The Seeker Book 1

Linsey Hall

DEDICATION

For Susan, Steve, Harvey, and Holly.

CHAPTER ONE

Consciousness came slowly as heat seared my skin. Every bone in my body ached, like I'd been stomped on by a dragon. Groggily, I forced my eyes open.

Walls of fire surrounded me, brilliant red and orange flickering up into the sky. My heart jumped into my throat, nearly strangling me. The flame was only a dozen feet away on all sides. I scrambled up, stumbling before righting myself on wobbly legs.

"No, no, no," I muttered as the flames flickered toward me.

There was only one place this could be. But I didn't want to believe it. "I am not in hell. I am not in hell. I am not in hell."

My sword lay on the ground. I stooped and grabbed it, comfort rushing through me as I gripped the smooth pommel of my sidekick. The ache in my chest tugged my gaze downward, toward the pain. My lucky black shirt had a puncture hole straight through it—right where the sword had sunk into my chest, who knew how long ago.

Dying was the last thing I remembered, and this black shirt was definitely no longer lucky.

My heart thudded, loud enough to deafen me.

If I was dead, should I have had a heartbeat? Just the thought made that wayward organ race. Was I dead?

"Get it together, Del," I muttered as memories flooded my mind. I'd been in battle, fighting with my friends and allies against an enemy so fierce that I hadn't had a chance. I'd died by the sword.

I touched the sliced fabric of my shirt and looked around at the flame.

Shit. With a wound like that, I had definitely died.

And was in hell. Or at least one of the hells. From what little I knew, there were multiple heavens and hells called underworlds, one for each religion.

Gingerly, I poked my fingers through the hole in my shirt. When I found only a raised scar, I almost collapsed in relief.

I had enough to deal with without gaping wounds. My chest hurt, but not enough to keep me from running for it.

And I *had* to get out of this place. Dead or not, I wasn't hanging out here.

I turned in a circle, eyeing the walls of flame. The heat seared my skin, which felt hot enough to start peeling off at any second. My head grew woozy from it.

I needed to lay down. For just a moment. The ground looked as comfortable as my bed back home, and it called to me.

I shook my head to clear the wooziness.

No. Not an option. Forward motion was the only way. After all I'd been through—*dying* for fate's sake—if fate thought I was going to lie down and give up, it had another thing coming.

I knocked on my head for good luck, then sucked in a ragged breath, tried to concentrate, and called on my magic. Before I'd died, I'd had the power to transport myself anywhere in the world with a thought. I'd lost that power in the battle—but perhaps I hadn't lost all of it?

I tried to call on the gift, imagining myself at home instead of here. I could almost see myself standing in my apartment. But instead of the usual tug, I felt nothing.

My heart clenched, disappointment dropping my stomach to my feet.

So I had lost it all.

That was gonna take some getting used to.

But I wasn't stuck. I wouldn't let myself be. I had a heartbeat, for fate's sake. I didn't belong here.

I might be one of the most despised species of supernatural—a FireSoul, one who shared the soul of a dragon and could steal other supernaturals' powers—but a seer had prophesied that I possessed a strange power related to death. It was magic I didn't understand and a power that could probably get me killed if anyone discovered I had it. But it was my only chance at getting out of here.

That meant adopting my Phantom form, and fast.

If that was possible in hell. Would my magic even work here? I'd never been to hell, and I didn't know the extent of my power anyway. The Order the Magica and the Alpha Council, the two magical governments on

Earth, imprisoned anyone with powerful magic they'd never seen before, so I only used it when absolutely necessary.

The flames flickered toward me.

Yeah, this qualified.

I closed my eyes and called upon my odd magic, envisioning my body turning pale blue and transparent as it did when I adopted my other form. A few months ago, I'd turned into a Phantom for the first time when another Phantom touched me. I'd learned a couple weeks later that I was a half blood, but that shouldn't even be possible. Phantoms didn't reproduce—not through touch or any other way. They were normally insentient beings that brought misery to anyone who touched them.

So fun. If I actually let others see what I could do, I'd be a real hit at parties.

As a Phantom half blood, I was something different, though I had no idea exactly what or the extent of my powers. But nothing could hurt me in my Phantom form, and I needed some of that right about now.

I let my magic rise within me, and a tingly chill followed it. Slowly, the heat licking at my skin began to fade. As the chill traveled over my flesh, my arms turned transparent blue.

Jackpot!

I moved toward the row of flames. Whatever was on the other side had to be better than this.

Right?

My heart climbed into my throat as I passed through the fire. I felt nothing, but it was so bright that it blinded me, forcing me to close my eyes.

When I opened them, I almost wished I hadn't.

A barren hellscape stretched ahead of me, jagged black rocks and crevasses reaching deep into the ground. More flames flickered up, dotting the miserable landscape here and there. Were they cages made of flames, holding other people as that one had held me?

The air shimmered with a weird gray haze. It was opaque in places, but the fog occasionally cleared to reveal a beautiful meadow. Like another world overlaid on top of this one.

Though there was beauty, it was mostly hell.

Shivers ran across my skin.

I wanted to go home.

Longing filled my chest as I reached up and touched the golden comms charm around my neck. My touch ignited the magic and I grinned.

"Cass? Nix?" I hoped either of my *deirfiúr* would hear me through their identical comms charms.

Deirfiúr was Irish for sisters, though they were my sisters by choice. My team. I prayed to magic that they'd survived the battle that had killed me.

And just because I was in hell didn't mean they wouldn't have my back. If they were somewhere in this godforsaken wasteland, I'd find them.

The charm crackled, its magic no doubt interrupted by the fact that I was *in hell*. I didn't even know where this particular Underworld was located, but it had to be far away from our home in Magic's Bend, Oregon.

The charm continued to crackle, but no voices came through.

"Nix? Cass?"

Still silence.

I was on my own. Okay. I could handle that.

"Escapee!" a deep voice roared.

I jumped, losing control of my Phantom form and turning back into my normal self. My heart thudded in my ears as I spun in a circle, searching for the voice.

Three massive figures charged toward me, leaping over the crevasses in the rock. They were some kind of demon, dark gray with massive horns. Weapons hung off their bodies, clipped to leather utility vests. As if they had so much killing to do they needed to dress up like deadly Christmas trees, with pointy things hanging all over them.

"Shit!" *Time to go!*

I spun and raced in the other direction, careful to keep my footing on the rocky ground. One fall and they'd be on me. My lungs burned as I sprinted, jumping over ditches and dodging rock outcroppings.

Damn, I needed to work out more. I was a mercenary and a treasure hunter—*I* normally did the pursuing. Being chased really wasn't working for me. Although to be fair, dying might have slowed me down a bit.

Something heavy slammed into my legs, wrapping around them so I tripped and crashed to the ground. My skull slammed against the rocks. Pain pierced my head as my vision turned gray. The jagged black rocks tore at the side of my face. Warm blood trickled down my skin.

Panic sent shivers through me. I needed to reach my legs and cut off whatever bound me, but my head was spinning like an overpriced ride at a carnival.

Through my hazy vision, I caught sight of a massive figure looming overhead. It bent down and grabbed the back of my jacket, yanking me up. I'd barely maintained my grip on my sword—an ingrained habit—but a big, booted foot kicked it from my hands.

"No!" I reached for it as it flew away and clattered to the ground.

"You don't need that where you're going," a deep voice growled.

"Jerk!" I thrashed in his grip, my head still spinning from my fall, but he had almost two feet and a hundred pounds of muscle on me.

When he swung me over his shoulder, my stomach slammed against his back, knocking the wind from my lungs. This close, I could get a sense of his magic. It smelled like rotten eggs.

Ugh.

"Take her to the Warden, aye?" a voice said from my side.

"Aye," said the demon who held me. "This one is strange. No one has ever escaped the holding cells."

I blinked, trying to get my wits about me, but it was slow going with my pounding head.

The demon shook me, probably for the sheer joy of it. My brain rattled in my skull.

"What were you expecting to accomplish, girly? Make a run for it? You want the Warden hunting you down?"

No, I really didn't want to be hunted by some dude called *the Warden*. But I wasn't going to hang out here, either.

The demon holding me started to jog, and I bounced against his back as I tried to catch my breath and get my bearings. My sword glinted silver against the black rocks, growing smaller and smaller in the distance.

Damn it, I loved that sword.

Even farther away, something blue swooped through the air. It was too big to identify, but probably just another hellbeast I didn't want to encounter. A distant shriek sounded and I shuddered.

Nope, I didn't want to run into whatever that thing was.

Or the Warden. I needed to get away from these bastards before they reached the mysterious Warden, whoever that was.

But my pounding head made it hard to focus on my magic. It wasn't easy to turn into a Phantom, but I'd been growing more practiced with it. If I'd ever needed to adopt my Phantom form, now was the time. I'd have to kill these bastards to keep them from telling anyone what I was, and I was willing to do that. But *could* I even kill them in the Underworld?

I had no idea. I'd have to worry about that when the time came, because I didn't want to end up wherever they were taking me.

When I caught the thread of my magic deep within me, I pulled on it, envisioning my Phantom form. The power flickered within me, growing stronger as I fanned the flames.

A headache pounded in my skull as I watched my arms, which hung down toward the ground, turn blue very slowly. Too slowly. Bright red blood dripped from my head wound, landing on my arms, stark against my pale skin. The sight of it relieved me, though. If I was bleeding and I had a heartbeat, I couldn't be truly dead.

"She's doing that weird thing again," a gravelly voice said.

"Don't let her."

Pain exploded in my skull, and the world went black.

When I came to, the world was just as dark and terrifying as it had been before I'd lost consciousness. Had the demon knocked me over the head? I still hung over his shoulder, his every footstep jarring pain through my middle. The same jagged black rocks passed beneath us as the demon ran.

But the magic in the air felt different. Stronger. Weirder.

I shivered.

Every supernatural's magic had a signature that was conveyed by one or more of the five senses.

Whoever possessed this new magic I was sensing was powerful. Really, really powerful.

Carefully, I shifted to see where we were going and to get a better sense of the exact nature of the strong magic. I moved a millimeter at a time so as not to alert the demons. I didn't want another knock on the head. If I was going to escape this, I clearly needed to do it through cunning rather than the brute strength of my Phantom form. My injuries made me too slow to shift.

Ahead, I caught the barest glimpse of a castle. It was a massive, hulking structure made of black stone. Tall walls gave way to a huge keep with towers at each of the four corners. Steam rose up from the base of the wall. A moat? Probably. I shuddered at the idea of what was in there.

The power came from that castle.

From the Warden.

Okay, I definitely did not want to meet him. His power was so strong that it cloaked the castle. Not everyone could sense another's magic, but strong supernaturals could. The more powerful you were, the more completely you were hooked into the magical grid. Some supernaturals worked to keep their signature repressed, like I did. No way I was gonna let anyone know the extent of my forbidden magic, and he was probably strong enough to sense what I was if I let my guard down.

Not this guy—repressing his signature wasn't on his agenda. This guy wanted everyone knowing he was the strongest dude in the land.

Weirdly, his magic didn't feel explicitly evil. Often, dark magic had a signature that fit—like the taste of death or the smell of rotten eggs, like the ugly bastards now hauling me across hell.

But the magic cloaking the castle smelled of fresh sandalwood and tasted like wine. Red wine. A nice one. Personally, I was partial to boxed wine, but I could at least identify a good one.

The Warden's magic was probably strong enough to register with more of my senses, but I'd need to be closer to find out.

I didn't want to get closer. Because sometimes, the greatest evil was cloaked in something palatable. Any guy who lived in a castle like this was probably one dark son of a demon.

We were nearing the moat now, and I could smell the brackish water that was letting off so much steam. I did my best to breathe shallowly. We were nearly to the main wall.

This close to the Warden, I couldn't use my Phantom power. Not where strangers could see me. I'd have to kill them if they witnessed that. And the Warden was too powerful to kill.

Normally, I threw myself at danger.

But this? This was enough to give even me pause.

So yeah, stealth was my best bet.

I called upon my dragon sense, hoping that I hadn't lost that magic when I'd died. The odd power that was a gift from my FireSoul half. FireSouls were said to share the souls of dragons, though no one knew exactly what that meant because dragons were long dead. FireSouls possessed the dragon's ability to find treasure.

Treasure could be anything we wanted badly enough—even another supernatural's powers—and what I wanted was a way out of this Underworld. There had to be a portal around here somewhere—most likely inside the castle.

I reached out with my magic, focusing on what I desired and letting my dragon sense flow through me. When the familiar tug about my middle pulled, I had it.

There *was* a portal within the castle wall. And wherever it led had to be better than this place.

As much as it made my skin prickle to think of going into the Warden's stronghold, this was the easiest way in. I forced myself to stay limp as the demons carried me across the wooden bridge. Through the wooden slats, the moat bubbled and hissed below.

I'd love to kick these jerks into it.

Instead, I darted my gaze between the three demons, taking stock of their weapons. An assortment of daggers and oddly shaped blades hung off them, more than enough to get the job done.

I was ace with weapons, considering that I didn't usually use magic on my mercenary jobs, but some demon weapons couldn't be wielded by any but their own kind. Probably why this guy was wearing them out in the open where I could grab them. Still, I hoped my weird death magic would allow me to manipulate his Underworld weapons.

I stayed silent and still as we passed under the massive gate into a courtyard. Dark gray cobblestones covered the ground, reaching all the way to the curtain wall. I caught a glimpse of the castle, which loomed large and dark.

"I'll get the Warden," one of the demons said before he jogged off.

This was it. I was down to two guards.

I sucked in a steady breath, then darted my hand out, grabbing the dagger strapped to the demon's thigh. I pulled the wicked-looking blade free. It burned in my palm, but I could hold it.

I jammed the deadly metal into his side.

He hissed, his grip loosening slightly on my thighs. I kicked out, pushing myself away from him. I crashed to the ground, pain streaking through my shoulder.

"What the hell?" the other demon said.

I scrambled to my feet and lunged for him, slamming the blade into his chest. His wide black eyes met mine. I shoved him backward, yanking the blade free. He collapsed to the ground, crashing like a great redwood.

I spun to see the other demon dragging a long dagger from his hip sheath.

His gaze darted to the blade in my hand. "You can't hold that."

"That's what you think." I threw myself at him, barely dodging the swipe of his blade as I plunged my dagger into his gut.

He grunted. I pushed him back, yanking my blade free and swiping it across his neck. Blood gurgled forth, and his eyes rolled. When you killed a demon on Earth, it went straight back to its hell. I didn't know what happened to demons when you killed them in their hell, but I didn't care.

I scrambled off him, calling on my dragon sense to help guide me to the portal. As I focused, I caught sight of the demon I'd stabbed in the chest. He was gasping his last breaths as his gaze met mine.

"He'll come for you," he rasped.

I shivered at the promise in his words, but sneered at him. "Whatever."

I left them lying on the cobblestones and ran, following the pull of my dragon sense. My *deirfiúr* and I used this gift to find treasure for our shop, Ancient Magic. Now, I used it to find what I valued most.

Escape.

It pulled me toward the castle, of course. Into the lion's den.

The building loomed ahead, a massive, hulking structure that threatened with its very presence. I sprinted up the expansive stone stairs and pulled on the heavy wooden door.

To my relief, it opened easily. I darted inside, careful to keep myself against the wall. The foyer was grand, a massive space done in rich woods and silk wall hangings.

I reached for my dragon sense, letting it direct me toward my goal. I followed it, skirting around the edge of the foyer to the other side of the massive room, careful to keep my ears alert for the sound of approaching footsteps.

Where was the Warden now? Had the demon found him already?

Windows glinted on the other side of the hall, beckoning me.

Outside, an oasis of a garden spread as far as I could see. Roses and other flowers bloomed in riotous color amongst the lush green, so different than the hellscape at the front of the house.

My dragon sense beckoned me toward the garden. The portal lay within.

A single wooden door caught my eye, and I raced to it, darting out into the garden. The air was cooler here, a delightful contrast to the fiery nightmare that I'd just left on the other side of the castle. The scent of flowers and recent rain permeated the place.

Did this Underworld have two sides—good and bad?—or was the Warden also a gardener? If it had two sides, why did I end up on the hell side? I wasn't a bad person.

Right?

I dragged my mind from the stupid questions and sprinted across the grass, losing myself in the hedges as I sought the portal. My time had to be running short. The Warden would see the fallen bodies of the demons any moment and know that I was gone.

Rose thorns scratched my arms as I raced by. I winced and kept going, my heart thundering in my ears. I came across a small blue pond. Black swans floated across the surface, their beady gaze clinging to me.

"Nice birdies," I cooed, eying them warily.

Swans could be bitches. Mean birds, those.

I skirted around the pond, following my dragon sense. Fortunately, the swans didn't pay any attention to me.

When I reached the other side, the pale green glow of a portal nearly made me weep with relief. I raced for it, not hesitating at the entrance.

I flung myself inside.

And bounced off, landing hard on my butt, the grass wet beneath me.

Pain sang through my face and chest where I'd slammed into the portal. I clasped my hand to my nose, hoping I hadn't broken it.

"Dang it," I muttered as I climbed to my feet.

It was locked. I scowled at the shimmering green air that marked the portal, trying to figure out why the heck I couldn't get through. Most portals just let you through, unless something was wrong with them. I'd seen a broken portal before, and it had caused some serious problems.

"Oh, you idiot," I muttered. Of course there was something wrong with this portal.

It led to hell. And out of hell. No way it'd be constantly open like a normal one. Demons would be flooding through to Earth all the time, which was totally not allowed. Most of them looked like such scary freaking monsters that they'd alert humans to the presence of supernaturals. No one wanted that.

Which actually made me feel better. If this portal was locked, it probably went to Earth. That was exactly where I wanted to go. Heading to another Underworld would do me no favors. I didn't know much about them—no Earth supernatural did—but I knew I didn't want to be in one of them.

So I just had to figure out how to get through this one.

The portal glowed a shimmering green, dense and impenetrable. But it was the edges that caught my eye.

They looked almost like seams, glowing a slightly brighter green.

I reached out and tried to stick my fingers through the seam. They hit a hard surface and stopped dead, glowing slightly green in the light of the portal.

Damn.

I glared at the portal, my mind racing. The green glow was a bit like the blue glow of my Phantom form. I glanced behind me, making sure no one was watching.

Idiot.

No one would be just watching me. Attacking me, maybe. But not just watching.

Still, it felt like there were eyes on me. Probably just paranoia.

I called upon my power, embracing my Phantom form and letting the shivery magic flow through me. It took longer to catch on because of my injuries, but it worked. The magic chilled my skin, turning me blue and transparent.

When I was fully transformed, I reached out again. This time, my fingertips sunk through, tingling where they touched the portal.

Jackpot.

I grinned as I gripped the edge of the portal like a blanket, and tugged. It resisted at first, but I yanked harder, giving it everything I had.

The portal tore away, peeling back to reveal a woodland scene in a place that was definitely not the Underworld.

I grinned, then knocked on my head for good luck, hoping that wherever I was going was close to home. As

I climbed through, my heart panged to leave my sword behind, but I was getting out of here, and that was all that mattered.

As I stepped into the woods on the other side, I couldn't help but shudder as the demon's dying words echoed in my mind.

He'll come for you.

CHAPTER TWO

The woods on the other side of the portal were definitely on Earth. The smell was so natural and distinct—dirt and trees and the fresh scent of water from the burbling river to my left. The sun was right where it should be— glowing orange and familiar. I didn't know if Underworlds had suns, but this had to be Earth. The trees were big, and thank magic, they looked like the ones native to Oregon, where I lived.

My muscles relaxed the tiniest bit, and my chest filled with bright, clear joy. I was almost home.

In the silence of the forest, I could hear my heartbeat.

I was grateful that the old ticker was still beating away, but it was also a reminder of how weird I was. I'd escaped hell *and* I was alive, complete with heartbeat.

That shouldn't be possible. And that was dangerous.

But I was back. And I was going to take it.

Somehow, I'd escaped the Underworld.

Did that make me immortal?

I shivered as goosebumps prickled my skin.

I didn't want to be immortal, watching all my friends die of old age. But I also didn't want to be in hell. And if I didn't get out of here soon and cover my tracks, I might be dragged back.

I turned to see what the portal looked like and winced.

A glowing green scar sliced across the air in front of me, a segment of the portal hanging loose like a torn curtain. Through it, I could see the beautiful garden.

"Dang it." There was no way this was how the portal normally looked. A human could walk right through it.

Still in my Phantom form, I grasped the edge of the portal and tried to tug it up so that it covered the hole in the ether that led to the unknown Underworld. If I could just knit the seam back together and return it to normal, it should be good.

The edges of the portal stuck together, kind of. It didn't look as neat as it had before, with the glimmering green seam outlining the haze of the portal, but it was better than before. If you didn't know what you were looking for, it could pass.

I stepped back and resumed my human form, delighting in the feel of the cool breeze against my skin.

As I turned to head toward town, something massive hurtled out of the portal and slammed into me. It plowed me into the ground, swiping out with its claws as it struggled to its feet.

Pain sliced through me where its razor-sharp claws had torn into my upper chest. I struggled up, my skin chilling as I caught sight of the massive demon in front of me. It was the biggest, meanest looking one I'd ever seen—pale gray with massive horns. His magic smelled like a garbage fire.

This was the Warden!?

He roared and surged toward me. Panic thundered in my chest as I called upon my power, desperately reaching for my Phantom form. The icy magic flowed through me, turning my body blue and incorporeal just as his clawed hand swiped out again.

It passed right through me. His eyes widened at the sight, something strange flashing through them.

He shoved his hand into his pocket, then threw something to the ground. Glittery gray smoke poofed up, and he stepped into it, disappearing.

A transport charm.

What the heck? Why would the Warden run from his prey?

Oh shit.

That hadn't been the Warden. It'd been some random demon, and I'd let him escape.

Some demon hunter I was.

Pain welled at my chest now that some of my adrenaline had faded. I staggered, glancing down at the wound.

Green fluid dripped from it, glowing bright despite my Phantom form.

Oh no.

Poison?

I sucked in a ragged breath, wincing. I had to get out of here.

I spun and hurried away from the portal, calling upon my dragon sense as I went. More than anything, I wanted to find my home in Magic's Bend.

Magic shivered through me as I ran through the forest. When my dragon sense latched on, I almost jumped. I hadn't realized how *close* I was. Not more than twenty miles. I must've been in the woods on the outskirts of town.

An expanse of brown caught my eye, and I glanced over. A beautiful house sat nestled amongst the trees, overlooking the wide, glittering river. It was a modern marvel of wood and stone, with massive windows that would provide a gorgeous view. The whole place was beautiful, and totally unexpected so close to a portal.

Not my business. Certainly not now. And no way I'd knock on that door for help. Who knew what lived there.

I raced away from the house and the portal, following my dragon sense toward town. I zipped up my jacket to cover the wound on my chest and resumed my human form. As I ran, I reached up to touch the comms charm at my neck, but it was gone.

Had it been torn off in the fight? Or during one of my many falls?

However I'd lost it, it looked like I'd be getting home the hard way.

When I finally staggered onto the street that held Ancient Magic, the shop I ran with my *deirfiúr*, tears prickled my eyes. I knew I'd be happy to see this place again, but crying? That was new.

The wound at my chest wasn't deep enough to cause massive blood loss, but the poison was becoming a problem. I could feel my limbs growing heavier and weaker.

It hadn't helped that I'd had to run the whole way home. Not a single car had passed me until I'd reached the city limits, where our shop was located. Though Magic's Bend was the largest city of supernaturals in the country, where fae walked around with their wings out and Shifters stalked around on four legs, it still wasn't big. We were hidden from humans by a massive spell, so the only traffic through town was supernatural. Hitchhiking wasn't easy when your town had so few cars going in and out. Most times it was impossible.

I stumbled down the main street of Factory Row, which was wide and nearly empty. Factory Row was usually pretty dead since we were at the edge of town. One side held a park, and the other a row of old factory buildings from the nineteenth and early twentieth centuries. They'd been converted into shops and apartments in the nineties. The shops were mostly antiques places, so our own shop, Ancient Magic, fit right in.

The rent was low and the company odd, which made it ideal for me and my *deirfiúr*. We rented the entire building above our shop, each of us taking a floor for our apartment.

The windows of Ancient Magic glinted in the light of the setting sun, welcoming me.

I was home. And not a moment too soon. My legs were starting to feel numb. I shoved aside the panic. It did no good in situations like this.

I shivered in the chill autumn air as I hurried toward Ancient Magic. When I stopped outside the window, my gaze immediately zeroed in on Cass and Nix, who stood behind the counter. Shelves stocked with all kinds of artifacts and replicas covered every wall. The treasures filling the space might draw most people's gazes, but I had eyes only for my friends.

They were *here*. Safe.

Cass, with her red hair and usual brown leather jacket, stood next to Nix, who was her opposite in many ways. Nix's brown hair was pulled into a messy ponytail, and she wore a T-shirt with a cartoon cat on it. She hovered her hand, which glowed blue, over an ancient Greek amphora. An identical vase stood by its side on the counter. In addition to being a FireSoul, Nix was a Conjurer who could also transfer magic.

Looked like they were transferring a spell from an artifact to a replica, which we would then sell. Selling only the decayed magic in artifacts was how we stayed on the right side of the law.

Cass glanced up, her gaze widening at the sight of me. Confusion was replaced by pure joy, a light so bright that I grinned.

Nix let out a shriek of delight. I stumbled into the shop, colliding with my best friends, getting lost in a tangle of arms.

"Del!" Cass cried. "You're alive!"

They squeezed me so hard that I almost saw stars.

"I'm so happy to see you!" Tears prickled my eyes.

Ten years ago, we'd woken in a field with no memories and only the ratty dresses on our backs. We hadn't even known our own names. Since then, we'd made our way in the magical world, three FireSouls lying low from the government that hunted them.

I pulled back, my gaze devouring them. They were alive. Really, truly alive, having survived the battle that had killed me. The magical world, which existed secretly alongside the human one, was a dangerous place. There were fights all the time. The one that had killed me had been a doozy, but only unusual in the fact that I had *died*.

"Where have you been?" Cass demanded as she shook me by the shoulders.

Pain streaked through my chest, and my knees weakened. I stumbled.

"I have a problem." In my joy, I'd temporarily forgotten my wound. I winced as I unzipped my jacket. The wound was still bleeding slightly, with the green poison oozing from the cuts.

"Shit!" Cass cried.

"Oh no." Concern clouded Nix's eyes. "That looks bad."

"Yeah." I gasped as my heart started to race. "It's poison."

Cass and Nix caught me under the arms and turned me to the door, helping me stumble along.

"Come on," Cass said. "We're getting you to Connor. He'll know what it is."

They all but dragged me down the dark street toward Potions & Pastilles, the coffee shop owned by our friends Connor and Claire. They were a brother and sister pair who had immigrated from England about six years ago. Claire was a mercenary, while Connor was a hearth witch with an extraordinary knack for potions.

Please know what to do about this poison, Connor.

Nix and Del helped me stagger up to the glass door. Massive windows on either side revealed the warmly lit interior of our favorite hangout spot. Mason-jar lamps and artwork of questionable quality completed the very hipster-Oregon picture, and it was perfect. I just hadn't thought I'd be in this condition when I saw it next.

By the time we stepped through the door, my head was spinning slightly.

"Del!" Claire hurried toward me, weaving through the small tables that cluttered the coffee shop. "Oh my gosh! You're back. How?"

"She's injured." Nix turned to the back of the shop. "Connor, get out here!"

"I'll shut the shop." Claire hurried behind us and locked the door, then turned the closed sign.

At night, P & P switched from being a coffee stop to serving craft beers and fancy whiskey. Fortunately, no one had yet stopped in for their evening drink besides our new friend Emile, who sat in the corner. I smiled wanly at him, or tried to, at least.

"Come, come." Claire's British accent had grown thick with worry. She guided us over toward my favorite corner of P & P, where the comfiest chairs were clustered.

Emile sat in one of them, gazing at us with concerned eyes. He was an Animus mage who had the power to communicate with animals. Two black and white rats—Ralph and Rufus—sat on his shoulders. I grinned at the sight of his furry little companions.

"Hey, guys." My voice sounded hoarse. The poison was really kicking in now.

"What's wrong?" Connor's concerned voice drifted from the other side of the shop.

He hurried closer, and I squinted at him through my blurring vision. His dark hair was flopped over his brow, and he wore a band T-shirt dusted lightly with flour. Today it was Jump, Little Children, a band I'd never heard of. As usual.

I clung to that inane detail, as if the normal would push aside the fact that I was succumbing to some mysterious poison.

Connor was about five years younger than my twenty-five, but he was a potions mastermind. I wouldn't trust anyone more when I was in a pickle like this.

He knelt by my side, inspecting my wound. "Looks like death didn't treat you so well."

"I'm back, aren't I?"

His gaze met mine. "And we're going to keep you that way."

I grinned, then winced.

Connor frowned as he leaned his head down and sniffed at my wound. He reared back, his eyes wild.

"What is it?" Panic laced Cass's voice.

"Ubilaz poison." He surged to his feet, then darted away, running through the door to the back of the cafe.

My heart thundered. "That sounds bad."

"You came back from the dead," Nix said. "This isn't going to get you."

"Though we're going to want answers on how you did that," Cass said.

"Yeah. Handy trick," Claire added.

"Neato," Emile added.

They were trying to distract me. I didn't know what an Ubilaz demon was, but it must be bad.

I tried not to hyperventilate while waiting for Connor to return. Ralph and Rufus hopped off Emile's shoulders and climbed onto mine, sniffing at my cheeks. Their little whiskers tickled.

"Ralph and Rufus have always been fond of you," Emile said.

I grinned. I was fond of them, too. Fond of all animals. "They're not saying goodbye, right?"

"Nah." Cass shook her head. "You're too stubborn to die."

"And it's not like dying stuck to you the first time." Nix grinned.

"I've got it!" Connor cried as he hurried out of the back of the cafe, holding up a small vial of dark green liquid. He knelt at my side and poured the stuff over my wounds.

It sizzled and burned, and I yelped. Ralph reached up with little paws and patted my cheek.

When I glanced down, the wounds were knitting themselves back together. Blood and poison had soaked into my once-lucky shirt, but my flesh looked entirely healed.

"Am I better?" I asked. It sure didn't hurt anymore, and I suddenly felt a lot stronger.

"No. Definitely not."

I jerked my head up. "What do you mean?"

His dark gaze was serious. "I've never seen an Ubilaz demon before. They aren't supposed to be able to leave the Underworld. But you can buy their poison on the black market for use in potion making. It's one of the strongest there is."

"Strongest as in deadly?" Cass asked.

"No," Connor said. "Worse. It's old school horror. In diluted forms, it does other things. But in pure form? It'll turn you into one of them."

"What?" I jolted up in my chair, and Ralph and Rufus tumbled into my lap. "Turn me into an Ubilaz demon?"

He nodded. "That's what's supposed to happen. The transition is slow. It'll take about a week. But there's an antidote. I can make it if you can get me some of the demon's blood."

Relief coursed through me, turning my muscles to jelly. "So I just have to get you some of its blood."

"Yeah. Or another Ubilaz demon's blood. Doesn't matter. And you have to take more of the potion I poured on your wound. Drink it every day, and it'll delay the effects of the demon's poison until we can make the antidote."

I sagged back against the chair, adjusting so that the sword scabbard strapped to my back didn't poke me.

"But you have to get the demon." Connor's voice turned grave. "The potion I give you will only last about a week before your body becomes immune to it."

Great.

"It's not a problem," Cass said. "We'll get the demon. It'll be fine."

"Knock on wood." I knocked on my head. "Don't jinx us."

Cass knocked on her head, too.

"Now that you're not staggering, I want a proper greeting." Claire threw her arms around me, careful to keep from touching my poison-stained shirt.

My heart leapt to see her again, and I hugged her tight. Claire was a Fire Mage, and she, too, was dressed in leather, her usual wear for her job as a mercenary. She worked part time at P & P with her brother Connor when she wasn't off killing monsters.

I pulled back and took in her familiar dark hair and eyes.

"How are you back? It's impossible," Claire said.

I opened my mouth to explain, but I honestly wasn't sure what had happened.

"Quit hogging her," Connor said.

Claire stepped back. "Fine. Fine. I'm going to get you a snack. You need to get your strength up before you go out looking for this demon."

Connor stepped forward and gave me a big squeeze.

"So good to see you." I hugged him tight.

"We thought we'd lost you." He mumbled against my hair. "Had us worried."

I pulled back. "Had myself worried."

"Well, you're back now." He grinned. "No idea how, but I'll take it."

"That's about where I am." My mind raced with what lay ahead of me. "Connor, do you think you could whip me up a couple defensive potions?"

I didn't have my sword, and if I was going to go hunting big game like the Ubilaz demon, I'd need some weapons.

Connor saluted. "On it!"

"Thanks."

He spun and headed back behind the bar.

Claire bustled past him, bringing a tray. She set it down on the table. "Vegetarian quiche and a cup of boxed wine. Your regular. Eat that now."

"Thanks. You're the best." P & P's specialty was the Cornish pasty, a savory treat usually made of meat and potatoes wrapped in pastry, but they tried to keep quiche on hand for me. It was my fave.

Ralph and Rufus had climbed back onto my shoulders, so I gave each of them a bite. I met Claire's gaze. "Thanks for the wine, but it'll have to wait since I need to track down that demon."

"How about an espresso?"

"Amazing. Thank you."

"Not a problem." Claire bustled off.

I went to work on the quiche, suddenly famished.

"Okay." Cass's voice drew my gaze to her. "Time for some answers. How are you here?"

"I saw you die." Nix's gaze was stark, sending a small streak of guilt through me at making her worry.

I'd had no choice—I hadn't wanted to kick the bucket, but I had. And I'd ended up in hell.

"Yeah, that happened." I swallowed hard, the memory making my skin prickle.

"Were you in the Underworld? How did you get out?" Nix asked. "That can't be possible."

"I don't really know. But I tore through a portal and ended up outside of town."

"That's so weird." Confusion coated Nix's voice. "That's not even possible."

It was. Somehow.

"What the hell took you so long?" Cass demanded. "We've been terrified. It's been two weeks!"

Two weeks? It hadn't felt like that long.

"We've been searching for you everywhere," Nix said. "We were onto our last clue back at the shop. If the spell in the amphora didn't work, we were going to go to the Order of the Magica and the Alpha Council for help."

"No!" The Order and the Council were the two factions of magical government. The Order oversaw the magic users—Magica—and the Council oversaw the magical beings—Shifters. The Order was a fine organization—they kept us hidden from humans and ensured law and order—but they weren't so fine if you were a weirdo with unknown powers. Then they thought *you* were the threat. And in that situation, you never came out ahead. Unfortunately, they would consider my *deirfiúr* and me to be a threat.

"We can't let them know what we are." I wanted to shake them.

32

We were all FireSouls, and we were all at risk. A few people knew about Cass, but we trusted them, unlike the Order and the Council.

"I know, dummy." Cass rolled her eyes. "I wasn't going to tell them the *truth*. Our secret's ours. And your new *can-escape-hell* talent is definitely a secret."

Emile's frightened gaze met ours. In addition to being an Animus mage, he was also a FireSoul and was hunted by the Order of the Magica. Just like us. He was one of the very few who knew what we were. We'd rescued him from the Prison for Magical Miscreants about a month ago, and he was still skinny from his time there. His eyes had a haunted look that twisted my heart every time I saw him.

Emile shuddered hard, no doubt remembering his time in prison. His bleak gaze met mine. "Don't let them discover that you're different. *Don't*. Being a FireSoul is bad. Coming back from the dead is worse."

"I know," I said. "I'll be careful."

Only the people who'd been at the battle with us knew that I'd died. They'd have my back. My *deirfiúr*, Connor, Claire, Emile, and Aidan definitely wouldn't turn me in. I even had faith in Aerdeca and Mordaca, our friends over in Darklane.

"Where is Aidan?" I asked.

Cass's boyfriend was a serious badass and respected by the magical governments because of his massive wealth and power. He descended from the first Shifter and could turn into any animal he pleased. Griffins were his creature of choice. Cass was just as tough as him, though. She was a Mirror Mage who could mimic any supernatural's magic, and she also had a whole bunch of stolen powers from her rocky past as a FireSoul.

"Aidan's okay, right?" I asked.

"Yeah." Cass nodded quickly. "He's fine. Everyone is fine. Connor, Claire, and Emile. Aerdeca and Mordaca, also. You were the only one who…"

"Died," I finished for her. Calm settled over me at the knowledge that all of my friends were okay.

Cass threw her arms around me again and muttered into my hair, "I was so scared. You were such a hero."

Nix's hand rested on my back, as if she couldn't help but touch me to confirm I was really back.

I squeezed Cass, then pulled away. "We all were. Another fight, another day, right?"

"Yeah, yeah, I know. Dangerous world out there." Nix tipped her chin toward the window. "But you went above and beyond. And now that you're back, it's safer for the rest of us."

I grinned. "It was easy."

Nix hugged me.

When I pulled back, I asked, "Where's Aidan?"

"Off following a lead about a portal to the Underworld, but I'll text him now that you're back." Cass pulled her phone out of her pocket.

"Yeah, I found that portal, thank fates." I swallowed the last bite of food and leaned toward Emile so that Ralph and Rufus could jump off my shoulders onto his. "We should get out of here."

Claire came over with a to-go cup and handed it over. "I figured you'd want to take this on the road. I added a boost."

"Thank you. You're a life saver."

In addition to the Cornish pasties they served, P & P's drink specialty was enchanted coffees. I didn't know what they added, but the special boost was like a shot of Red Bull in your coffee, without the jitters. I didn't always add it, but today… Totally necessary.

"No, that would be me." Connor approached from the back. He handed me a small black pouch. "There are a few helpful potion bombs in here. Red are Portlothian acid bombs. Deadly. Gold are freeze bombs. Blue unfreezes whatever you've frozen. The dark green is your potion. Take it every day. They're labeled, so you don't get them confused. *Do not* drink the acid bomb."

"No problem." I grinned and took the bag. "Thanks."

Connor looked at me hard. "Don't forget to take it every day. The poison is still in your system. You'll start looking like an Ubilaz demon if you don't take it, and that's just the beginning of the transition."

Okay, yeah. I wouldn't be forgetting this potion.

"Thanks. You're a life saver. Literally."

"Come on," Cass said. "You need a shower, then we'll come up with a plan for getting that demon."

"Yeah." I looked at Claire, Connor, and Emile. "Thanks again, guys."

"Let us know how we can help," Claire said.

I felt almost entirely normal as we said goodbye and left P & P. The night was cool and dark, the silence punctuated only by crickets.

"The best thing we can do is split up," Cass said. "Use our dragon sense to try to find a different Ubilaz demon. That increases our odds of catching one."

Nix nodded. "Smart."

We neared Ancient Magic and Cass said, "Let me duck inside and get my bag."

"Yeah, I left mine too." Nix followed her in.

I trailed them into our shop, soothed by the familiarity of the place. It was filled with all sorts of magical artifacts that we sold to the highest bidder. But we were totally legal.

My *deirfiúr* and I might hunt ancient artifacts for a living, but we didn't keep them. Our goal was to retrieve the magical spells encased in the artifacts. The magic decayed with time, becoming unstable and dangerous. We removed the spell from the artifact and transferred it to a replica, which we then sold. Once it was all done, we returned the artifact to its original resting place.

It was how we stayed on the right side of the law and kept our consciences in the clear. None of us wanted to steal from the dead, or disrupt archaeological sites.

Cass held up her bag. "Right! I've got it. We can go."

As I turned to leave the shop, the air vibrated around me, something I'd never felt before. I snapped my mouth closed and glanced around.

"You feel that?" Cass asked, her green gaze darting.

"Yeah," I muttered.

It thrummed against my skin, a strangely soothing feeling. At least, it'd be soothing if it weren't so unusual.

Then the power hit me. The signature of a supernatural who was so strong it made my breath come short and my ears hum with a low buzz. The scent of sandalwood filled my nose, and the taste of a fine red wine exploded on my tongue.

"Ohhh shit," I breathed as I turned toward the door.

The man who walked into the shop made my heart pound like I'd run a marathon.

This was the Warden. No question. His power was so immense I felt like I'd been hit by a truck.

I just couldn't get a break. First the Ubilaz demon, now this guy.

Worse, he was everything I'd feared and nothing I'd expected.

For one, he was too damned handsome. Probably the best looking guy I'd ever seen, which would normally make me say something stupid. Particularly since his was the strong, dark type of handsome. Like a freaking fallen angel.

But I couldn't focus on his looks when his power was sucker punching me. His magical signature was so strong that all five of my senses registered it.

The scent of sandalwood and the taste of wine were familiar, but the feel of his magic—a caress that made me shiver—was entirely unexpected. And the sound—a low growl that was as seductive as it was threatening—was a signature I'd never heard before. His aura was bright blue, a rare cobalt that I suspected was unique to him. Few supernaturals had auras—those who did were one some of the most extreme magical signatures.

With it, this guy hit up all five of my senses. No, *six*, I realized. He was lighting up my dragon sense, which only picked up things of value.

My heart raced as my dragon sense pulled me toward him.

No, no, no. This guy was not valuable to me. He couldn't be. I didn't even know him.

But my dragon sense did. And it didn't seem to care that he was the Warden, come to drag me back to hell.

CHAPTER THREE

Quickly, I dug into my pocket and pulled out a freeze bomb, then chucked it at his feet. The golden vial crashed to the ground and exploded in a flurry of glittery gold dust.

The Warden froze in his tracks, his foot partially lifted to continue his walk toward us.

"Freeze bomb?" Cass asked.

"Yeah." Didn't take me long to break into Connor's stash.

"Quick thinking," Nix said.

My gaze raced over the Warden's features. It made my breath come short just to look at him. Though maybe that was a bit of fear as well.

"Why is he holding your sword?" Cass asked.

"And why does he have a magical arsenal like the entire Order of the Magica combined?" Nix asked.

He gripped my beloved sword loosely in his fist. My heart leapt, and I started forward to snatch it back.

"Stop!" Cass cried. "Don't approach. You could be frozen too."

I halted in my tracks. She was right. The golden freeze dust still glittered in the air around the Warden. I just wanted my sword back *so dang much.*

I dragged my gaze from my sword back up to the Warden's dark eyes.

Nix wolf whistled. "He's hot."

"Yep." And I didn't like it.

I didn't like his perfect face or the black hair that waved back from his forehead or his blazing dark eyes. I certainly didn't like that he was well over six feet, nor the muscle that lurked beneath his dark shirt and jeans. It'd be pretty much impossible to resist him at a bar if he tried to pick me up, because *hello, handsome.*

"Powerful, too," Cass said.

"Yep." I was eloquent, as usual.

Even without his magic, I'd have a tough time beating him in a fight. If he got ahold of me, he could tear me apart.

Would he, though?

The fact that he could was unusual since I could hold my own against just about anyone in hand-to-hand combat. It was a point of pride.

"Who is he?" Nix asked.

"I think he's the Warden," I said.

Nix met my gaze. "Of what?"

"I don't know. He's some kind of badass from whatever hell I was in."

"He's come for you?" Cass asked. "First the demon, then this guy?"

"Yeah. My luck hasn't been so hot lately. Don't know how he tracked me, but he's definitely here for me."

"His magic doesn't feel evil," Cass said.

I reached out for his magical signatures, trying to get a better feel for them. The aura had faded, as I'd heard they did after a first encounter, but the rest were still evident.

Cass was right—he didn't feel evil. And I'd felt evil before. Plenty of it. This wasn't it. True evil made your heart race and your skin chill. You could feel it, like an animal sensed danger. But his power was so strong that I *did* sense danger. He might not be outright evil, but he was big trouble for me.

"Just because he manages an Underworld doesn't mean he's necessarily evil," Nix said. "It's probably better if someone with that kind of power is fair minded."

"I guess so." I wished I knew more about the power structure of the Underworlds. Death was as mysterious to supernaturals as it was to humans. I was probably the only supernatural to ever see one of the hells and come back.

"Now that we know he's not a super baddie, should we unfreeze him and see what he has to say?" Cass asked.

I eyed my sword, but decided I didn't want to risk being frozen along with him. Cass and Nix would unfreeze me, but if it happened at the same time as the Warden, I'd lose the upper hand. I had a few seconds head start on him. I wouldn't use it to run. He'd found me here; he would find me again. Better to face this head on.

"Yeah, unfreeze him." I spotted a thick iron chain piled on a shelf nearby. "Wait! Let's immobilize him first."

"Good thinking," Nix said.

I ran to grab the enchanted chain. When I reached the shelf, I hefted it, then called, "Give me a hand here."

Nix joined me, and together, we carried the thing toward the Warden, stopping about six feet away.

"On three," I said.

Nix nodded.

"One, two, three."

Nix and I heaved the chain toward the Warden.

The artifact's enchantment took over, directing the chain toward the Warden like a heat-seeking missile, albeit a slow one. The ends stood up like snakes and wrapped around his broad chest and muscled arms, pinning them to his sides. Finally, the ends met, turning bright orange as they welded together.

"Whew, that thing is cool," Cass said.

"Can't believe no one has wanted it yet," I said. When we'd set our eye on that enchantment, I'd been sure it would sell quickly. It could contain anything.

"I can." Nix glanced around at the wares that she protected and sold. "People are mostly interested in ancient beauty potions and the occasional enchanted weapon. That thing is a bit too weird for the common Magica or Shifter. And it's heavy."

"To our benefit." Cass met my gaze. "Do you have another freeze bomb so you can run for it if you don't like what he has to say?"

I nodded as I dug into my pocket for the blue unfreezing potion. "Yeah. Good thinking."

I pulled the vial out and confirmed that it wasn't the acid bomb—it'd be totally unfair to kill him while he was frozen. We didn't normally deal in potions, but we'd recently started to see the benefit of their subtlety. Normally we just beat up whoever threatened us.

I made sure that I had another freeze bomb in hand—just in case—then chucked the blue vial. It didn't explode like the gold one had. Instead, the Warden suddenly snapped to attention, his trance broken.

He glanced down at the heavy chain that wrapped around his chest and upper arms, his gaze confused. Then he reached up and tugged the chain away as if it were made of butter. Briefly, the muscles in his forearms bulged, but that was the only evidence that he'd just torn away a hundred pounds of iron chain.

Whoa.

Nix coughed, clearly attempting to cover some kind of noise, while I tried desperately to recover from the surprise.

"Looking for me?" I finally choked out.

Smooth. Real smooth.

His gaze met mine. A slow smile curved the corners of his mouth. I tried desperately to ignore the fluttering of my heart.

"I am." His voice was deep and warm, and I hated the shiver that raced across my skin. "You're good with the surprise attacks. Freeze bomb and enchanted chain?"

I nodded. Too bad the chain hadn't really worked on him. "I wasn't expecting you. How'd you find me?"

He pointed to his forehead. "You've left a trail of blood."

I reached up and touched the wound at my head. From falling on the rocks in the Underworld. Right. It was mostly dried by now, though. The blood may have been from my chest wound. But even that hadn't bled much.

"Not a lot of blood," I said.

"I'm a good tracker."

Something in his eyes looked a little off. A lie?

"I'm here to take you back," he said.

"Too bad. I'm not interested."

"I hardly think that matters. You're dead. I don't know how you escaped the Underworld, but you're subject to my laws now. And you'll be returning with me."

"Um, no." I shook my head and spread out my arms. "I'm not dead. I've got a heartbeat and everything. So you might as well forget any crazy ideas about dragging me back to the Underworld."

No way I was letting him take me back. Then I wouldn't find the Ubilaz demon, and I'd be stuck as one forever. They probably lived in the worst parts of the Underworld. That was not going to be my fate.

"And we're kind of a package deal." Cass gestured between the three of us with her finger. "You come for her, you're coming for us."

His gaze darkened, and he reached out a hand, beckoning. I sensed the tug of his magic. Was he compelling me? That was an uber-rare magical gift that would force the listener to comply. So much more subtle than using the crazy muscles I'd just witnessed.

When he spoke, his voice had deepened even further, turning into a massage that made my muscles feel like pudding. "Come, Delphine Bellator."

Shock lanced through me at the name. I sucked in a ragged breath. "I'm Delphine Hally. That's not my name."

I tried to ignore the feeling of rightness in my chest. It was too weird.

"Delphine Bellator is your name." Certainty filled his voice. "I know the true names of all my subjects. You are Delphine Bellator."

I chucked the freeze bomb at him. When it exploded at his feet, he froze again, dead solid.

"You gonna run for it?" Cass asked.

"No." I shook my head, hardly able to breathe. "He knows my name. My real name."

Startled gazes met mine.

"Are you freaking for real?" Cass asked.

"You're sure?" Nix asked. "He could just be confused."

"Yeah. It feels *right*." My chest felt shivery at the knowledge. My head felt shell-shocked. "Bellator is my real last name."

I'd never known my true last name before. When Cass and Nix and I had woken in that field ten years ago, we'd known nothing. Not even our names. We'd named ourselves for the constellations above. Cassiopeia, Phoenix, and Delphinus. Since Delphinus would have been ridiculous, I'd modified it to Delphine. We'd picked our last names at random. I'd been going by Del Hally for the last ten years, having no idea what my true name was.

But this guy knew it. He *knew* it. How?

"Do you think he knows more?" Cass asked.

She'd recently learned a bit about her past, but Nix and I were still totally in the dark about our lives before we'd woken at fifteen with no memories. Information was worth more than all the gold in my trove.

"I don't know," I said. "But I want to find out."

"You're not thinking of going with him!" Nix's face was pale. "You have to find the Ubilaz demon."

"I know. We don't have time for this. But I do want to know more. I *have* to know more. Maybe I can grill him later or something. Trade him for information."

"We don't even know what he wants," Cass said.

"Yeah, I may have jumped the gun by chucking the freeze bomb so soon," I said. "I just freaked."

"Understandably." Wistfulness tinged Nix's voice. "He knows your real name."

I nodded, desperate to hear more from him. "Can you unfreeze him, Cass?"

"Yeah, but that's the last of the freeze bombs."

I nodded and she dug into her pocket, then chucked a small blue vial at him.

He unfroze, shaking his head as his vision cleared. His power swelled on the air, knocking me back several feet. Nix and Cass as well.

"You need to stop freezing me." His voice vibrated with command, but it was his power that had me nervous.

It'd *pushed* me backward. That was nuts. Since we hadn't chained him this time, he shouldn't have been able to tell we'd frozen him. It was a very subtle potion. But he'd sensed it.

I shivered. "What are you?"

"The Warden."

"I know that. But what kind of supernatural?"

"Were-demon. What are you?"

Half demon, half Shifter? "They don't exist."

"Apparently they do." He stretched out long arms, displaying himself. I tried not to stare too hard at the muscles that were so obvious beneath his dark shirt and jeans.

He was really a demon? But they were evil. Maybe I hadn't felt it in him, but if he was right about what he was, that made him even more dangerous than I'd thought.

"And it's time for you to return." His gaze darkened again, and his voice deepened. "Come, Delphine Bellator."

His voice tugged at me, but I shook it off. "No. You're trying to compel me, but it won't work."

A scowl creased his brow. "No, it doesn't seem to be effective on you. And it always works. The dead are compelled to obey me."

"I'm not dead, so I'm not your minion."

"No." His gaze moved over me, appreciative but fortunately not sleazy. "You are not."

"And I'm not going back to that Underworld with you."

"I can make you."

Cass gestured between the three of us again. "Package deal, remember?"

No way was I letting this dude drag me back to hell, no matter how hot and not-sleazy he was. That combination was a rare one, but not rare enough to go to hell for it.

"That'd be a fight," he said.

"I imagine it would." He lifted the blade in his hand, gazing admiringly at my beloved sword. "Any woman who dies with this in her hand isn't to be underestimated."

"You've got that right." I sensed he could fight us and probably win, but he didn't want to. He seemed the sort to only use violence when absolutely necessary.

I liked that. And I liked him. I shouldn't, but I did.

"Since I'd prefer not to fight you and your friends, how about a threat? You're the only supernatural to ever escape an Underworld. That should be impossible."

"What about demons?" And I wasn't just thinking about the Ubilaz demon. Other kinds showed up on Earth all the time, usually as mercenaries for some jerk who had bad intentions.

"You're not a demon. And they don't escape on their own. A wizard or mage must assist them. And only weaker demons can escape that way. But you…. A non-demon supernatural who shouldn't be able to escape under any circumstance. You escaped without any help. How is that?"

"Nothing special. I just wasn't supposed to be there. It's fate."

"No. There's something very odd about your magic. Odd enough that the Order of the Magica would take interest. What are you?"

I shuddered at the mention of the Order, my stomach dropping. "Nothing special, like I said."

"The Order doesn't like the unusual," he said. "Unknown magic is exceedingly rare. And dangerous. If you escaped an Underworld, you possess some power related to death. Something never before seen. What kind?"

Beats me. And that was the scary part. "I have no idea what you're talking about."

His gaze turned thoughtful. "Informing the Order is the smartest thing I could do. The responsible thing."

My heart thudded. "You don't want to do that."

A bit of surprise flickered in his gaze. His expression turned solemn. "No, surprisingly, I don't. You'd be out of my control then, subject to whatever horrors the Order deems necessary for a rarity such as yourself."

I shivered, wondering what they might do to me. If they knew I was a FireSoul, they'd throw me in the Prison for Magical Miscreants merely for existing. As a weird deathling Magica, I was subject to mysterious *horrors* as they tried to figure out my species. It wouldn't be good, that was for sure.

"So, since you don't want to turn me in and I don't want to go back to the Underworld with you, we're at an impasse." I didn't even mention the info I wanted to get from him. I needed to keep that on the down low. It was too early to show my hand. Especially since I held almost no cards.

"Duty frequently requires that I do things I don't want to do."

The seriousness of his expression made chills race over my skin. He didn't want to turn me in, but if he had to…

A buzzing noise sounded from his left wrist. I glanced down to see a wide copper band wrapped around it. He raised it close to his mouth. He wore a couple other metal bands on his right wrist, too, and I wondered what they were for.

"Yes?" he said into the comms charm.

"An Ubilaz demon has escaped," a rough voice spoke through the charm. "Through your personal portal."

Oh shit.

His brow creased. "Ubilaz? You must be mistaken. They can't leave the Underworld."

"I'm not, my lord. It is an Ubilaz, and it has been on Earth for at least an hour. Your personal portal was malfunctioning, and it escaped right before you departed the Underworld."

Oh no. I met Cass and Nix's gazes, and they looked as freaked as I was.

"Do you have any idea where it went?" the Warden asked.

"No, sir."

"Do you know anything else about it? Name? Origin? What it's after?"

"No, sir. We know nothing else."

"Fine. I'll deal with it." The Warden lowered his arm and looked straight at me. "This is your fault."

Yep. Totally was. "No. It's not."

"Ubilaz demons are Cat 5s. You've heard of Cat 5s?"

I nodded. The Order categorized demons from one to five, like hurricanes, with five being the absolute worst. Totally catastrophic. In my side job hunting demons for the Order, I *never* came across Cat 5s. Cat 3s at worst.

"A Cat 5 shouldn't even *be able* to escape the Underworld," he said. "Their dark magic is too strong. Even the most powerful mage can't get them out. Whatever you did to my portal allowed that demon to escape."

Oh shit, oh shit, oh shit. My mind raced. Now I was poisoned *and* I was going to get in huge trouble for this.

"Can't you track it like you tracked me?" I asked.

"No. Unless it's bleeding and leaving a trail."

"I'll help you find it." I'd get some of the demon's blood, and he could have the demon. "We'll trade. Once I find the demon, you forget I was ever in the Underworld. It was a fluke. And forget any weird, incorrect suspicions you have about me. And give me my sword back."

His dark brows rose. "You can see how that might not be a fair exchange."

I scowled. "'Course it is."

"You want three *huge* favors in exchange for solving a problem you created."

When he put it that way… I had revealed my hand too early. I glanced at my *deirfiúr*. Their gazes confirmed my fears. Always jumping too fast at things, that was my problem. Good intentions, poor execution.

"It's a Cat 5," I said. "You need my help. You can't track the demon, but I can."

"How can I be assured that you are even any good at finding demons?" he asked.

I laughed. "Oh, I'm good at it. I'm a mercenary for the Order. A demon hunter, to be precise."

Fortunately, it was a job that didn't put me in the way of the Order hardly ever, since I got my assignments by phone. I also liked to think I'd be on their good side if they ever discovered what I was. Wishful thinking, probably.

"More importantly, I'm a third of this operation"—I waved my hands to indicate the shop—"that identifies and locates the artifacts that contain magic we want to sell. I'm the Seeker. So, you see, I'm perfect for finding your lost demon, because I can find anything."

Maybe if I helped the Warden, he'd let me off the hook.

"She's the best at what she does," Nix said. "Best Seeker I've ever seen."

Cass said nothing, but I could see the worry in her eyes. She didn't want me to work with him, I'd bet.

The Warden's thoughtful gaze skimmed me as he considered. I tried not to fidget, but I wasn't often the recipient of such an intense stare.

He stepped closer to me, his eyes widening. "What's wrong with you?"

"What do you mean?"

"I can sense demon magic on you." His gaze traveled over me, landing on my upper chest.

Shit. I hadn't zippered my jacket.

His brows drew together over his eyes. "Your shirt is covered in your blood and…" He sniffed the air. "Ubilaz poison."

I said nothing. What was there to say?

"Damn it." His brow creased. "It scratched you, didn't it?"

Reluctantly, I nodded.

"You're going to have to come with me. You need the demon's blood for the antidote. I can't have another Ubilaz demon on my hands. You'd spend eternity in the Underworld as a Cat 5 demon. That's the last thing I need."

"Okay, I'll help you. But what about my requests?"

"Undecided. But if you get the demon back, I'll give you your sword."

"What about the other stuff? I'm not going back to the Underworld."

"Don't push your luck."

"That doesn't sound promising."

He shrugged. "You haven't got much choice. Your first priority needs to be getting the antidote."

He was right. And he held all the cards.

"Fine." I nodded sharply. "How do I contact you once I have the demon? Through your comms charm?"

"Why would you need to contact me?" He smiled, too handsome for my own well-being. "I'm going with you."

CHAPTER FOUR

Great. I'd have to spend who knew how long with this guy.

But maybe it wasn't all bad. I needed to convince him I was trustworthy and shouldn't be dragged back to the Underworld. This was the perfect opportunity.

"Okay." I tried not to sound begrudging. "We work together."

Cass and Nix glared at the Warden. If they'd been dogs, they'd have growled. We'd never been any good with honey instead of vinegar.

"Del will help you," Nix said. "But don't even think about trying to take her back to the Underworld. She doesn't belong there."

Cass's green eyes blazed. "We'll stop you if you try."

The Warden said nothing, which was no surprise. He was definitely the strong, silent type. He turned to me. "We should get started."

"We'll come," Cass said. She and Nix stepped forward.

"No," the warden said. "I can only take one when I hunt the demon."

"*I'm* hunting the demon," I said.

"You're leading me to it. I'll do the hunting. He's escaped my Underworld, so he's my responsibility."

"We can still come," Cass said.

"If we need you, we'll ask." The Warden's tone made it clear that would be a cold day in hell.

I glanced at the Warden. "It's fine, guys."

If he wanted to take me back to hell, he would—it wasn't like we could kill the Warden of the Underworld. Even if we could manage it, how would we cover it up? And I didn't want to get into the cold-blooded murder game, anyway. Demons were one thing. They just went back to their Underworld when you offed them. Supernaturals—that came with more guilt. It was why I'd never stolen another's power, even though my FireSoul gift would allow me to. I'd have to kill to take the power, and that was something I wasn't interested in.

"Fine," Cass said. "But give her any trouble, and we're coming after you."

He nodded sharply. At first glance, one might think it silly that someone as physically slight as Cass and Nix would threaten the Warden. But they were massively powerful supernaturals. I was glad the Warden respected that. Respected *them*.

"What's your first step in finding the demon?" The Warden raised his wrist as if indicating a watch. His dark brows rose. "Time is ticking."

No kidding.

"First, I need to wash the poison off myself. I'm a mess. Then, I'll use my seeker sense to find the demon. It's kinda like meditating until I feel a tug leading me to its location."

"Fine. Where are you going to shower? I'm coming with you."

My heart thudded. "No, you're not."

"I'm not letting you out of my sight."

"Well, you're not getting in the shower with me."

"Then I'll wait outside the bathroom."

I sighed and pointed to the ceiling. "Fine. My apartment is upstairs."

"I'll come with you."

"Right, then." I nodded at my *deirfiúr*. "See you later."

Their gazes were skeptical, but they nodded. I'd find a way to sneak out and see them one last time.

I hurried from the shop, giving the Warden a wide berth as I passed him. But I could tell when he followed me. The heat of his gaze on my back burned.

It was dark when I got outside, the yellow streetlamps shedding a golden glow on the damp pavement. Sprinkling rain fell from the sky, cold on my face. It'd been too damned long since I'd had a shower. Or clothes not covered in my own blood. Or demon blood.

Honestly, I just needed to get away from blood for a while. It was a hazard of the job, but everyone had a limit.

I glanced back to see him close on my heels, towering behind me. I swallowed hard, then stopped at the green door punctuating the brick wall beside Ancient Magic and dug deep into my pocket, grateful to find the single key. I unlocked the door, then pushed it open and started to climb.

"I'm the next floor," I said, too aware of his gaze on me and the fact that it was level with my butt. The leather was practical fight wear. It was also tight. And revealing.

Normally I wouldn't mind that, but with this guy...

I reached the small landing that held the door to my place and gripped the handle. Before I could push it open, a big hand appeared on the door above my head, pressed flat to the wood. My gaze darted to it, then up and behind to where the Warden stood at my back.

He lowered his hand and nudged my shoulder to turn me around to face him. Anger flared inside me. No one pushed me around, certainly not literally. I growled as I swung back my fist and pelted it toward his face.

He caught it, faster than I'd expected, stopping me about six inches from his perfect jaw. So I struck with my other fist, nailing him in the ribs.

The bastard grinned.

I'd expected a grunt or a grimace. And my fist hurt, like he was harder than your average supernatural.

My heart fluttered, stupid traitorous thing. Apparently it liked strength.

"What the hell are you?" I whispered. His sandalwood scent wrapped around me, fogging my brain.

"More than you expected." His voice was low and rough enough to send a shiver through me. "Just as you're more than I expected."

"That's kinda my thing." I shook myself. There was chemistry here, no doubt. I was attracted to him with a capital A. Hell, all the rest of the letters were capitalized too.

But he was half demon, and they were evil and untrustworthy. How could I be attracted to someone like that?

I didn't know what to do about it. Use it to my advantage? Normally not my style. However, he might try to drag me back to the Underworld. So maybe I should give it a try.

I rejected the thought almost as soon as it occurred, annoyed with myself, and demanded, "What the hell are you, really?"

"Were-demon, like I said."

"I don't even know what that means. I've never even heard of it." But if it was real, it meant a demon was hunting me, the demon-hunter.

"I'm one of a kind. Half shifter, half demon."

"What kind of shifter? What kind of demon?"

"Don't know. Never knew my mum or dad."

Same, I wanted to say. And I'd only learned my true last name today. From him. "You've got weird powers."

Like super strength and the ability to compel the dead. I didn't even want to know what he looked like when he shifted. Because in this form, he looked about a thousand times different from any demon I'd ever met. They were all ugly and scary.

"I'm not the only one." His dark gaze turned intense. He loomed over me, too tall, and looked like a fallen angel who'd seen too much. Just the sight made my heart flutter.

"*What* are you?" His voice was gravelly and deep, intrigued.

Wish I knew. "Nothing special. Just a seeker like I told you."

"That's hardly all. You're different."

He'd tried using that as a threat earlier, but it was clear that deep down, he liked that I was different. But if he learned what I really was, that I was a FireSoul and had some strange power related to death that even I didn't understand—he wouldn't like that. I'd be budging into his territory, and no supernatural appreciated that. Not to mention that my power was one hundred percent against the law, and this guy seemed to like the law.

My mind scrambled for something to distract him. "Uh, what's your real name?"

"Roarke."

Sexy. "That's a weird one."

He grinned.

"What's your last name?" I asked.

"Fallon."

Roarke Fallon. I liked that. My gaze skated over his handsome face. I couldn't help but like it.

Oh, I needed to get my head in the game. There was too much at stake here, and this guy was too much of a distraction. I was about to push him away when a thin leather cord around his neck caught my eye. Whatever was attached to it hung down beneath his shirt.

"What's that?" I reached up and snagged it, pulling the familiar cord out from beneath the fabric.

He let me. I had a feeling that if he hadn't wanted me in his space, he'd have stopped me. It was rare that I met a supernatural as strong as me. Stronger, even, which was unsettling.

"My comms charm!" I cried.

"I thought it might be yours. I found it in the garden." He reached up and fiddled with the cord at the back of his neck, then pulled the whole thing away and handed it to me. "Here. A gesture of goodwill."

I eyed him suspiciously as I took it, confusion ricocheting through me.

"How about my sword?" I glanced down at the blade.

"Not yet."

I frowned, but couldn't help but like his gesture of goodwill. "Hmmm. Well, I've got to go get a read on your demon. So if you'll excuse me…." I arched a brow.

He stepped back.

I turned and opened the door, then let him inside.

My skin prickled uncomfortably. Having a stranger in my house was *weird*. And dangerous.

Though I rented the whole floor, only a tiny front portion was my apartment. The rest was my trove, hidden behind a wall cloaked with enchantments. Like all FireSouls, I had a place where I stashed my treasures. We just couldn't escape our dragon nature.

I couldn't let him anywhere near that space. Fortunately, it was hidden and protected. I had to keep reminding myself of that as I let him into my little apartment. It was done all in jewel tones. My clothes and hair might be black as an Ubilaz demon's soul, but my home was a technicolor paradise.

"You can sit on the couch." I pointed to the bright red couch. "I'll take a shower."

"I'll check the bathroom first. Just to make sure there are no windows for you to crawl out of."

"There aren't."

I stalked to the tiny bathroom and let him look in.

"See?" I gestured. "No windows."

He leaned in, then nodded. "Fine."

I sighed. "Now sit on the couch. Don't go in my bedroom."

He inclined his head, then moved to the couch.

I went into the bathroom and slammed the door, then slumped against it, leaning my head back against the wood.

Okay, I'd gotten myself into a mess with this one. No two ways about it. Not only was I in trouble with the Underworld and had only a week until I turned into a demon, but Roarke made my brain go foggy. A half demon.

Great.

So now I just had to find this Ubilaz demon, keep my secret, and convince the most powerful Supernatural I'd ever met to give me everything I wanted. All while trying not to drool on him.

Easy peasy.

What I wanted was a long shower, a mug of boxed wine, and a nap. But I wasn't going to get that.

Instead, I turned on the shower, then touched the golden comms charm and ignited its magic.

"Cass? Nix?" I whispered.

"Del!" Cass's voice cried.

"Shhh!"

"Everything all right?" Nix asked quietly, worry in her tone.

"Yep. Tall, dark, and deathly hasn't tried to drag me off yet. I'm in my place. But can we meet at Nix's in five minutes? Ask Aidan and maybe Dr. Garriso for any dirt they've got on the Warden. His real name is Roarke."

"Sure. Aidan just got back. I'll ask him and meet you there," Cass said.

"I'll call Dr. Garriso," Nix added.

Dr. Garriso was our friend, a historian who worked at the local Museum of Magical History. He knew just about everything, and I hoped he'd know about this.

"And can you bring me a sword, Cass?" Her trove was full of weapons. "Something that might fit in my scabbard. I don't know if the Warden will give mine back."

"Sure."

"Thanks, guys." My friends were the best.

"No problem. See you soon," Cass said.

"Will do." I broke the connection with the comms charm and yanked off my clothes, sadly tossing my old lucky shirt on the ground.

I glanced down at my chest to see if there was a scar from the sword wound that had killed me and grimaced at the sight.

About two inches long and raised, it wasn't exactly pretty.

Ah well, at least I was alive.

How? No idea. I'd figure that out after dealing with the demon.

I jumped in the shower, scrubbed myself off in record time, and hopped out three minutes later. I left the water running while I grabbed the robe off the back of the bathroom door and put it on, then called upon my Phantom magic, doing my best to keep my magical signature contained. This plan would only work if I was quick, and if Roarke thought I was still in the shower.

Once I'd completed my transition to Phantom, I climbed up on the tiny vanity that held the sink. The mirror reflected my bright blue glow, and I looked eerie as hell. With minimal effort, I reached up through the floor and pulled myself up into Nix's bathroom above. One of the great perks of being a Phantom half blood was the ability to walk through walls but still interact with the physical world on my terms, unlike ghosts, who just passed through things.

I let myself return to human form and hurried out into the living room to find Nix, Cass, and Aidan sitting in the living room. He was a massively tall, dark-haired Scot who also happened to be the most powerful Shifter in the world.

Though he was handsome, he wasn't my type. Maybe because he lacked the dark fallen angel air that Roarke possessed. And he was Cass's.

"Hi, guys," I said.

"That was quick," Nix said.

"Yeah. Not sure I got all the shampoo out of my hair, but whatever. I only have ten minutes, max."

Aidan stood to hug me, then pulled back. "Can't tell you how glad I am to see you alive and well."

"And we're going to keep it that way," Cass said.

"I've called my contact at the Order of the Magica," Aidan said. "I thought this guy sounded familiar, and I was right. He's called the Warden of the Underworld. *All* the Underworlds."

"That sounds bad."

"It is," Aidan said. "At least if you want something different than he does."

I frowned. "Like me."

"Exactly. He's the most powerful figure in the Underworld, but his position is kept quiet because he likes it that way. It's one of his rules."

"But the Order of the Magica doesn't follow anyone else's rules," I said.

"They follow his. They need him. He keeps the peace in a place that no one else has access to. He keeps Underworld problems from spilling over onto Earth."

"How?" A lot of underworlds made up what we collectively called the Underworld.

"I don't know. But he appeared on the scene about ten years ago after convincing all of the kings of the different hells to report to him."

"Holy shit," I breathed. How did one man accomplish that? He wasn't even thirty yet. Late twenties, max.

"The dead obey him," Aidan said. "As for how he convinced the kings of hell to do the same, I don't know. But because of it, he's now a liaison between the Order of the Magica and the Underworld."

"So he's government," Cass said.

Aidan nodded. "In a sense. He doesn't work for them, though they pay him a fee. But he's ruthless about law and order. It's the only way to keep the different Underworlds in control. If he discovers what you are, he will turn you in to the Order. It's in his nature. It's how he's maintained his power—constant adherence to his rules. He's notorious for it."

"Dr. Garriso said he even turned his own brother in for some infraction," Nix said.

"What?" My stomach dropped. I couldn't imagine such a thing. His own *brother*? I'd never do that to Nix or Cass.

"That's it. I don't like it." Cass gripped my hand. "You should run, and we'll do this on our own. It's not worth the risk. You're a FireSoul, and your power over death is too unknown. You're as different as they come."

"I can't run." The idea made me ill. "Then I'd never stop. I don't want a life away from you guys. And I need to figure out what I am. He might be able to help."

Cass looked at Aidan. "You can keep her hidden, Aidan. Your wealth could hide anyone. And we could see her."

He reached for her hand, the love in his eyes so clear it made my heart clench. "If I thought it would work, she could have all of it. But the Warden makes me look like a pauper. There's no resource he doesn't have."

My jaw slackened. Aidan was the richest guy I'd ever met. He owned a freaking plane, for magic's sake. A big one. The Warden was wealthier than him? And powerful enough to cow the kings of hell?

I couldn't hide from a guy like that. Not that it was the right thing to do with this demon on the loose, anyway.

"He's going to go after the Ubilaz demon," Nix said. "What if he catches it before we do? Then we won't get its blood. It's best if Del tracks that demon with the Warden, and we try on our own to find another one. We'll double our chances of getting what we need."

"And he's not outright evil," Aidan said. "Not according to my sources. He adheres strictly to the rules and has a strong sense of honor. Find the demon, make him beholden to you. After that, his honor will demand that he help you. It's the best way."

"But he's half demon," I said. "How could he have such a strong sense of honor? They're known for being untrustworthy."

"Maybe he's different," Nix said. "Remember— people judge us harshly because we're FireSouls. But we're not evil."

Shit, she was right. I hated stereotyping people. It was a jerky thing to do.

Still, unease tugged at me. He was part *demon*. Every other one that I'd met—that anyone had met—had been an evil killer. I tried to shove the thought aside.

"You can kill two birds with one stone this way," Nix said. "Cure yourself, and maybe get the Warden off your back."

Cass frowned. "Fine. I don't like it, but fine." She reached down on the other side of the couch and pulled out a short sword, then handed it over to me. "This was the closest to your sword. Think it will fit?"

I hefted the short steel blade. The weight was off and the balance weird, but it was a quality blade. Cass only collected the finest. "Yeah. It's great, thanks."

"It's not great because it's not yours." Understanding glinted in Cass's eyes. "But it's better than nothing."

"Exactly," I said.

Cass tugged the chunky, pale stone ring off her hand and handed it to me. "Here. Take my lightstone ring. I know you normally light up your sword with your Phantom glow to help you see in the dark, but you can't do that around the Warden. So you'll need this."

I took the ring from her, my heart swelling. It was one of Cass's favorite treasure-hunting tools and came in immensely handy. "Thanks. You're the best."

"Okay, you're good to go," Nix said, nodding sharply like she was convincing herself. "You've got weapons and a plan. You'll help him find the demon. Just like finding an artifact. A big, ugly artifact."

"An artifact with poison claws," Cass added.

"I'd rather look for an enchanted sword," I said.

Cass grinned. "Wouldn't we all."

But they were right. This would be business as usual, with a few extra bits and pieces to worry about.

"Go," Nix said. "We'll try to find another Ubilaz demon. If you need us, just call."

"Thanks, guys." I hurried to the bathroom, turning back just long enough to say, "Love you."

"Love you more," they said.

When I reached the bathroom, I called upon my Phantom form and dropped down through the ceiling, landing lightly on the floor.

When I saw that the bathroom was just as I'd left it, I grinned. It'd only been fifteen minutes total, but still… It was going to be hard to get things past Roarke.

I turned off the shower and stashed the sword next to the toilet, out of sight of the door. After a moment, I walked out of the bathroom.

Roarke glanced over from the couch, his eyes taking in the short robe I wore. Immediately, his gaze darted up to mine and stayed there.

Well, that was polite.

He stood. "Have you located the demon?"

"I'll get dressed and do it." I turned and hurried into the bedroom. He followed, peeking in long enough to see that there were a couple of windows on one wall.

"Hang on." Quick as a snake, he pulled a metal band off his right wrist and snapped it around my own.

"Hey!" I raised my wrist and studied the slender silver bracelet. "What is this?"

"Tracking charm. In case you decide to go out those windows."

I scowled. "You sure come prepared."

He shrugged. "It's my job."

I scowled and shut the bedroom door, then tried to tug the bracelet off.

It stuck solid.

Great.

Quickly, I went to my dresser, not even hesitating over jeans or leather. I definitely had a fight ahead of me, so leather it was.

I tugged on the pants, tank, and jacket. Though the pants and jacket were black leather, the tank was cotton because I wasn't a masochist. The leather itself was a special enchanted variety, made specifically to be flexible and comfortable. It was my fighting uniform.

I took a deep breath and called upon my dragon sense, using my deep desire to find the demon as fuel. I needed one of two things for my dragon sense to work. Desire or information.

I had both. I knew what the jerk looked like, what his magic smelled like, and I *really* wanted to find him.

Almost immediately, I felt the familiar tug around my middle, but it stayed indistinct. The demon was far away. No surprise, considering the fact that he'd had a transportation charm.

My dragon sense wasn't quite as strong as Cass's or Nix's. It used to make me feel really inadequate, but I've tried to get over it. Being jealous of my friends sucked. I didn't want to be that person. So I just reminded myself that I had other talents. It worked.

Mostly.

Cass and Nix could find most things with just desire alone. I, however, usually needed a bit more info. That's where my books came in handy. By now, I was a heck of a fast reader.

I glanced toward the door to the living room. I just needed a minute. Enough time to get into my trove and get a book. I wouldn't have to go far, so his tracking charm likely wouldn't pick up much.

And I really wanted one of my lucky pendants now that my shirt was trash.

I turned toward the empty wall in my bedroom. I loved my technicolor apartment, but it wasn't even the best part of my home. The trove behind the wall really made this place shine.

I sucked in a shivery breath of anticipation and called upon my Phantom power. Once I had transformed, I walked straight through the wall. Normally, I pressed my palms flat against the paint, igniting the magic in the secret door. But I didn't want to leave the door there for Roarke to find.

When I walked out of the wall into my trove, calm and joy suffused me. Spread out before me was the biggest library in Magic's Bend. Also the biggest collection of golden trinkets and lucky talismans that I'd collected from my travels around the world. My good luck charms could be anything from clothes to jewelry, but each meant something special.

FireSouls had one major weakness—like the dragons with whom we shared a soul, we coveted treasure. It was a compulsion, one that could be debilitating if it got out of hand. We could spend all our money and all our time on our trove if we weren't careful.

For each of us, treasure was a different thing.

For me, it was books, gold, and lucky talismans. The gold was an obvious choice—my dragon soul just couldn't help it. The shiny yellow stuff made my heart sing. I didn't care if I was a FireSoul cliché—I wanted to roll around in it like Scrooge McDuck. But the books and lucky talismans were my more unique treasures.

Nix, Cass, and I spent all of our extra income on our troves, which we kept hidden behind secret walls in our apartments. It meant we were all perpetually broke, no matter how much money the shop brought in. But we were cool with it.

My trove wasn't laid out like a library should be. I knew I should put my books and trinkets on nice neat shelves, but that never suited me. Cass's trove was organized to within an inch of its life. Not mine.

Instead, my treasure was piled up in towers all around me, a haphazard arrangement that was artful and lovely to my eyes. I knew where everything was, so why did I need shelves?

I hurried toward a pile of books about ten feet away, weaving around the other piles. The space was nearly four thousand square feet, so it was big. Fortunately, the book I needed was close to the door.

When I reached the pile of old tomes and treatises, I dropped to my knees and began sifting through the books. It took only a few seconds to find the one I sought.

"Bingo." I grabbed the massive leather-bound tome and returned to the exit, grabbing a golden feather necklace on the way. I'd gotten this talisman from a fae in New Mexico. It was both gold and lucky, so it was extra perfect. Just holding the thing made me feel better.

I listened at the wall, straining my ears to hear if Roarke had entered my bedroom. All was silent. I'd been gone less than a minute. It'd been a risky move, but necessary.

I knocked on my head for good luck, then stepped through the wall and shed my Phantom form. The room was empty, as I'd expected. Thank goodness.

Once I was human, I put the golden feather necklace over my head and left the bedroom. I stopped by the bathroom quickly to get my borrowed sword and the potions that Connor had given me. I strapped the scabbard over my back and put the tiny potion vials in my pocket. The weapons potions went in the left pocket; the ones that kept me human went in the right. Carefully, I zipped the pockets closed. I could *not* lose those potions.

Finished, I grabbed the heavy book and went out into the living room.

"What have you got there?" Roarke asked.

"My handy book of demon dealings. Information helps my seeker sense. And this"—I held up the book—"has information. You can tell me what you know about the Ubilaz demon, and the rest…I'll look it up in my book."

"Okay."

I sat on the couch with the book and looked at him expectantly. He was the Warden, after all. "You start."

"Ubilaz demons are considered Cat 5s because they attract other demons to them by their very nature, creating a demon army. Growing like a massive demon cloud."

Oh crap. "So they're demon catnip."

"Exactly. Lower level demons that have been illegally taken out of hells by mages on Earth to work as mercenaries often leave their posts and flock to the Ubilaz, compelled to join the strongest of their kind."

"Oh, that's bad. Humans will notice that."

"Not to mention the damage they could cause. Those mercenary demons need to be reined in by their masters. If they aren't, they do what demons do best. Kill."

Great. I'd released a mini apocalypse.

But something he said caught me. "Do what demons do best? *You're* a demon."

"And I work hard to be different." His gaze was deadly serious.

Hmmm. How hard did he have to work at it?

"See what your book has to say."

I nodded and flipped open the heavy cover, the scent of old paper and ink wafting toward me. I sucked in deeply and grinned, then started to sift through the pages.

My grin faded once I found the Ubilaz demon. He looked just like I remembered. Scary as hell.

I skimmed the text.

Bingo.

"They're ancient demons," I read. "Prone to congregating at the oldest sites in the Underworld because they like the old magic that hovers at those places. The Underworld version of archaeological sites, essentially."

"So he'll go to an Earth archaeological site? Or someplace ancient."

"Probably. If anything, the information will help my seeker sense get a lead on him."

I skimmed the text, reading a bit more about their grooming—negligible—and their powers—super strength, speed, and poison. I could confirm that.

Now that I was armed with more info, I might have an easier time finding the demon.

The image of the Ubilaz demon didn't fade as I closed my eyes. I used that, and the memory of the portal it'd escaped from, to try to get a feel for where it was. My dragon sense reached out, seeking.

I got ahold of it almost immediately this time. "It's in England. Cornwall. Probably the north coast, near Devon."

"Cornwall?"

"There's a lot of history there. And the demon had a transport charm, so getting there was no problem."

"We can take an Underpath. Once in Cornwall, we'll get a car and track down the demon."

"What the hell is an Underpath?" I asked.

"A series of portals and pathways that travel through the hells, connecting different places on Earth."

"I've never heard of that."

"Because only I can access them."

"Okay." That was crazy. "I have a friend who could pick us up when we arrive and take us wherever we need. Melly. She's a mercenary with a British firm. She'll know the lay of the land."

Roarke opened his mouth like he was going to refuse, but then closed it and nodded. "We'll exit the

Underpath in Plymouth. It's fairly close to Cornwall. If she can meet us at the Hanged Man Pub, that'd be ideal."

"Right, then. Shall we get started?" I asked. "We've got a demon to find."

CHAPTER FIVE

We left the apartment after I called Melly and told her where to meet us, heading out into the dark night to get to his car. As we crossed the street, I couldn't help but glance at Roarke out of the corner of my eye, noting how the yellow light from the street lamps glinted off his midnight hair. When his head tilted toward me, I snapped my gaze back toward the park on the other side of the road.

"Where exactly is the Underpath?" I asked.

"Everywhere. But I access them at graveyards or places where the dead reside. The older, the better."

"But *how* do you access them?"

"I tear through the ether."

Holy magic. That was an insane power. "That's possible?"

"For me. In Magic's Bend, I've created an entrance at a tea shop called Mad Mordecai's that was built over a graveyard. It's in the Historic District."

The Historic District had been the first part of town established back in 1712 when supernaturals had settled Magic's Bend, so that made sense. But it wasn't my part of town, so I wasn't familiar with the tea shop.

He gestured to a sleek sedan, and I climbed inside. I did my best to keep my stolen glances subtle. Not just because I was dumb enough to have the hots for him, but because I was trying to get a feel for the guy.

I shifted as I sat so that my borrowed sword strapped to my back fit comfortably against the seat behind me. The blade was short like my own, but it still felt weird.

"You don't carry a weapon?" I asked, glancing at my real sword, which he was setting on the back seat. He'd kept his hand on it the whole time I'd been with him, which had driven me nuts.

"Don't need one." He ran his fingertips over the hilt of my blade and I shivered. "Though your blade is very nice."

"Ah, thanks." I couldn't help but feel like he was talking about more than my sword here, but that was crazy.

Roarke started the car, which was one of those swanky electric ones that was entirely silent. When he pulled out into the street, it felt like a weird spaceship taking off.

"Do you only use swords?" he asked.

"Why do you care?" I asked.

"You're interesting. I'd like to know more about you."

That was bad. I wanted him to not give a damn about me and leave me alone. Though my ego wanted him to be intrigued, my sense of self-preservation wanted him to be positively bored to death.

"I wouldn't say that," I said. "Just your garden variety mercenary and treasure hunter."

"That's hardly a boring combination, even in our world."

My gaze darted around outside of the car, looking for a distraction. I pointed to the tall buildings on either side of the car. "So, this is the business district."

"Is this a tour?"

"Maybe."

"Trying to change the subject from the fact that I think you're intriguing?"

So maybe I hadn't been that smooth. "No. Just thought you might be interested."

I could feel the heat of his gaze on me as he drove. "Oh, I'm interested."

No question—he definitely wasn't talking about the buildings. Fortunately, we were now in the Historic District, our destination. The ornate, old buildings were distinct from the shiny glass office towers. Their bright paint was cheerful—perfect for the part of town that had most of the good restaurants and bars.

"Where is this place?" I asked.

"Up on the left." He pointed toward a blue shop with wide glass windows.

He pulled the car into a spot alongside the road and climbed out, grabbing my sword off the back seat.

"What are you going to do with that?" I asked.

"Lock it in the trunk."

My heart sank as I watched him lock my beloved blade in the trunk of his car. "Are you sure no one will steal it?"

"Who would steal from the Warden of the Underworld?" He patted the trunk of the car. "But don't worry, there's excellent security. No one will get in."

His confidence was a bit soothing, though I still wanted my blade back.

We waited for a few cars to pass, then hurried across the street. This part of town was busier because of the club scene, with supernaturals of all shapes and sizes scattered about. The ones who didn't look human were required to live in all-magic cities like Magic's Bend, which gave our town an interesting flair.

A pretty fae girl with pink wings and a smoking cigarette dangling from her fingertips smiled at Roarke and said, "Hey, handsome."

I scowled at her, then almost stumbled, horrified at myself. I was *jealous*? Ugh. I needed to get it together. Fast.

Roarke just nodded at her, then turned toward me and gestured to the tea shop next to the bar. The windows were brightly lit, despite the fact that the place was closed. Tiny tables covered with floral tablecloths cluttered the inside, and every chair was different. I'd bet big money that the proprietor wore a crazy hat.

"It's closed," I said.

"Not a problem." He pointed toward the edge of the building, where a narrow alley extended back into the darkness. "There's a side door."

I followed him, but pulled up short when I stepped inside the alley. "There's no door."

There was nothing but an expanse of brick. My heart thundered in my ears. Roarke could have hurt me long before this, but no girl had ever been led into an alley by a man and not gotten a little nervous.

He held out his hand.

I stared at him like he was crazy. "What?"

"You can't see the door. Take my hand."

I eyed him suspiciously, then did it, biting my lip at the warm strength of his palm. A shiver ran right up my arm as his grip closed over mine.

Focus!

His gaze turned serious. "Whatever you do, do *not* let go."

I swallowed hard, trying not to imagine what it would be like to be lost in an Underpath. "I won't."

He nodded, then tugged. I followed him toward the wall, my fingertips itching to draw my blade.

When he reached for the expanse of brick, a light glowed at his palm. I could feel the magic pulsing, forcing outward to tear through the ether.

A pale gray glow shined from the wall like a passage, and Roarke tugged me through. I followed, stepping over a threshold that sparked against my skin.

Darkness enveloped me and gravity disappeared. A second later, I hurtled through space like I was riding a runaway train. My heart jumped into my throat, and I clutched at my only connection to the familiar—Roarke's hand.

The strangest comfort flowed through me, and I took it, not caring where it was coming from.

A moment later, we slowed to a halt. A glowing doorway appeared, and Roarke dragged me through into a bustling old bar.

Disorientation slammed into me.

Strong hands gripped my shoulders and I blinked, clearing my vision. Roarke supported me, leaning down until his gaze was close to mine. Concern was clear in his eyes.

"Are you all right?" he asked.

I nodded, slightly woozy.

"Sorry, I should have warned you. I don't often take people through Underpaths."

"It's cool." I pulled back and glanced around.

Patrons were crowded around little tables in a windowless bar that looked like it'd last been decorated during Henry VIII's reign. The Hanged Man was in Plymouth, a bustling harbor town on southwest England's coast and the country's biggest supernatural city. None of the patrons—many of whom sported horns or wings—spared us a glance.

"Was this built on a graveyard, too?" I asked.

"No, it's haunted."

Where the dead reside. "You come through here often?" I gestured to the revelers. "These guys don't seem to think it's weird that you popped out of nowhere."

He looked up, his gaze meeting mine. "No. But the Underpath entrances are enchanted to obscure activity. They sense we're here, but an enchantment keeps them from really noticing us."

"Nice." I stepped back, shaking off the effects of Roarke and the Underpath. "Lead the way. Melly should be pulling up any minute."

Roarke nodded and turned, weaving through the crowd and walking up a short flight of steps to the main part of the bar. It was just as small and cramped as the bottom floor, but somehow looked even older.

A ghostly silver figure peeked out from behind a wooden beam that supported the ceiling. She was wearing an old-fashioned dress and a lacy cap. Her gaze met mine and she waved.

"Roarke." I tugged at the back of his shirt. "Do you see the woman over there? The silver one?"

He glanced over, his gaze searching. "There are no women over there."

Uh, yeah there were. But I didn't want to make this weirder. The girl smiled.

"Can you see ghosts?" Roarke asked.

"Must be my imagination."

Most supernaturals couldn't see ghosts. I never had before. But if this was another unexplained power involving death, I didn't want to share it with Roarke.

Roarke turned, his gaze sharp. "You sure?"

I nodded, probably too enthusiastically. "Yep. Just woozy from the Underpath."

He didn't look like he bought it, so I said, "Our ride is waiting."

He gave me one last suspicious look, then led the way out of the bar.

I followed him out onto a narrow cobbled street. The buildings rising on all sides were made of dark timber and white plaster, the kind of Tudor construction that I always associated with England. We were definitely in the old part of town.

I squinted against the bright sun that hovered overhead.

Roarke gestured to the left. "This way."

I followed him down the narrow street, onto a wider thoroughfare that had just enough room for one lane of cars. A bright green mini screeched to a halt in front of us, and a pretty, dark-haired woman rolled down the window.

"Del! And Mr. Death!" she said.

"Melly!" I hugged her through the window. "Good to see you."

"Wouldn't miss a chance to see you. Hop in."

I glanced at Roarke, who was about as big as Melly's tiny car. There was no way he'd fit in the back. "You can have the front."

"Thanks." He grinned wryly at me.

As I climbed into Melly's car, I had to move aside a pile of weapons to make a little space for myself.

"Just shove that stuff over," she said. She was a telepath, so she preferred a good pair of daggers when hunting down a demon.

The familiar scent of Melly's magic drifted to the backseat. The smell of lilacs and the taste of honey. Lovely, and as strong as I remembered, which was good. Hopefully it'd cover my own signature as I tried to locate the demon using my dragon sense.

Melly zipped into traffic, driving along a large bay filled with sailboats. We were on the left side of the road, which was disorienting, especially since Melly drove like a bat out of hell. Every time I thought she'd hit a light post or another car, she zipped nimbly around. I'd have bet she had killer aim with her daggers, too.

"You're still hell on wheels, Melly," I said.

"Only way to get around. Now where are we off to?" Melly asked.

"Give me a sec, and I'll let you know." Now that we were closer, I could get a better feel for the demon's location.

I closed my eyes and called on my dragon sense, careful to keep my magic contained. I'd practiced that a lot in my life, trying to hide what I was. Now that I was more used to Roarke—though honestly, I'd never be truly used to him—it was easier to do.

After a moment, the familiar sense tugged at my middle. Fortunately, it didn't seem as if the demon had moved since I'd last checked. "North. Near the coast."

"North it is," Melly said and put her foot on the gas.

"This is it," Melly said as she pulled the car to a stop on a quiet road. We'd been driving for hours, sometimes through moorland, sometimes on narrow roads surrounded by hedges. "Tintagel castle."

I peered out the window at the winding path that led up the craggy hill on the coast. "This is where King Arthur lived?"

"So they say," Melly said. "Though no one has been there in years. Haunted."

Excellent. Just what I'd been hoping for. "How so? Ghosts or what?"

"No one's seen any ghosts that I know of. But some ancient places protect themselves."

Wasn't that the truth.

"Thank you, Melly." Roarke climbed out of the car. "We'll call you if we need a lift."

I followed, turning back to Melly.

"Thanks." I waved and she sped off, her little car bumping down the narrow road back to the village.

"Why would the Ubilaz demon be here?"

I turned at the sound of Roarke's voice. The wind whipped at his dark hair and shirt while the setting sun illuminated his fallen-angel face.

I scowled at my stupid poetry. What was this guy doing to me?

"Honestly, I don't know," I said. "It's a weird place."

We were on a high cliff overlooking the sea. A path led upward toward the castle ruins, which I could just make out ahead.

"There's nothing here."

"Maybe that's the point." I reached up to touch the hilt of the sword that was strapped over my back, a habit when I was feeling uneasy. "Let's go. It's getting dark."

Roarke nodded and turned, starting up the path. I hurried to join him, keeping pace with him as we climbed. Every now and again, I'd catch a glimpse of the sea and the setting sun.

"This silence is eerie," I muttered.

Roarke grinned. "Good thing you broke it."

"I try to be helpful." I smiled up at him, then slammed straight into an invisible wall.

"Ouch!" I reached up and rubbed my nose, then peered forward. "There's nothing there."

Roarke reached out and pressed his hand flat against something. "Magical barrier."

I frowned. There'd be a way around, but it would take time to find. "I wonder if there's a way to break the enchantment."

"There is." Roarke's magic swelled, hitting my senses with the scent of sandalwood and the taste of wine. My head went a bit woozy, it was so strong.

He drew his fist back and slammed it into the invisible wall. Brilliant white lines, like cracks in glass, radiated out from his fist as the enchantment crumbled.

"Whoa." Tentatively, I reached my hand out. It passed right through where the barrier had been. "How'd you do that?"

He shrugged. "Same way I break through to the Underpath. I can disrupt the ether, which destroys this kind of protective barrier."

"So you can break through enchantments."

"Some enchantments. Mostly just protective spells that are placed upon the ether."

"Whatever the case, it's handy." I eyed him appreciatively. Not only was he all kinds of brute strength, but he could break through ether itself. Talk about a useful skill. "You ever need a job, you can come work for Ancient Magic. It'd sure be easy to get into protected tombs and temples with you around."

He grinned. "That's a kind offer, but I've got a job."

"Oh, yeah." I frowned. I hadn't forgotten, but the joking had been nice. "Boss of the Underworld."

"Something like that." He glanced up at the sky, which was now a dusky gray as the sun dipped below the horizon. "Let's get a move on. Night's falling."

I nodded and followed him up the path. Or at least what I thought was the path. It was overgrown with grass. "Apparently not many people get past that barrier."

"No. It was a strong one."

Like you. I kept my mouth closed for once, though.

We hadn't made it very far when the earth started to tremble beneath my feet. It was a subtle vibration, but enough to be worrisome.

"You feel that?" I asked.

"Yeah." Roarke's sharp gaze traveled the landscape. "We've triggered something."

Suddenly, the ground beneath my feet dipped away, surging like a wave. A tsunami of earth to my left rose up, a gaping maw of dirt and grass. I lunged to the side as it crashed down, but didn't make it far enough. The earth enveloped me, sucking me down into the dirt.

Instinctively, I shrieked, but my mouth filled with soil. I choked on the foul stuff, trying desperately to claw my way free. But the dirt was so heavy that I couldn't move my arms. Panic made my mind buzz and my chest feel hollow.

Buried alive.

How deep in the earth was I? With a frantic burst of strength, I tried one more time to claw my way free.

Nothing.

And I couldn't hear Roarke. Air was running out. Alone. I was alone.

But not helpless.

No way I was going to die again and go back to the Underworld. I called on my magic, envisioning turning blue and transparent. I needed my Phantom form now more than ever. There was no way to know if it could get me out of this, but I had to try.

Chilly magic tingled through my limbs as they grew weightless. I couldn't see, but I felt it when I'd fully adopted my other form. I directed myself upward through the dirt, passing effortlessly through it. When the crown of my head broke through the last layer of earth above and I felt cool air on my forehead, I forced myself to turn back to human so that Roarke wouldn't see me pop out of the dirt in the wrong form.

The panic returned immediately, but I shoved it aside and clawed my way free. I was close enough to the surface that the dirt wasn't too heavy, but I felt like a freaking zombie as I crawled out of the ground and sprawled on my back, gasping.

I glanced around, searching for Roarke, but saw only the quiet expanse of night. The ground even looked normal, as if the wave of earth had devoured us and returned to business as usual.

I scrambled up, calling, "Roarke!"

But he was nowhere to be seen. My heart thundered, and my skin chilled.

To my left, something burst from the earth in a massive explosion, shooting into the sky. Dirt flew everywhere. I stumbled to my knees, pushed by a massive wind. When I could finally look up, my jaw dropped.

A dark figure shot high into the air, propelled by huge wings. It looked human—mostly. In the moonlight, all I could make out was a dark gray form and dark wings that would shame an angel's.

Roarke?

"Whoa." I watched as he returned gracefully to the ground, getting a better look at his demon form. He was bigger than he had been—probably over seven feet tall—and his skin and wings were a dark, silvery gray.

He had no horns, but black claws tipped his fingers. His features had changed too, turning almost leonine, and his eyes were a pitch black with no whites. His shirt had disappeared, no doubt blasted away by his wings, but his pants had stayed on. His muscles were all harsh lines and obvious strength, like some kind of crazy Olympic swimmer.

Wow. Even in his demon form, he was hot.

"Uh, hi," I said.

He grinned, giving me a peek of bright white teeth, then a black mist swirled around him like a mini tornado. A moment later, he'd shifted back to his human form. His shirt had returned, as clothing did when a powerful Were shifted. But I could still see the demon in him, in his strength and dark eyes, even though the whites had returned.

He was one scary dude in his demon form. And pretty dang scary in this form too.

He stalked toward me, concern in his gaze. "Are you all right?"

"Yeah." I brushed dirt from my hair and shook out my shirt. "Clawed my way free."

His brow creased. "How? I had to shift to even move the dirt. No way you were strong enough."

"Um, don't underestimate me." *Also, don't ask too many questions.* "Speaking of shifting, are you what humans were thinking of when they came up with the legend of Lucifer?"

Because it fit. Fallen angel looks, massive wings, incredible power. Boss of the Underworld.

"Too young. And I'm not the devil."

No, he wasn't. If he'd been evil, I'd have felt it in his magic. Especially when he shifted. But I'd felt nothing except his usual magical signatures. And those were pretty nice, actually. Powerful, but nice.

"Do you know what kind of Were your non-demon parent was?" I asked. Because it had to be something crazy if he had wings. A demon/Were pairing was a weird one.

"No." He glanced around, clearly not wanting to discuss his parentage.

I couldn't blame him. I didn't know who my parents were either, and I wasn't usually keen to chat about that.

"We should get moving. I don't know what else is coming at us."

"Okay."

We headed up the path, silence cloaking us, but I couldn't help but glance at him occasionally. Weirdly, I felt a kinship with him. We both had strange, unknown parentage and had scary, death-related alternate forms. Demon-angel dude meets ghosty-Phantom girl.

The stuff dreams were made of.

The sun had fully set by the time we neared the broken walls of the castle. Fortunately, we hadn't run into any more enchantments.

"Melly said this place was built in the thirteenth century," I said. And it looked it, with tumbled-down walls made of massive blocks of stone. The shadows cast by the wall were eerie patches of blackness. But it was the magic that was oddest.

"Feel that?" I whispered.

"No."

I glanced at him. "Really? I feel some crazy strong magic."

It prickled against my skin like sand blowing on the wind. Ahead of us, the air shimmered, obscuring the walls.

I didn't want to go through the castle grounds. Something was off there, but we had to go. My dragon sense pulled toward the castle, which was built on a tiny strip of land that connected to a larger piece out in the sea. The castle crouched on the bridge of land, protecting the little island from intruders. Or it would have when it wasn't in ruins.

There was no going around, only through.

"Let's head in." I started toward the empty archway where there would have once been a massive wooden door.

The interior of the castle was as eerie as the outside, with shadows and tumbled-down stone everywhere. Moonlight gave it a creepy look.

Magic hummed against my skin, but so did something else. Something almost…alive. I rubbed my arms with my hands and considered drawing my sword just for the comfort of holding it.

My dragon sense directed me toward the right side of the castle where the sea crashed against the cliff wall. We'd been climbing steadily upward to reach the fortifications, and now that we were here, it was clear how well-built the castle had been.

"This is great land for defense." Wind whipped my hair back from my face.

"It was." Roarke gazed out at the sea, which was a dense black in the moonlight. Cliffs marched into the distance, rising steeply from the ocean.

He turned to me. His eyes widened. "Get away from there!"

The urgency in his voice made me jump. Instinct took over, propelling me toward him. I glanced back. A strange shimmering glow extended out from where I'd stood. It crept along the ground, turning it from grass into cobblestone.

"What the hell?"

The glow crept up the castle wall, faster and faster. As it traveled, the wall grew, rebuilding itself from ruins. No longer were the walls tumbled down and broken. Now they rose high, soaring into the dark night sky. The empty archway that had permitted us entrance was now covered by a massive wooden gate.

"The castle is coming alive," Roarke said. "You tripped an enchantment."

An oinking sound echoed in the dark night. A pig? I searched the courtyard until I caught sight of a pig sty against the castle wall. Four fat pigs all stared at me, their black eyes glinting in the moonlight. Their scent rolled across the courtyard, all too real.

But what hit me next was worse. Magical signatures of all varieties. Not just the castle's latent magic that I'd felt when we'd approached, but the signatures of many magical beings. Were they coming alive like the pigs had?

Unease shivered along my skin.

A shout sounded behind us and I whirled. A man had appeared. His back was turned to us, and he was yelling at a young boy who was carrying a basket. Torches flared to life all around, lighting up the castle courtyard. The air shimmered as more figures appeared.

"Hide!" I hissed and dove behind a pile of barrels near the wall.

Roarke followed, but not before shouts lit up the night.

I reached for one of Connor's potion bombs when I glanced up at the castle wall, just in time to see two bright green objects dropping from the sky. I dodged, but one of them hit me on the shoulder and exploded in a cloud of green dust.

My mind went foggy. I swayed on my feet, blinking rapidly. Through hazy vision, I saw Roarke collapse to the ground like a great oak tree. His hair was coated in a dusty green color.

Direct hit. He was out like a light.

I tried to brush the green potion dust off my shoulder and reach back for my sword, but the potion bomb had turned my mind to mud.

Shouts sounded from all around. Before I could reach my sword, a heavy arm clasped around my middle and threw me over a shoulder.

Oh, this *so* wasn't going my way.

CHAPTER SIX

This was too real.

Definitely not just an illusion—the castle had come alive.

Pain sang through my middle as I bounced along, thrown over someone's shoulder. I was being carried like this far too often lately.

I blinked, trying to clear my blurry vision and make out what was going on.

Everyone was dressed in old-style clothes. Like, really old style. But unlike the ghostly girl at the pub in Plymouth, these folks looked as real as me or Roarke. And they all smelled. *Bad.*

Where was Roarke?

I craned my neck, peering around, but the movement felt so slow and awkward, almost like I was underwater. Finally, I found him. Four men were carrying him, and still they struggled. Roarke was out cold, but he was a big guy.

Before I could formulate a plan, the man carrying me stopped abruptly next to a stone wall. A door creaked open, and suddenly I was flying. I slammed to the hard ground, knocking my head against stone.

The four men dragged Roarke inside. Before I could make it to my feet, a heavy wooden door closed, locking us in darkness. The air smelled stale, like this room wasn't used often.

"Roarke!" I hissed as I wobbled to my knees.

The potion had me woozy, but I staggered toward him. When I bumped into his solid body, I finally had the presence of mind to raise my hand and ignite the lightstone ring that I wore.

The golden glow illuminated Roarke's still face and the powdery potion in his hair. My heart thundered, and worry made my breath come short as I tried to brush the powder out of his dark locks.

"Wake up!" I shook his shoulder, still seeing double myself. This damned potion was strong.

Eventually, his eyes cracked open and he groaned, then sat upright. He loomed over me, and I reached up to pat his cheeks.

"Wake up, big guy."

He blinked, his gaze finally focusing on me. It sharpened almost immediately as he threw off the effects of the potion.

"Where are we?" he demanded.

"Locked up. No windows." I shined the light around the room, revealing a small square space with one door. There was nothing else in the room, but there was a strange sense of residual magic with a thousand different signatures that I couldn't identify. Like potions had once been stored here.

"So this wasn't just an illusion," Roarke said.

"Nope. The place came alive."

"That's a strong enchantment."

"Damned good hiding place for the demon. He's got his own security force and everything."

Roarke nodded and stood, then stalked the room, searching the walls and finally the door.

"We're stuck."

"Not for long." He turned to me. "Try to figure out where the demon is. We need to head in the right direction when we get out of here."

I nodded and sat down hard on my butt. I needed all the focus I could get since I was still a bit off from that potion bomb. Even standing wasn't super easy at this point. As I drew a deep breath, I focused on keeping my magical signature repressed while I called upon my dragon sense.

It thrummed inside of me as I envisioned the Ubilaz demon's ugly face, and I let my dragon sense roam. It tugged me from behind. And lower. Near sea level.

I opened my eyes and looked at Roarke, then pointed to the wall opposite the door. "He's on the other side of this wall. Low, near the sea, I think. Though I've no idea why my seeker sense led me here instead of there."

Roarke walked to the wall and pressed his palms to it. "This could be an exterior wall."

"That makes sense. When we first arrived, I wasn't sure the demon was even in the castle. But he could be on the other side. On that piece of protected land that jutted out into the sea."

"Or down at sea level, right?"

"Yeah."

"Okay. Give me a moment, and we'll be out of here."

"A castle this age, the walls are at least three feet thick and made of stone."

"Not a problem."

All right. I stepped back instinctually as black mist swirled around Roarke. When it faded, the dark demon stood with his back to me.

Up close, I could see that his wings were a million shades of gray and black, shimmering in the glow of my lightstone ring. Really pretty, actually.

He reached up and gripped the stones like one would grip elevator doors to pry them open. A second later, there was an explosion of rock as he tore his way through the stone wall.

"Whoa." I stared, wide-eyed, at the gaping hole in the wall.

In the distance, the black ocean roiled on the other side. He'd been right. This was an exterior wall built along the cliff.

I approached slowly and peered left and right. In both directions, the castle's outer wall was built up directly from the cliffside, which plunged into the sea below. When I peered down at the waves crashing into the rocks, I caught sight of notches in the stone wall. Like a narrow staircase.

My dragon sense pulled hard, indicating that the Ubilaz demon was at sea level.

The only way to access it was exactly the way that Roarke had—by blowing a hole in the castle wall. Maybe in present day, without the magic that had brought this place to life, this wall wasn't even here.

"Go." His voice was far deeper when he was in this form, like gravel scraping against gravel. "The noise may have alerted the guards."

"Okay." I climbed out the hole in the wall and stood at the precipice.

I knocked on my head, then made my way gingerly to the stairs that were carved into the cliffside. One wrong move and I'd be headed straight for the sea, going way too fast.

A door slammed, and I looked up, back into the room. Four figures streamed through the door.

"Go!" Roarke yelled. "I'll hold them off."

He grabbed one by the throat and threw him into the wall of the cell. Any hesitation I'd had about leaving him to fight four against one disappeared. He could handle himself, and someone needed to find this demon.

Anyway, Roarke could just fly out of there if he didn't like the situation.

The wind whipped my hair around my face as I scrambled down the stairs as carefully as I could. I strained my ears to hear sounds of the battle above, but got only the sound of crashing waves. Wherever possible, I gripped stones that jutted out from the cliff wall. Dirt wedged under my fingernails as I clung on.

By the time I made it to the narrow beach at the bottom, I was sweating. My boots splashed in the waves, and I hopped off the step. Roarke landed next to me, looking scary as usual, but completely calm. The moonlight glinted off his shimmering gray skin.

Scratch that thought about him being scary. He was, but he also looked pretty damn good. In a monstery way.

Apparently I was weird.

"Get them?" I asked.

"Yes. And I rebuilt the wall. They won't be able to follow for some time." Golden light swirled around him, and he shifted back to his normal form. "Lead the way."

I nodded, then followed the tug of my dragon sense along the beach. It was more of a narrow strip of pebbles than a beach. It wasn't long before we turned a small corner in the cliff face. Ahead of us was the gaping mouth of an enormous cave, and my dragon sense went wild.

"Of course," I muttered. "The demon is hiding out in the creepy cave."

"He'll know I'm after him. He'd want a good place to hide and a better place to defend. Be ready for him to have accumulated some demon followers."

"Not many, I hope."

"No, it hasn't been long. There shouldn't be many."

Magic spilled from the cave mouth, seething and riotous. There were many signatures, both good and bad. The smell of grass, sulfur, rock, wind, cookies, and perfume all competed.

"There's a lot of magic in there," Roarke said. "Merlin's Cave."

"Merlin?"

He nodded. "Arthur was supposedly conceived at Tintagel. I'd heard there was a cave here called Merlin's Cave. This must be it, considering the magic that surrounds the place."

"Yep. I don't like it."

He grinned, then started forward. I followed. As we neared, the prickle of magic grew stronger.

"Protection charm," I said.

When Roarke neared the mouth of the cave, he reached out, his face tightening as he did so. I'd bet being that close to the barrier was pretty uncomfortable.

"It's penetrable," he said. "Uncomfortable, but we can make it through."

"You can't break it?"

"It's strange. I don't think it will shatter like most charms."

"So it's meant to encourage you to stay out, not force you to."

"Yes."

"Okay, then." I gritted my teeth and started forward, pushing through the miserable feeling of the protection charm fighting me. Tiny knives stabbed me with every step, not leaving a mark but sure as heck feeling like they did.

As I entered the cave, the dim light of the moon faded almost entirely. I blinked as my vision adjusted and raised my lightstone ring.

It glowed, illuminating the huge space. The walls were uneven slabs of rock, with recessed, shadowed areas that made my muscles tighten. Wariness flooded me as Roarke stepped up beside me.

"I feel the demon," I said. "Sort of. He's near."

"Perhaps—"

Roarke's words were cut off as figures leapt from ledges and crevices of the walls—two, four, eight of them. More. Demons of all shapes and sizes

"Shit!" I drew my sword, fighting the urge to adopt my Phantom form.

Roarke's magic swelled beside me as he shifted. He grew larger and stronger, his wings flaring wide at his back.

"Retreat," he said. "I will handle them."

"No!"

He pushed me backward, trying to force me to leave. I stumbled and hit a solid wall. My skin prickled fiercely. Surprise flared and I glanced behind me, expecting to see solid stone.

I saw nothing but the rolling ocean waves crashing on the beach outside the cave.

Shit. The protective barrier didn't protect the cave from entry. It kept you inside.

My heart dropped to my feet. "It's a trap."

"Smart demon," Roarke muttered.

In front of him, demons surged forward. I counted more than a dozen. Some wielded magic as glowing light in their palms, and others were armed with wicked looking weapons.

All looked ready for a fight.

"Party time," I said.

Roarke turned and shot into the air, his wings carrying him toward the oncoming demons. He was massive and powerful as he grabbed two by their shirts and picked them up, then threw them into the walls of the cave as if they weighed nothing.

I charged, my sword at the ready. One of the demons hurled a fireball toward me. I ducked, lunging left as it hurtled past me. The heat seared my skin.

Damn. If I wasn't careful, I'd get flamed.

The fire demons had skin of a burnished red, and their eyes were pits of flame. I leapt toward one, dodging the fireball that he threw, and sliced out with my sword.

It severed the demon's neck, spraying me with blood. I gagged as the warm stuff hit my face and lunged toward another demon, severing its head. My borrowed blade felt awkward, but it was effective.

In the air, Roarke swooped and dodged, taking out demons left and right. I spotted another demon and raced for it, dodging the icicles that it threw. It was a pale, icy blue color, not unlike my Phantom form.

From the grin on its face, I could tell he was enjoying himself.

Freaking demons. I hated the things.

It danced backward, so I followed.

It drew back a massive arm, then hurled a spear of ice at me. I lunged to the side, but it threw another ice spear.

Damn, it was fast! I needed to shift into Phantom form, but Roarke would see.

I barely dodged the second icicle when the demon laughed and hurled a third. The projectile was nearly to me when a huge dark form swooped down and knocked it out of the air.

Roarke.

I surged to my feet and leapt toward the demon, swiping out with my sword. I cut through his waist, spraying blood, and he staggered, shock plain on his face. I lunged again, piercing his chest. I kicked him in the stomach to dislodge him from my blade and whirled at the sound of footsteps coming from behind me.

Two more demons charged, both armed with wicked serrated swords.

My favorite. I loved fighting sword to sword.

My mind cleared as they approached, the kind of eerie calm that was the product of years of practice. Whatever they were going to try, I'd seen it before.

"Careful!" Roarke yelled.

I laughed, and he growled in frustration.

The demons struck at the same time, one going low and the other high. The low one came sooner, so I leapt over his blade, then ducked under the blade that aimed for my neck. Their hisses filled my ears as I crouched and spun, sweeping out with my sword at shin level.

I sliced both their legs. As they staggered, I leapt up and finished the job with two well-placed slashes to their throats.

This time, I even managed to dodge some of the blood.

When I whirled to find more prey, I was feeling pretty good.

The sight of another dozen demons hopping off the walls of the cave wiped that feeling away real quick.

Behind the horde surging toward me stood the Ubilaz demon, bigger and meaner looking than any of his minions.

The magic that swelled from him smelled like a garbage fire and made my stomach heave.

I swallowed bile and raced toward the oncoming wall of demons. In the air, Roarke destroyed a demon with his bare hands, then whirled and dove for the demons who charged me.

I'd nearly reached the closest demon when an unholy shriek sounded from behind me. It tugged at my memory, but before I could turn to see what had emitted the noise, something swept me up into the air.

The world turned a shimmery blue as I was lifted, spinning high into the cavern.

Panic closed my throat. What was happening? I could barely see. I was flying. I was lost.

I thrashed, trying to break the hold of whatever had caught me.

The sound of an unholy roar ripped through the cavern.

Roarke.

I screamed, trying to break free of the blue cloud that had enveloped me. But it was spinning faster and faster. I caught a glimpse of what looked like shimmery blue scales. Almost like dragon scales.

Magic trapped me. Magic that almost looked like a dragon, with fangs and brilliant blue eyes.

At the corner of my vision, I could barely see my arms, which began to slowly turn a transparent blue. Something tugged at my soul, a familiar sense.

No! I was being transported. While turning into a Phantom.

My heart thundered as I struggled, watching my arms fade even more. The tugging sensation grew as I spun and spun, like the magic was trying to pull me somewhere.

A powerful force sucked me into the ether and hurtled me through space. I crashed to the cold, wet ground a moment later. My head spun.

The blue light was gone. Darkness all around. Whatever force had thrown me here had disappeared as quickly as it'd come.

Where was I? I struggled to clear my mind, but it continued to whirl. My vision blackened entirely as I lay flat on my back, unable to banish the image of the blue force that had stolen me from the cave.

It'd been familiar. Strange, but familiar.

Memories dragged at me. I fought them, but a vision clouded my mind, sending me back in time to three months ago.

My *deirfiúr* and I were on an abandoned island off the coast of Scotland, fighting our way through a village to reach a huge manor house on the other side of town. The village was abandoned, full of creepy old houses that looked like the inhabitants had just walked out one day, leaving all their possessions behind. Magic seethed in the air. Wild, dark, scary magic that sent shivers across my spine.

As we crept through the empty streets, ghostly forms drifted from the walls of the houses.

Phantoms.

I shivered. I'd never seen a Phantom before—only heard of them from Cass. They were horrible creatures who fed on the misery of others. Their touch made you live your greatest fears. It was a terrible agony.

As they drifted out from the houses, the scene around us took on a haunted air. The sun had just dipped below the horizon so that the only light on the street came from the Phantoms' ghostly blue glow. They crowded around us, dozens of them converging on the street.

"Hurry!" Cass yelled.

We needed to get past them.

But they barricaded the street, blocking our way. My heart thundered in my ears, my skin going chilly as we became prey. When one of them grabbed Nix, she shrieked in pain.

A Phantom dressed like a farmer swayed toward me. I swiped out with my blade, but it passed right through him. I tried again.

Nothing.

No!

We couldn't fight them. Our weapons did nothing to their ghostly forms.

"We have to run through them!" Cass said.

"We can't." Aidan's face was etched with pain. "It'll tear us apart."

The Phantoms surrounded us like a horde of zombies, their faces ravenous for misery and their claws outstretched. My *deirfiúr*'s faces were twisted with the agony of being near them, but I felt nothing. Why?

"Turn into a griffin!" Cass shouted.

"Can't." Aidan's voice was tight with pain. "The Phantoms stop me."

One reached out, snagging my shirt and pulling me into the crowd. Its arms wrapped around me, enveloping me fully.

It felt amazing.

Like coming home. Pleasure buzzed in my head, comfort and joy.

All around me, my friends cried out in fear and pain. But what were they complaining about? This felt great.

"No!" Cass screamed, lunging toward me.

My friends hacked at the Phantoms with their weapons, trying to free me from their grasp. Cass's gaze was fixed on my chest, horrified.

I glanced down, my head woozy with pleasure. My chest was a transparent blue.

Shock snapped me out of my daze.

No! I didn't want to be a Phantom. That was impossible! Terrible.

But my body had turned a silvery blue, and my sword glowed like cobalt flame.

My friends attacked the Phantoms that surrounded me, but their blades did nothing. The Phantoms were impervious. And more were converging on Nix, Cass, and Aidan. One of them grabbed Cass, and she shrieked in pain. They grabbed Nix and Aidan as well. Tears poured down Nix's face.

These bastards wouldn't take them, too!

Rage took over, clearing my confusion. I raised my fiery blue sword and sliced off the arm of a Phantom who held me. It howled, then collapsed.

My blade worked against them now!

It was in Phantom form, like me, and it made all the difference.

I whirled on the Phantoms surrounding me, slicing and jabbing. New speed and strength rushed through me as I cut down the monsters who had turned me into one of them. The Phantoms shrieked and fell.

I lunged for the one holding Nix, severing its ghostly head. *Take that, you bastard.*

With the heat of rage coursing through my veins, I plunged my sword into the shoulder of the Phantom who clutched Aidan, then jabbed at the side of the one who held Cass. It was surreal to watch my transparent blue arm and cobalt blade hack down the Phantoms.

"Run!" I screamed.

"Not without you!" Cass yelled.

"I'm coming." I beheaded another Phantom. My friends were still human. I was the only one who could fight them. "Go!"

Indecision warred on Cass's face, but she nodded sharply, then turned and ran. Aidan and Nix followed.

Good.

This was my fight now. I spun through the crowd of Phantoms, faster and more graceful than I'd ever been before. My silvery blue hair whipped around my face as I cut down my enemies. Anger filled my chest every time one laid a hand on me. Because it felt good when they touched me.

I didn't want to be one of these monsters that fed on pain and misery. But they'd made me one of them.

I killed them all, filled with joy every time one of them fell.

When their ghostly blue forms littered the ground around me, some fading, some still intact, I turned to join my friends.

Cold dragged me back to the present. I blinked, staring up at the dark night sky. A chilly breeze whipped over the hill upon which I lay. There were no stars and just the faint glow of the moon behind some clouds.

Why had I just remembered the time I'd first turned into a Phantom? I'd never remembered it in such clarity before. When it had happened, I'd been so panicked that it had gone by in a blur.

But now I remembered. With a level of detail I never had before.

And it sickened me.

I'd *liked* being with the Phantoms. I'd been enraged that they'd changed me and afraid it was permanent, but I'd *liked* them. What kind of person liked such horrible beasts?

The memory of the ghostly blue force that had dragged me here flashed in my mind.

What had that been? It'd looked almost like a dragon, though it'd been made of wispy blue smoke. Not real, but made of magic.

And where had it taken me? Was it really gone?

My breath grew short and my skin chilled. The grass was wet beneath my hands as I struggled to my feet, and my burns ached. Damned fire-throwing demons.

I was in the middle of nowhere. But there was no ghostly blue force. A light rain fell, cold and damp on my face. I shivered, sheathing my sword and clutching my arms around myself.

Roarke was stuck back in Merlin's Cave. He could handle himself, which was a good thing, since I had no way to get back there. And I had no idea where I even was.

Still, worry for him dogged me. Which was annoying. It'd be a good thing for me if he got offed by some demons. Right?

Logically, yes. I wouldn't have the Warden of the Underworld on my tail.

But I really didn't like the idea of him getting killed.

Fortunately, it was unlikely. And standing here worrying wasn't going to do any good. I fiddled with the tracking bracelet on my wrist as I took in my surroundings, so desolate and dark.

Moonlight shined on the land that rolled gently into the distance in all directions. The ground cover was scrubby and hard to distinguish, but it was clear that there were few trees and no houses or roads. Here and there, massive piles of stone punctuated the horizon, crouching on top of hills like giant beasts.

They looked vaguely familiar. I had to be on a moor somewhere, and the rock-topped hills were tors. Possibly Dartmoor or Exmoor, both of which were close to Tintagel. Or I was all the way up in Yorkshire.

A wolf howled in the distance.

Right. Great. I was on Dartmoor, and that was the Hound of the Baskervilles. Even in my Phantom form, I didn't want to run into some giant hellbeast.

I reached up and rubbed the golden feather charm at my neck for good luck, then pressed my fingertips to my comms charm to ignite the magic.

"Nix? Cass?"

"Del!" Cass's voice came through clearly. It was so good to hear a familiar voice. I might throw myself at demons, but hanging out alone on a dark moor was creepy.

"Where are you?" Nix demanded.

"No idea. On a moor somewhere. I lost Roarke."

The wolf howled again.

"Dartmoor," Nix said. "That's got to be the Hound of the Baskervilles."

I laughed. "I made the same joke. But I don't think that hound is real."

"I don't know. Sherlock was pretty clued in, for a human," Nix said.

"Want us to use our dragon sense to find you? We can come get you." There was a pause on the other side of the line for just a moment. "I think you're still in southeast England."

"It's cool," I said. "I'm too far for you to determine my precise location, so give me an hour to see if I can find my way to civilization. I'd rather not sit around out here waiting for you. If I can't, I'll call."

"Fair enough," Nix said. "In that case, you need to head downhill. Find a river and follow it downstream. That will lead you off the moor."

"Then find a road sign and tell us where you are," Cass said. "We'll come get you."

"And hurry," Nix said. "Weather can turn foul real quick on a moor. You don't want to get caught in a storm."

She was right. I could take on my Phantom form and be protected from the worst of the elements, but it would still suck.

"Okay," I said. "I'm off. Wish me luck that I find the shortest river."

"You've got it under control," Cass said.

"Call us when you know where you are," Nix added.

"Thanks, guys."

The connection broke, and I was once again alone. If only I had a tour guide to get off this freaking moor. It was cold and wet, and the desolate beauty was hidden by the darkness. This was going to be one miserable hike.

I set off downhill, disoriented by the lack of stars and the moon that kept hiding behind the clouds.

The wolves' howling grew closer, sending goosebumps over my skin. There was more than one now.

But it was no big deal.

Two shadowy figures appeared on the next ridge. The wolves.

I stiffened as they headed toward me, ready to take on my Phantom form so that their fangs couldn't sink into me. But when they neared, I squinted.

Those weren't wolves.

They were dogs.

Two collies. A brown one and a black one. Their tongues lolled out of their mouths in what I assumed was a doggy smile.

Apparently I'd just been paranoid.

"Hi, guys," I said.

This was the second time in recent memory I'd had dogs show up when I was in a pickle. About a month ago, I'd met a hellhound named Pondflower. Now these two were here. Dogs liked me, it seemed. And I liked them back. Better than most humans, in fact.

They weren't as obviously magical as Pondflower had been. She'd smelled like brimstone. These two just smelled like wet fur and looked up at me happily. But there was something special in their eyes.

"Think you could lead me off the moor?" I asked.

They looked at each other, then turned and trotted down the hill. I shrugged and followed. Since they were headed downhill, I assumed they were leading me to safety. I'd been heading in this direction anyway.

"You guys are pretty nice," I said.

They distracted me from my injuries. With the adrenaline fading, I could feel the burns more. The dogs trotted at my side, slightly ahead of me, glancing back every now and again to make sure that I was keeping up.

When we reached the valley between two of the tors, the dogs stopped at the river that ran between. They bounded toward it and slurped up water.

The water glittered in the moonlight, which made it look inviting. I reached up to touch my cheeks and felt the stickiness of demon blood. While I bent down to wash it from my face, the brown collie waded right into the stream, wallowing happily. When I stood, he bounded out again and set off downstream.

I smiled and followed, grateful that they headed in the same direction I did. I really didn't want to leave them behind. Why were two collies on the moor in the middle of the night anyway?

About twenty minutes later, I caught sight of a glow in the distance. The dogs picked up the pace, and so did I, loping along in my wet boots. I prayed to magic that someone friendly lived in the house where the windows glowed brightly.

But when I neared, I saw that it was a pub.

Oh, thank fates.

A wooden sign blew in the breeze. I squinted and read the name *Royal William Arms*. Through the windows, I could make out the golden light of the lamps and the bar that was nearly empty save for a few hearty souls sitting near the crackling fire. They had the distinctive pale eyes of one of the nocturnal, supernatural species. Magic hummed around the place.

Jackpot. I'd stumbled on a pub owned by a supernatural. That'd make things even easier. Particularly since it was probably nearly morning. If this had been a human pub, it probably wouldn't even be open.

The dogs ran right up to the wooden door, nudging it open with their noses, and I followed.

"Harvey and Holly!" a voice boomed. "What have you found on the moor?"

I stepped into the warmth of the pub. My clothes were clinging wetly to my skin and my nose felt red as an apple, so the heat from the crackling fire felt amazing. The interior of the pub was all dark wood and heavy, antique furniture upholstered in faded red velvet. This place had probably been here for five hundred years.

A rotund barkeep draped in a white apron was grinning at the two dogs, who grinned right back, their tongues lolling. The man's friendly gaze met mine. His gaze was the same pale shade of gray—almost white—as that of the men sitting in front of the fire.

"I see our local fairy dogs found you?" he said.

"Fairy dogs?" I took a seat at the bar closest to the fire.

My injuries were now making themselves apparent, and standing was no longer an option. My shoulder ached from where I'd landed on the hard stone when those medieval jerks had tossed me into the cell, and my burns were stinging.

"Aye. They live in the village with a human couple. But they let themselves out at night to roam the moor. They've got a bit of magic in them and like to dance with the fairies on the tors at night. They go between that world and this world. Been around as long as anyone can remember. Immortal, probably."

"The humans know about this?" Humans knowing about magic was strictly against the rules.

"Not a clue, bless them. But Harvey and Holly seem to like them, so they stick close by. Except at night, when they go out and find stragglers such as yourself."

"Lucky me."

"You shouldn't be wandering at night."

"No kidding. Where am I, by the way?"

"Merrivale. West side of Dartmoor."

Dartmoor, with my two Baskerville hounds. I was living in a novel.

"Can I get you a pint?"

I nodded. Might as well, if I had to wait for Cass and Nix to show up. And it might dull the pain of the burns. I eyed the taps, noting a selection of real ales popular in the region. Good. None of that wimpy stuff Cass drank.

"Anything is fine."

While he poured me the pint, the dogs gave me one last look, then headed out into the night again.

"Thanks!" I called after them. I pushed aside my worry over Roarke and reached up to touch the comms charm at my neck. Time to get the heck out of here.

But before my fingertips made contact, the barkeep put the pint on the bar.

"Thanks." I dug into my pocket for my slim wallet. This place was old, but I'd bet they took a card.

"First one's on the house, if Holly and Harvey approved of you."

"Thanks extra, then." I grinned and took a sip. Warmer than American beer and a bit flatter, but lovely all the same. Though my fave was boxed wine, I was a beer snob at heart when I actually drank the stuff. The weirder and stronger, the better, and this fit the bill.

"Not a problem. Now you warm up. Do you need me to call you a lift?"

"I've got it, but thank you."

He nodded and turned. I reached up to touch my comms charm, but the door swung open.

I turned to see Holly and Harvey trot in, leading a tall, wet man.

Roarke.

He was okay. Tension flowed out of my shoulders.

Which annoyed me. I shouldn't like him.

I looked at the dogs instead of him. "I thought you were on my side, guys."

They grinned at me.

"You found another one, eh?" the barkeep said. "That's a record!"

The dogs gave a bark, then turned around to head out into the night, probably to dance with the fairies. I smiled after them, but it slipped from my face as I looked at Roarke.

He strode toward me, back in his human form with his hand pressed to his side and his gaze worried. He stopped in front of me and lifted his other hand to hover it near the burns on my face. He didn't quite touch, but the so-close sensation made my heart race.

"Are you all right?" he asked.

"Fine."

He lowered his hand. "Then what the hell was that? You disappeared."

"He giving you trouble, lass?" the barkeep asked.

"Yeah, but it's okay," I said. "We're pals."

The barkeep nodded, satisfied, and turned to answer a call from the back of the pub.

Roarke huffed a small laugh. "Pals?"

"What would you call us?" I asked.

"Not pals." His dark gaze met mine, and it definitely wasn't cruel. It was... *interested.*

"Uh." My mind scrambled, then righted itself. "What happened back there? Did you see what carried me away?"

He frowned. "It was a strange blue cloud. Wispy. There was a pattern to it, almost like scales."

"But did it have a shape?"

"Not that I could see. Though it was hard to get a good look during the battle."

So he hadn't thought it looked like a dragon. Which made sense, because no one had seen a dragon in centuries. Cass had four dragonets who occasionally helped her, but they were the size of cats and made of magic, not flesh and blood. Entirely different.

"Whatever it was, it was weird," I said.

"Part of the protection spell on the cavern, maybe?"

I shrugged, though I didn't believe it. That cloud had felt familiar. And if that wasn't a weird sentence, I didn't know what was.

"What happened with the demons?" I asked.

"Killed most of them before the Ubilaz demon escaped. He had a transportation charm."

Damn. "It'll take him time to collect another army, right? He only had a couple dozen."

"Yeah. We're good to recover for the night, then start tomorrow. He'll have more on his side, but we should be able to handle it."

"Not like we could handle him now, anyway." My whole body ached. Roarke looked pretty beat up too. I rubbed the tracking bracelet on my wrist. "Then you tracked me here?"

He nodded. "To Dartmoor. Then the dogs met me."

"How'd you get to Dartmoor so quickly? Was there an entrance to the Underpath at Tintagel?"

"No. But I made one."

Wow.

I was about to ask how when the barkeep approached. "What will you have?"

"Whatever she's having." Roarke took the stool next to me, grimacing as he sat.

We were going to need a bit of recovery time before we picked up the hunt again. He accepted the beer from the barkeep, but his movements were a bit stiff. Again, the barkeep turned down payment.

"You okay?" I asked.

"Just a flesh wound."

"Okay, Monty Python."

"It'll heal quickly. I just need to sit a moment."

"Advanced healing?"

"A bit."

"Nice." Some supernaturals had the gift. I wished I did. But Roarke's powers seemed to hang out in the realm of super strength and physical superiority, so it made sense that he had it.

"So, exactly how many did you off?" I asked.

He shrugged. "Maybe a couple dozen."

"All in a day's work."

"Exactly. Though I'm concerned. He accumulated a larger following than I would have expected."

"He's strong. And smart. He trapped us there."

"Yeah. He knew I'd come for him."

"Smart, powerful, and popular," I said. "Among demon-kind, at least. Dangerous combo."

"Yeah." He drank half his beer in one long gulp. "They call them Cat 5s for a reason."

I flinched, guilt streaking through me. I'd let that demon escape. Using powers I didn't understand. I didn't love that the Order was so suspicious of unknown magic, but they had a good reason. I hadn't even intended to cause problems with mine, but look where it'd gotten us.

Roarke finished his beer and stood. "All right. Let's get out of here."

"How?" I polished off the last few sips of my own ale and hopped off the barstool, wincing when I hit the ground.

"I'll create an Underpath entry." He glanced around, his hand still pressed to his side. "I find I'm keen to return home."

"Nuh-uh," I said. "No way I'm going back to the Underworld with you."

"My home isn't in the Underworld. I live outside Magic's Bend. On the river."

A memory tugged at my mind. "Wait, you mean the house near the portal in the woods?"

"Yes. I commute to the Underworld for work."

That was way less creepy than I'd thought. "I still don't want to go there. I don't know you. I'm not going to a strange dude's house. I'm going home. Tomorrow, once we've recovered, we'll start the search again."

Understanding lit his gaze, and he nodded sharply and turned for the door. I followed him out into the dark night, both of us limping slightly. He walked to the edge of the building.

Tombstones stuck up out of the uneven ground within a small, fenced area. A graveyard.

"Is there an Underpath entrance here?" I asked.

"Not yet." He held out his hand, and I took it, trying to ignore the shiver that ran up my arm.

The wind whipped across the moor, blowing my hair away from my face. This time, when Roarke held out his hand to create the passage, the magic that surged from him almost made me stumble. It was stronger than before, probably because there hadn't already been a portal here.

He reared his arm back, then punched the air. His fist stopped dead, like it was hitting a wall, and a burst of light exploded as he ripped into the ether. The air glowed with light, and Roarke tugged me forward. I stepped in behind him, immediately caught by the rushing train feeling of the Underpath. Gravity disappeared and my head spun as we were sucked through space. I squeezed Roarke's hand. He squeezed back.

Seconds or hours later—I couldn't tell—Roarke tugged me out onto a dark city street. I blinked until my vision cleared, leaning on Roarke's arm.

"That went better," I said, though I was still a bit queasy. At least we were back in Magic's Bend in the gross alley near Mad Mordecai's. "Thanks for bringing me here."

"No problem."

We left the alley and exited onto the bustling street. It was night here, too. We needed to stop hopping from continent to continent and avoiding daylight.

On the way to the car, Roarke moved more slowly, his limp more pronounced.

"Are you okay?"

"Fine." His voice was gruff.

Hmmm. Doubtful. He'd expended a lot of magical energy creating the Underpath entrance—I'd felt it. If I had to bet, he'd weakened himself temporarily.

All supernaturals, except for my *deirfiúr* Cass, had a limited amount of magical power. Some had more than others, and I'd bet Roarke had a lot, but once it was used up, even he would likely have to wait a while for it to regenerate. The waiting time was different for everyone depending on their strength. That must be why he went through Mad Mordecai's—to preserve his power for whatever battle waited on the other end of the Underpath.

By the time we made it to the car, I was dragging too. This had been a *long* day.

It didn't take long to drive back to Factory Row, and we made it in silence.

When I climbed out of the car, Roarke grabbed a small duffle bag from the back and followed.

"You're just walking me to my door, right?" Like this had been some weird, violent date?

"Something like that."

Hmmm. I reached the green door, withdrew the key from my pocket, then let myself in. I turned to say goodbye to Roarke, but he stepped through the door, crowding me.

"Um, goodbye," I said.

"No."

"I'll see you tomorrow."

"I'm staying. No way I'm letting you out of my sight."

"I promised to help you tomorrow. You're not coming up."

"We aren't partners, Del." His voice was firm. "You're still a fugitive. I've put that on hold so that we can catch the Ubilaz demon, but once we have, you're coming back to the Underworld with me. I've never let a fugitive escape, and I'm not about to start now."

My heart thundered. "I don't belong there."

"Then how did you end up there? There's only one way to get to the Underworld, and that's death."

My brain stutter-stepped. I didn't have an answer that would convince him to let me stay free, so I said, "Fine. But you're sleeping on the couch."

He nodded, satisfied for now. But as I climbed the stairs, my skin chilled. I'd started to like him. To think that maybe he liked me, too, and that he wouldn't make me go back to the Underworld.

Apparently I'd been wrong.

CHAPTER SEVEN

I let myself into my apartment, then held open the door to Roarke. I couldn't help but scowl as he entered. He just grinned.

"You're a pain in the ass." I wearily dragged a hand through my hair.

He grinned wider, then winced when his side nudged the doorknob.

"How's the wound in your side?" I asked.

"Delightful. But really, I'll be fine."

"Suit yourself. I'm going to take a shower." I nodded toward the kitchen. "Food's in there. Help yourself. Don't go in the bedroom."

He nodded, then headed toward the kitchen, looking far too big in my tiny apartment. I watched him disappear into the small space, then turned and headed toward the bathroom. On my way there, I pulled the bedroom door shut. He wouldn't be able to find my trove because there was no visible door, but no reason to invite his curiosity.

I flinched at the sight of myself in the mirror. Burns on my neck and the side of my face stood out starkly against my pale skin. Fortunately, they looked to be just first degree. They'd fade soon enough. The rest of me was filthy. Dirt in my hair and all over my clothes. Demon blood speckled over my shirt and jacket and a bit on my neck.

Ew.

At least my face was mostly clean. And it really had been a good thing that pub in Dartmoor had been run by supernaturals. Walking into a human pub like this wouldn't have gone well for me.

As I turned toward the shower, I caught sight of a weird lump on my head right under my hair. I reached up and poked it, then almost yelped.

A horn.

I was starting to grow horns. And my face wasn't just pale from exhaustion. It was turning slightly gray.

My stomach dropped to the floor and a cold sweat broke out over my skin. *No, no, no, no, no.*

My heart started to thud, pounding in my ears like drums. With a shaking hand, I dug into my pocket for one of the vials of potion that Connor had given me. The one I pulled out was dark green, but I squinted at the tiny, handwritten label to make sure.

Temp. Ubilaz Antidote.

Bottoms up.

I knocked on my head, avoiding my horns, and drank the foul-tasting stuff. *Please work, please work, please work.*

I stared hard at myself in the mirror, almost collapsing with relief when the bumps on my head receded. I poked them, grateful to find only my normal scalp. My skin even looked a tiny bit pink.

Oh, thank fates. A reprieve.

My muscles were shaky as I turned on the water to the shower. I made quick work of cleaning up, because frankly, it felt like hell. Hot water was too warm on my burns, and cold just felt miserable on the rest of me. By the time I made it out of the shower, I was aching and starving.

With the towel wrapped around me, I darted from the bathroom to the bedroom and changed into PJs decorated with penguins, then made my way to the kitchen.

The sight inside made my jaw drop.

Roarke stood in front of the stove, a spatula in his hand, looking as domestic as June Cleaver.

He turned to look at me. "Nice pants."

I glanced down at the dancing penguins. "I'm not all black leather." In fact, I had a serious fondness for cartoon pajamas. "What are you doing?"

He turned. "Making dinner."

"I just figured you'd pop a frozen pizza in the oven or something."

He shrugged. "You looked pretty beat. I thought you could use a decent meal."

He was making me dinner? While wounded?

Huh.

That was really nice of him. But the guy was gonna give me whiplash. One second, it was all *I'm going to drag you back to hell*, and the next it was like *Here's a nice, home-cooked meal.*

He was strong, deadly, mostly silent, and… *domestic*? He'd make sure I followed the rules of the Underworld, but he'd take care of me while doing it.

"Thanks," I said. "What is it?"

"Stir-fry."

"Like, with vegetables? Where'd you find those?" I was a beige vegetarian, sticking primarily to the easier, less healthy veggie options like cheese pizza and pasta.

"Back of the freezer. A mixed bag."

Huh. Who knew? Not my usual thing, but I'd been on a few failed health kicks over the last few years.

I sniffed, getting a hint of soy sauce and garlic. I hadn't expected that whatever he scavenged from my kitchen could smell so good.

"So, you're kind of a good cook?" I asked.

"Not bad. I needed a hobby. Life can't be all managing the Underworld." He picked up a sweating brown beer bottle that had been sitting near the stove and took a sip.

Just the sight made me thirsty, so I grabbed a chipped coffee mug and headed to the fridge. I kept the beer on hand for when I visited Cass at her place, but I always had boxed red wine on hand. Cheap and tasty.

As I was filling my coffee mug from the box in the fridge, Roarke spoke. "I just want you to know, however this works out, I'm not sending you back to hell."

I stood and glanced at him, surprised. "You're not?"

"Not to hell." His gaze met mine, unwavering. "But you do have to go back to the Underworld. You shouldn't be in hell, though. You're obviously not a bad person. There will be a decent place in one of the heavens for you." He scrubbed a hand through his hair, looking weary. "But I didn't want you to worry about ending up in a shitty place like hell."

So he was worried about me? But not enough to spare me. "Uh, that's not exactly what I'm looking for. I belong on Earth. With my friends."

His gaze turned dark, almost tormented. "There are rules, Del. Good rules for good reasons. Following them keeps the Underworlds in line. I can't make exceptions."

There was something on his face, both sad and terrible. "Did you once? Make an exception for someone you shouldn't have?"

His face closed off, but I had him. I totally did. Roarke, the consummate rule follower, had once broken the rules for someone.

And been hurt because of it. Or hurt someone. Had it been the brother that Aidan had mentioned?

Whoever it had been, it seemed that now he wasn't going to break the rules for anyone else. From the pain on his face, I'd guess he was bound by the rules as strictly as I was bound by my secrecy.

My stomach growled, but I ignored it and studied him as he did something chef-like with the veggies in the skillet. Roarke was stiff as a board, and not from his injury. He clearly didn't like where this conversation had gone.

So I'd save my questions for later. I could be patient if it suited my end-goal. Though it made me twitchy.

But something had really been bothering me about where I'd ended up in the Underworld.

"Why did I end up in hell, if I'm not a bad person?" I asked.

"It wasn't really hell. It was an abandoned part of the Underworld that's been used to temporarily hold souls who don't go straight to a specific Underworld. Some souls automatically go to an Underworld, particularly if they adhered to a religion on Earth."

"So, ancient Romans go to Elysium, and the Vikings went to Valhalla? Modern Christians go to heaven or hell? That kind of thing."

"Exactly. But if you didn't practice a certain religion, you might end up in a holding Underworld before you're sent to a permanent Underworld. That's where you'd end up. There's good parts to it as well."

I remembered flashes of the beautiful meadow that had appeared through the haze. And his garden at his Underworld fortress. Ugh. I didn't like this subject.

"How's the food coming?" I asked. "I'm famished."

Roarke turned back to the stove and poked the contents of the skillet with the spatula. "Looks about done."

"It smells great."

He smiled, and my stupid heart beat faster. When he turned back and started dishing up the food, I pinched myself.

Get it together. This guy was dangerous. No liking his food. No getting swoony over his smile *or* his muscles. *Definitely* no falling for him.

When he turned to me and handed me a bowl, I tried to smile like a normal person. I think it came out pretty weird, but my voice sounded mostly normal at least. "Thanks."

"No problem. Hope it's decent."

"I have a feeling it will be."

The smell made my mouth water. I went to the tiny table pushed into the corner of the kitchen nook. Roarke sat across from me, his legs bumping mine. I ignored the awareness that prickled along my skin. But there was no way to ignore him. He was way too big for my place.

I tucked into the food, shoving a giant bite of broccoli and carrots into my mouth.

"This is great," I mumbled around the mouthful.

"Glad you like it."

"Love it." I spent the next several minutes scarfing down the food. When I finished, I took a sip of beer and met his gaze. It dropped to my bowl and then back up to me.

"Impressed?" I asked.

"Very."

"I'm even faster with ice cream."

"I'd like to see that."

"Um." Did he mean, like, we go on a date and get ice cream? Because that was real date material. Nah, I was probably reaching. "So, how did you end up as Warden of the Underworld? And I hear you're rich as Croesus?"

Nicely done. Distract him with rudeness. I might not remember my past, but I would bet big money it hadn't involved any kind of finishing school.

"Worked my way up, like any job."

I laughed. "It's not exactly any job. You're like the boss of millions of people."

"Dead people. And demons." He ate a bit of stir-fry, much more elegantly than I had. "At this point, it doesn't involve much work. I laid the groundwork with intimidation, and now everyone pretty much follows the rules."

"You love rules."

"I do. Keeps things running smoothly. Most people like rules, or at least, the calm that they provide. Except for Rogue demons like the Ubilaz and his fire-throwing friends. That's one loophole I'm working on closing."

I leaned back in my chair. "Hang on—let me get this straight. The only folks in the Underworld who don't follow your rules are the Rogues? Even the Kings of Hell do what you say?"

"Pretty much."

"How?"

He shrugged. "When I figured out what my powers were, I realized two things. One was that I could use them for good. Ten years ago, many of the Underworlds were at war. The hells primarily, which is no surprise."

"But you didn't like that."

"Not particularly." He looked around my apartment, but I had a feeling he was seeing more than the tiny space. "I like Earth. But I don't fit here. I also don't really fit in the Underworlds."

"Because you're half demon, half Were."

"Exactly. An anomaly. I needed to find a place for myself. Given my half-demon parentage and my ability to cross between the Underworlds and Earth, I realized there was a space for me there to do good."

Huh. Roarke was a good guy. Who would throw me back in the Underworld. Just like he'd turned his brother in. I wanted to ask about that, but it wasn't the time. "You said you realized two things. What was the other?"

"The Order of the Magica and the Alpha Council don't like anomalies. Not powerful ones, at least. We're wildcards who could wreak havoc or alert humans to our presence."

"I never thought you'd be at risk."

"Of course I was. No one has ever seen a Were-demon before. I've seen how the government treats the unknown."

Like FireSouls. They tossed us right into the Prison for Magical Miscreants. "So what'd you do?"

"I realized that if there was nowhere I fit, I had no choice but to make a place…try to straddle the bridge between the afterlife and this one. But I needed a position of power so strong that the Order of the Magica and the Alpha Council couldn't threaten me. They had to *need* me."

"So you stopped the wars in the Underworld."

"Pretty much. It took me a few years, but the result was worth it."

"Just peace for peace's sake?"

"That's a worthy goal. But no. What's valuable to the Order and the Council is that I keep the Kings of Hell in line. The hells aren't great places. There are revolts. People and demons try to escape and return to Earth through portals or magic."

"How can you keep a handle on that?"

"I don't have to keep an eye on everyone. Just the Kings of Hell. I stopped the wars by going to each king individually and scaring the shit out of them. My ability to access the Underpath meant that I could get straight into their inner chambers."

"Even though they might not be built on graveyards or haunted places."

"Yeah. It just takes more power."

Like I'd thought. He had been weakened by creating the new portal earlier tonight. "Then what?"

"It took me a few years to visit each king of each hell—there are a lot. And with some well-placed threats, they all agreed to stop their wars and keep a better eye on the dead and demons in their realms who were trying to get to Earth."

"Just like that?"

"I made it clear that I could tear through space, enter their bedroom, and rip their heads off any time I liked."

"Fair point. But I can't imagine the Order or Council like knowing that you can do that."

"No, and they don't know exactly *how* I keep the peace. Just that I do. And they pay me well for it."

I put down the mug of wine I'd been holding, suddenly dumbfounded. "So with all that on your plate, why did you come after me, specifically? I'm no big deal."

His gaze turned serious. "But you are, Del. You're a very big deal. I don't know why, but you are."

Of course I couldn't sleep.

Not after what Roarke had said. Or after the weirdness with the blue cloud thing that had swept me away.

I spent the night tossing and turning, only getting an hour of sleep here and there. By 6:00 a.m., I was going out of my mind. Roarke was out in my living room, sleeping on a too-short couch while my brain did the whole dog-chasing-its-tail routine.

I had answers about Roarke, but not very many. I had almost no answers about myself and even more questions than before. Why had the Phantoms turned me and no one else? Why had I *liked* it? And why had the blue cloud swept me away instead of Roarke?

When I'd turned into a Phantom for the first time a few months ago, I'd thought maybe it was just a cool new power. But it was more than that, and my magic was related to death in a way that I didn't understand. The seer who'd prophesied it had said almost nothing about it. And never directly to me. Only to Cass.

I needed answers.

Unable to take it anymore, I climbed out of bed and pulled on some clothes, then debated whether to write a note for Roarke or not. But what if he was a super light sleeper?

I didn't want him coming into my bedroom, so I settled on posting a sticky note on the outside of my bedroom door—*Gone for coffee at P & P.*

Hopefully he'd sleep another hour and find me at Potions & Pastilles with an espresso when he woke.

I grabbed a jacket and my borrowed sword, then searched the dresser for the keys to Scooter, my motorcycle. They peeked out from beneath a T-shirt that definitely had to go in the wash.

Jackpot.

I grabbed them, then realized my helmet was out in the living room. Dang. I couldn't go get it with Roarke out on the couch. I'd just have to be careful.

I climbed out the window and hopped down to the ground silently. It was still dark out as I raced through the alley between the buildings and out onto the main street.

It took me a moment to remember where I'd parked Scooter. Up past Potions & Pastilles, because it'd been the only spot available. As I hurried up the street, I reached up and pressed my fingertips to the charm at my neck.

"Cass?" I asked.

"What?" Cass's groggy voice sounded through the charm.

"I want to go see Aethelred to get some answers. Can you tell me where he lives?" Cass had been to see him a few times, but I only knew about him through her.

"In Darklane, three doors down from Aerdeca and Mordaca. Blue house."

"Thanks. And can you call Connor or Claire for me? Tell them to stall Roarke if he shows up looking for me?"

"Yeah. Good luck with Aethelred," Cass said. "Promise him some Cornish pasties if you have to. I've bribed him with those before. It works better than money."

I grinned, thinking of the savory treats that Connor made. "Will do."

I broke the connection with my comms charm when I reached Scooter, the Harley that I'd saved up for when we'd first moved to town. The thing was a beast, but I liked the name Scooter.

I climbed on, cranked the engine, then took off, navigating through the business district and the Historic District, both of which were still dead this time of night. The same couldn't be said of Darklane. Like its name, the dark hours of night were usually the busiest for this neighborhood.

Ramshackle buildings rose three stories tall on either side of the street as I turned onto the main thoroughfare in Darklane. Ornate gas lamps shed a golden glow. The buildings were as old and ornate as the brightly painted ones in the Historic District, but these were coated in a layer of grime that obscured the bright paint. I'd long been convinced that the layer of dirt and soot had been there since shortly after the buildings themselves had been built.

Darklane housed those supernaturals who worked with magic's darker side. The kind that harmed as well as helped. But it wasn't entirely bad. It was all up to interpretation.

While a lot of these supernaturals occasionally bent the law, they weren't total criminals. The Magica would crack down on that. They walked the line with things like blood magic—illegal if you did it without the consent of the donor, but otherwise acceptable. It was still danged creepy here, though.

I slowed the car as I passed the Apothecary's Jungle, our friends Aerdeca and Mordaca's shop. They were both sitting on the steps leading to their door. Aerdeca, blonde and dressed in a white silk robe, was drinking what looked to be a mug of coffee. Mordaca, dressed in a black evening gown with a midnight bouffant, was drinking a Manhattan. I waved, and they waved back. We weren't close, but they'd had our backs when my *deirfiúr* and I had needed them.

When I reached Aethelred's house, a skinny building that had once been blue, I pulled over and parked on the side of the road. I hurried up the narrow wooden steps and banged on the falcon door knocker.

"Who is it?" a cranky old voice called.

Shit. The sun hadn't even risen. I really should have brought coffee or something, because this was seriously rude.

"Um, it's Del Hally." But that wasn't even true, was it? I was Del Bellator, according to Roarke. Who I still had to grill for info about myself. After I convinced him to let me stay out of the Underworld. But that was a problem for another day. "I'm friends with Cass Clereaux. I have some questions."

"Don't they all," the voice muttered.

But the door creaked open, thank fates. On the other side stood an old man with a long white beard that he'd tucked into the pants of his blue velour tracksuit.

I smiled. "Hi."

"Harumph." He stared at me through shining spectacles. "So you're friends with Cass. And you have questions. Important ones, too, if you're coming before dawn."

"Yeah, important."

He scowled. "I don't work for free, missy."

I winced. He was a seer, so he probably knew I was broke. Sure, I had a trove full of treasure, but that didn't leave a lot in the old bank account to pay off seers.

"I could, ah, ask Connor to make you any kind of pasty you want. For a week."

"Hmmm…." He considered it as I writhed inside with guilt. Connor was not going to be happy. In fact, I'd probably be the one making the pasties just to make it up to him.

Oh man, maybe this had been a bad idea. Aethelred would *not* like my pasties, then he'd be pissed at me. He was the only seer I knew, and I didn't want to lose his help.

"All right," Aethelred said. "Pasties for a month."

My shoulders sagged in relief. I could deal with the pasty dilemma later.

"Great! Thanks."

He stepped back and let me into the dimly-lit foyer, then led me toward a living room crowded with shelves of books and trinkets. A tiny iron hearth crouched at the side of the room with its fire burning low.

Aethelred gestured to a couch as he took the old armchair near the fire. I sat, but just as I opened my mouth, he waved a hand, cutting me off.

"Give me a moment." He closed his eyes. "I'd like to see what I can get from you before you speak."

I snapped my mouth shut and waited. His magic swelled on the air as he accessed his power. I got a hint of allspice and whiskey before he spoke.

"You are part of the Triumvirate. Three women who represent life, death, and magic. The three legs upon which the world stands. You were prophesied to do great things."

"Me specifically?" I asked. A seer had once told Cass that we'd been prophesied to do something great, but *me* specifically?

I didn't really feel qualified.

"Yes. You."

"Not just the Triumvirate?" Triumvirate was Latin for three of power. I represented death, Nix life, and Cass magic. Together, we could accomplish a lot. On my own? Not so much.

"No. You have a role to play. Though I cannot see what, exactly. Not at this moment." His brow creased as he searched for more answers in the mist of his mind. Seers could not see all, but what they did see was true. "But your power is growing. I can feel that. And you must use it to fulfill your role in the prophecy."

"How? What does it even mean that I represent death?"

"That your powers come from the Underworld."

Great. That sounded fantastic.

"Is that why I turned into a Phantom when they touched me three months ago?"

He nodded. "They were a trigger. And there may be more triggers. More power, possibly. You must be ready."

Oh, that didn't sound ominous at all. "Is that why I can see ghosts?"

"Yes. And it won't be the last new power you develop."

"But Phantoms are evil. They feed on misery and despair."

"Do you?"

I shook my head. "I don't think so. But I don't want to be like that. They're awful creatures."

He shrugged. "You do have a dark past."

My heart raced. "Do you know anything about it? I learned that my true last name is Bellator."

He shook his head. "No, my dear. I do not know about that."

Dang. "The other day, a blue cloud that may have been shaped like a dragon swept me up and spit me out on Dartmoor."

Aethelred's brows rose, climbing all the way up to his hairline. "Dragons are dead."

"I know."

He frowned, then closed his eyes. His magic welled, but he continued to scowl. His eyes popped open. "I do not know. That is strange."

"Yeah. You're telling me."

"Your questions are finished?"

My shoulders slumped. I had some info, but not all that I had come for. "Yeah."

"Then a word of warning. Be wary. This is a dangerous gift. The Order of the Magica would not like you to wield it. There is too much unknown."

"I know."

"That is the best I can do for you, my dear."

"Thank you. It helps. And if you think of anything else… anything at all, I'd love to know."

"I will tell you. But be alert. Things are changing for you now. The way is unclear. It is up to you to determine your path."

CHAPTER EIGHT

When I stepped out onto the street, Roarke was pulling up in his fancy sports car.

Caught.

I'd pushed my luck.

He got out and glared at me, looking back to his usual self. No limp, thankfully. And a clean set of clothes, which I guessed he'd gotten from his car. Once again, he looked like a million bucks.

"What are you doing in Darklane?" he demanded.

"I had to see a friend."

"About what?"

"None of your business."

"This isn't a good part of town. And I don't remember us agreeing that you could wander off."

"I was coming right back."

"Sure." From the look on his face, he wouldn't be letting me out of his sight anytime soon.

"Seriously, I'm not going to ditch you. I know you can find me." I held up my wrist to show the tracking band he'd snapped on me.

"Exactly." From the determined set of his brow and the expression in his dark eyes, he looked like he'd cross heaven and earth to find me.

"Come on, let's go get a coffee and then find that demon."

"Where exactly are we getting coffee?"

"Wherever you want." I'd have liked to go to P & P, but I didn't want to press my luck after sneaking out.

Anyway, we needed to get a move on with finding the Ubilaz demon. I was almost out of Connor's potion, and once that was gone, I was going to turn into a demon real fast.

Though I should have been used to the Underpath by now, I wasn't. Roarke had driven us there in no time, zipping through traffic in his futuristic super-car, and the journey to the The Hanged Man in Plymouth had taken even less time. But the moment we stepped out of the Underpath, I was woozy.

My head swam as I followed Roarke out of the bar and onto the street. Midday sun shined brightly on the cobblestones and Tudor buildings, while the scent of fried fish wafted from the fish and chip place next door. A moment after we reached the main road, Melly's little green car zipped up to the curb.

"Hello!" she called through the open window.

"Hey, Melly." My head had cleared enough that I felt human again, and I climbed into the cramped back seat of her car.

"Where to this time?" she asked.

"Somerset," Roarke said. "Central part, right Del?"

I closed my eyes and cleared my mind, focusing on my dragon sense, careful to keep my signature repressed, then said, "Yeah. I'll know more once we're closer."

"Somerset it is!" Melly stepped on the gas. Hard.

It took us a couple hours to reach Somerset, during which time the demon's location changed slightly. Eventually, I pinpointed it to the city of Glastonbury.

"He's definitely moving," I said. "I can feel his location changing slightly."

"Slowly?" Roarke asked.

"Yeah. I think he's on foot. Or in traffic. We're close, though."

Melly had entered the bustling city streets of Glastonbury a few moments ago. We'd taken a few false turns, so by the time we entered the city, it was late. Whoever was still out on the sidewalks staggered as they headed from pub to pub. I directed Melly through the streets, following my sense of the demon.

Fortunately, Glastonbury was a supernatural city. Smaller than Plymouth, but still good-sized.

When we reached a stretch of parkland, I called out, "Stop! We're here."

Melly stomped on the brakes. After we screeched to a halt, she turned to look at me. "Here? It's a park."

I nodded and peered at the expanse of open grass and woodland, then climbed out of the car into the chill night air.

I turned to the car. "He's in the park somewhere."

"Good," Roarke climbed out of the car and leaned down to peer at Melly. "Thanks, Melly. We'll call you if we need a ride back."

"Not a problem!" She waved, then zipped off.

"Let's go." I set off across the grass.

Roarke followed and we made our way quickly across the park and through a small patch of woods. When we popped out on the other side, a massive ruined cathedral appeared in the moonlight.

I grinned. "Bingo."

"Makes sense considering they prefer ancient sites. But why this one? It's not well protected like the cave."

No, it wasn't. The cathedral was a shell of a building and sat in the middle of the immaculately tended parkland. Its broken stone walls and massive arches soared up into the night sky, leaving a hollow shell in the middle.

"Weird," I muttered as we moved forward. As we neared one of the doorless entrances, I caught sight of a small iron plaque.

Glastonbury Abbey, Est. 712

"That's familiar." I searched my brain for why, but came up empty. "You know anything about this place?"

Roarke shrugged. "No. I like the History Channel, but old churches aren't really my thing."

"Okay." I peered inside at the expanse of grass that looked like black carpet stretched between the broken walls of the cathedral.

Roarke stepped over the threshold and I followed, my skin prickling as I stepped inside. The ruins ran on forever, tumbled down stone walls creating a hundred hiding places. The abbey had once been huge. It was deathly quiet, just the sound of distant revelers on the other side of the park. Kids partying, no doubt.

Magic thrummed, though, rich and strong. There were a lot of different signatures here—too many. Scents, tastes, even sounds. The demon had grown his army in the short time we'd been recovering.

But there was even residual magic in the cathedral. Something ancient. It vibrated along my skin, familiar.

"Del!" Roarke's low voice was intense. "Move."

I jerked, then hopped away, glancing back at where I'd been standing. Horror opened a chasm inside my chest.

Where I'd been standing, a shimmering blue glow was stretching across the ground. Just like back at the castle. As it grew, flat stone slabs appeared on the ground in place of the grass. Some were inscribed with names and dates.

The cathedral floor.

The glow extended up the broken-down cathedral walls. When it reached the top, it kept going. So did the walls, growing into their old form. Stained glass filled the hollowed-out windows, glinting in the moonlight.

My head buzzed as I tilted it back, watching as the glow raced overhead, leaving behind a ceiling supported by ornately carved stone arches.

Candles burst to life in their sconces on the wall, lighting the place with a golden glow. A partial wall appeared between us and the massive central part of the church. We were behind the altar now. Maybe. My understanding of cathedral architecture was a bit lacking.

"What the hell is going on?" Roarke asked. "The same enchantment as the one at Tintagel?"

Magic shivered along my skin. My mind raced. "Yeah."

My magic roared inside me, like it was responding to the enchantment. It thrummed in my chest, vibrating like a massive engine ready to take off on a race to my destruction.

Was I doing this?

Roarke's skeptical gaze met mine. My heart pounded. "Maybe that's why the demon is here. He's attracted to ancient places with this type of enchantment."

It sounded slightly like bullshit. Maybe a lot like bullshit.

A shout sounded, distracting Roarke.

Thank magic.

Roarke whirled to locate the noise, and I did the same, drawing my sword from the sheath at my back. I nodded toward the pathways on either side of the obstruction in front of us.

We took the one to the right, creeping around. I looked up, satisfied to see that I was correct. We'd been behind the raised altar. Ahead of us, the cathedral stretched long and tall, a massive space dedicated to worship.

Two demons, both with burnished red skin like the other fire demons we'd seen, were standing in the main aisle, their heads craned toward the ceiling. Shocked, no doubt, by the sudden appearance of the abbey in its entirety.

A shout sounded from my left. "Oy! Come on, then!"

I glanced up at the altar. Two demons were shoving golden holy items into sacks. My dragon sense tugged toward the glittering gold, and my fingertips itched.

No. No matter how much my dragon soul coveted those golden treasures, they weren't mine. And they sure as hell didn't belong to those demons.

Beside me, Roarke's magic swelled on the air—the scent of sandalwood and the taste of wine the most distinct. Swirling black mist surrounded him, and he shifted into his demon form. He took off into the air, his massive wings carrying him toward the demons in the aisle.

I leapt up the steps to the altar, charging the demons who were sweeping the holy relics into their bags. They were so distracted by the loot that they didn't hear me coming.

"Resorting to petty thievery?" I swiped my sword at the neck of the tallest demon.

His head tumbled to the ground, and I whirled to see the other with his hand raised. Flame swirled around the big mitt and I grinned.

"Go on," I taunted. "I bet I'm faster."

He scowled and hurled it. I dodged, avoiding the firebomb by inches. It exploded into the stone wall behind me, as I'd hoped. I didn't know if this cathedral was here to stay, but if it was, I didn't want him firebombing anything flammable.

Before he could gather the magical energy to hurl another, I charged, leaping off a low bench and swinging my sword down on his shoulder. It cleaved him straight to the heart. Blood sprayed as I tried to leap out of the way, but it hit me in the neck.

Ew.

The demon tumbled like an oak, landing hard on the ground. I left him and his treasures on the ground. In a few minutes, his body would disappear, returning to the Underworld. I didn't know what would happen to the golden artifacts, but I didn't want to touch them. No reason to get my dragon soul even more excited.

I raced down the steps toward Roarke, who'd just broken the neck of the second demon. He stood between the pews, looking like a fallen angel, the cathedral soaring high above him.

Oh boy. Now I was getting poetic again about the Warden of the Underworld. That was no good.

I hurried to his side, jumping over the fallen body of one of the demons. His black gaze met mine, scary in its intensity. He was well into demon-lord mode now.

"Come on." I pointed down the church, which was even longer than a football field. "The big one is that way."

"He's got more minions." Roarke's voice sounded dark and gravelly once again. He cracked his knuckles, looking ready to kill something.

I shivered. "Then we'll get them, too."

We hurried down the main aisle, our footsteps silent on the stone. Pews stretched out on either side of us, candles propped on the end of each. I hadn't seen any ancient monks come back to life yet, thank goodness. Perhaps it was too late at night.

A whistling sound was my only warning before something grabbed me around the middle. The ground fell away beneath my feet. I shouted as it carried me into the air.

A winged demon! Its pale arms were wrapped around my waist as it dragged me up, higher and higher. My heart pounded. We were in the tallest part of the cathedral, the tower that was right in the middle.

On the other side, four winged demons dropped down from their perches in the rafters, headed straight for Roarke. They were pale where he was dark, their skin an eerie white pierced by red veins. Their wings were the same blood red as their eyes.

Roarke soared into the air, all grace and fury, headed straight for me.

I stilled my struggling. We were high enough that if the demon dropped me, I was dead.

What that actually meant, I didn't know. But dying the first time had hurt, and I didn't want a repeat. I also didn't want to turn into a Phantom.

It killed me to await rescue, but I wasn't an idiot.

Most of the time.

The demons charged Roarke as he flew, but they couldn't get a hand on him. He was faster and stronger by a mile. All it took was for him to grab a single body part of theirs, and he'd heave them into the walls. They flew wings over ass, tumbling through the air until they crashed against the stone.

When Roarke was nearly to us, the demon who carried me hissed, then loosened his grip. I fell, my stomach leaping into my throat, but managed to grab his ankle.

He kicked, but I tightened my grip. I was still over forty feet in the air, which was well within *splat-like-a-pancake* distance. And no way was I going to let this bastard get away.

Roarke hurtled toward us, a vision of strength and fury as his massive wings ate up the distance. In one graceful move, he grabbed me by the waist and gripped the demon's calf in his massive hand. I released the demon, and Roarke spun in a circle, gaining momentum as the demon swung around us like a whirligig. Right as my vision went blurry, Roarke let go of the demon too. It hurled into the wall, colliding with a stone archway before plummeting to the floor below.

Roarke stopped spinning and held me tightly against his side, his skin so hot it nearly burned me. We hovered in the air for a moment, so high it should've made me nauseous, but I'd never felt safer.

"Thanks," I wheezed.

He nodded sharply, then lowered us to the ground.

I stumbled as he set me down, but he gripped my shoulder gently to steady me. My mind narrowed in on the feel of his hand.

"What the hell were those things?" I asked.

Winged demons were rare. Roarke was the first I'd ever seen.

"Hellspawn. Quite literally. They come from the deepest hell in the Underworld. Cat 3 demons that are rarely on Earth. They don't make good mercenaries."

"They did all right."

He grinned. "They're good fighters, but they don't follow orders."

"So they're just attracted to the Ubilaz demon's evil."

"Most likely." Roarke glanced around at the now-quiet church. "Where the hell is that thing, anyway?"

I turned toward the far end of the church, where the entrance would normally be. "That way. And possibly underground."

"The crypts."

"Yeah."

We hurried down the nave. I kept my sword at the ready and my gaze darting. This place was crawling with demon magic, though the church was now silent. Candlelight flickered on the jewel-toned figures in the stained glass. I swore their eyes followed us as we passed.

When we reached the main entryway of the cathedral, I stopped.

"We're above him," I whispered.

"There." Roarke pointed to a narrow doorway. The wooden door was open to reveal a winding set of stone stairs that led down.

"Of course the creepy demon hides out in the crypt."

I followed Roarke to the stairs, my skin prickling from the magic that flowed up from below—the distinct garbage fire smell of the Ubilaz demon, along with the scent of mold and rot and the feeling of ice against my skin.

Roarke insisted on going first, so I followed. Our footsteps were silent on the stone stairs. The hair on the back of my neck stood up at the sound of something scraping against stone. When we reached the base of the stairs, I knocked on my head for good luck.

The crypt was dark and low ceilinged with many nooks and crannies. The symmetrical order of the cathedral above was not mirrored down here. This was a labyrinth of stone walls and tiny rooms. Stone sarcophagi were aligned neatly against the walls. Some were ornately carved, some plain. But it was the small ones that broke my heart.

I shook my head and focused on the hunt, searching the dark space around us.

A ghostly silver form rose up from the sarcophagus to my left. A regal looking woman with an ornate gown, she looked to be about forty. She inclined her head toward me, then pointed to the left, deeper into the crypt.

It was the same direction that my dragon sense pulled me.

She then held up both hands and showed me nine fingers.

Demons. She had to be talking about the number of demons.

I nodded my thanks.

The ghost's mouth moved, like she was trying to speak. *Hurry.* She made a shooing motion. Her gaze was desperate.

I pointed. "That way."

His quizzical gaze met mine, but I didn't tell him how I knew. He hadn't seen the ghost, and I wouldn't confess to having seen it.

My heart thundered in my ears as we hurried toward them. Why did we need to hurry? What would I find? Some terrible ritual in the crypt of an ancient cathedral?

I shuddered and gripped my sword tight.

We turned a corner in the crypt, immediately coming upon a long, low-ceilinged room that was filled with demons. We pressed ourselves against the wall and peered in.

Nine demons.

Shit. The ghost had been right.

Worse, they were massive, at least a foot taller than Roarke while he was in his Were-demon form. Their magic smelled like dust and felt like paper cuts.

In the middle of the room, there was a pit. Dirt flew out of it, like someone was shoveling. Must be the Ubilaz demon.

I sheathed my sword at my back and reached into my pocket for three of Connor's potion bombs. The glass vials were red, which meant they were deadly

Portlothian acid bombs. I could take out three demons from a distance with these.

I looked at Roarke and mouthed, "Let's move."

His black gaze met mine and he nodded.

We raced into the room, each taking one side of the pit. I hurled the potion bombs in quick succession, taking out three demons in a row. They collapsed to the ground, shrieking. I drew my sword and headed straight for the demon who stood at the edge of the pit.

He looked even bigger up close. I leapt, swinging my sword for his neck. But he reached out with one massive arm and swatted me away. I crashed against the ground, skidding on stone until I could see into the pit. Inside, the Ubilaz demon shoved the top off of a massive stone coffin. Within lay a skeleton dressed in tattered robes. A gleaming golden pendent lay on her chest.

The Ubilaz demon reached for it and yanked it off. The skeleton's head tumbled to the side.

That bastard!

I heaved myself to my feet and spun to face the demon who had hit me. He approached, his massive fists clenched and ready to strike. This time, I went low, hurling myself at the demon's legs and swiping out with my blade. I landed a blow that made him stagger, so I capitalized on it, leaped up, and planted my feet in his chest. He stumbled backward. I leapt upon him and plunged my blade into his heart.

His mouth opened on a snarl as I yanked my sword free and jumped back. Just as he was about to fall, he swung his massive arm, knocking me in the chest and hurling me into the pit.

I crashed to the ground. I scrambled to my feet, but before I could raise my sword, the Ubilaz demon spotted me.

His muddy eyes flared with rage as he backhanded me.

Pain exploded in my cheek as I flew through the air and crashed against the side wall of the pit. Instinct alone kept my blade in my hand. My head spun as I lurched to my feet, briefly catching sight of the carving on the top of the stone coffin's lid.

Gwenhwyfar.

I called upon my magic, desperate to shift into Phantom form. Roarke couldn't see me here in the pit, and I'd need everything I—

The Ubilaz demon jumped on me before I could shift. His clawed fingertips slashed against my front. Pain fired through me, whiting out my vision. Another clawed blow pushed me off him. More pain flared in my side.

I had to shift or he'd kill me!

The demon's heavy form crushed mine as he landed on top of me. His claws raked down my arms. Acid pain shot through me. I shrieked.

It didn't matter if Roarke saw me. I couldn't survive this in my human form. I struggled to throw the demon off as I tried to shift, but I was too weak.

My magic stayed dormant, crushed by the debilitating pain that roared through me. I was thoroughly human, and I was staying that way.

Because I'd waited too long.

Blood coated my hands, and I lost my grip on my sword. Through blurry vision, I could make out the demon's enraged face.

He was going to kill me.

Help!

The demon raised a massive clawed hand, ready to swing the death blow that would break my neck. I thrashed, my motions now weak as my blood pooled around my broken body. Too weak.

His arm swiped down. Death coming.

A transparent blue cloud swooped into the pit. But instead of encompassing me as it had the last time, it swirled around the demon and lifted him up into the air.

Magic sparkled, familiar and warm. It smelled sweet, something I recognized. The blue light whirled around the demon, keeping him suspended. It whirled faster and faster, then began to coalesce. Taking shape.

Blackness crept in at the corners of my vision. I struggled to stay conscious as the blue cloud rose up, away from me. Through my blurry gaze, just before I passed out, I thought I saw the blue cloud form something recognizable.

But impossible.

A dragon.

Definitely a dragon.

CHAPTER NINE

Light flickered in the distance, pale gold and beckoning. Pain seethed through me as I struggled toward it. Heaviness weighted my limbs.

Trapped. Blind.

I struggled, or tried to. I couldn't move. Something held me down. Through the morass of pain and exhaustion, I pulled myself toward consciousness.

When I first opened my eyes, I saw nothing. Blackness all around. Then light filtered in, revealing a high wooden ceiling. A figure leaned over me. Pale, slanted eyes and a pair of tiny horns stood out starkly in my vision.

A demon!

I shrank back.

"It's okay, it's okay." Roarke's voice, rough with concern. "She's helping you."

My neck ached as I turned my head. Through blurry vision, I saw Roarke, hovering behind the demon. His clothes were blood-soaked and dirty, and concern shadowed his eyes. My gaze dropped to his hands which were clenched into fists.

I opened my mouth, trying to ask what had happened, but my head swam. Something cool flowed over the wounds in my chest, followed immediately by a searing, molten-iron agony.

Blackness took me.

I floated in the dark, free of pain. Visions flashed across my mind. Memories. Me, lying in the pit. Roarke, tall and strong in his Were-demon form, jumping down beside me. Blood poured from wounds piercing his chest and stomach, but he bent and picked me up, cradling me to his chest.

His wings spread wide, and he lifted us both gracefully into the air.

When I woke again, the healer was gone. So was most of the pain.

Golden sunlight filtered in through the cracks between the wooden blinds, sending an orange glow across the wooden floor. My head felt like it weighed a million pounds as I turned it to search the room.

Roarke sat on a small sofa near my side of the bed, his head tilted back and resting against the wall. His broad chest rose and fell slowly. He slept. The shirt he wore was cleaner than the other had been, but patches of fresh blood dotted it.

He hadn't let anyone tend to his wounds.

Stubborn man.

But otherwise, his face looked peaceful in slumber.

My gaze darted around, taking in my surroundings. The room was rustic-chic with a heavy wooden bed and fireplace on the far wall. The ceiling was high with wooden rafters hung with iron lights. Paintings of the forest dotted the walls, and through the windows, I could make out the faintest sound of a rushing river.

We were at his place by the river in the woods. It had the feel of *Expensive Mountain Retreat* rather than *Cabin*, but that didn't surprise me. Between his car and clothes, Roarke was used to the best.

"You're awake." His sleep-roughened voice made me jerk my head toward him. A slight pain pierced my skull at the quick movement, but it faded.

Relief was stark on his face. Happiness as well. It made his expression look lighter, as if a weight were lifted off him.

Huh. I wouldn't have expected that.

He stood, then knelt by the bed. Concern darkened his eyes. "How are you?"

"Okay." I struggled to sit, my muscles aching and pulling. Though I felt like I'd been hit by a bus, there was no sharp pain like I would have expected from the kinds of deep wounds the demon had given me.

"My healer mended your wounds. The poison is still in your system, but you'll survive. She gave you another dose of the potion that wards off the transition, but we still need the demon's blood to cure you."

And we hadn't gotten any. Not in that fight, at least. But he'd gotten someone to heal me? "Is that why we're at your place?"

"Yes. It's closest to the portal she uses to leave the Underworld."

"Thanks." I glanced down to see that I was wearing an overlarge T-shirt. His. My arms weren't wrapped in bandages. They weren't even scarred.

I peeked under the neckline of my shirt. My chest was the same, except for the scar from the blade that had killed me.

"Did you put these clothes on me?" I asked. Nerves skated through me. I definitely didn't want him seeing me naked.

"No. Lofta did."

"The healer?" An image of her face flashed in my mind. "The demon healer."

He shrugged. "She's good."

"Yeah. She was." I should be far more injured than this. Dead, even. Though I did feel vaguely disgusting. "But I could use a shower."

Roarke nodded and stood, wincing.

"You should have let Lofta tend to you."

"She was tapped out. Are you hungry?"

"Famished."

He strode to the door, then turned back. "Del? I'm glad you're all right."

I blinked stupidly. His words were one thing, but his tone…

So grateful. He really cared that I was all right. He'd taken care of me before himself, letting the healer use up all her magic healing my wounds instead of his. And he'd sat by my bedside this entire time.

The gruff Warden of the Underworld was hell of a lot kinder than I'd thought.

Roarke's shower turned out to be even more amazing than the bedroom. It was a massive slate-tiled thing with the biggest showerhead I'd ever seen. It looked and felt like an actual waterfall. There was even a window overlooking the river and forest, like I was a part of nature.

This guy showered in the forest like a freaking woodland nymph. Albeit a large, scary woodland nymph.

Once I'd cleared some of the cobwebs from my mind, I called upon my dragon sense. What had happened to that demon when the ghostly dragon had carried him off?

And had it actually *been* a dragon? It sounded crazy. Real dragons had been gone for centuries. And that hadn't even looked like a real one. It'd been transparent. And blue. Like I was when in my Phantom form.

Too weird.

When I finally climbed out of the magic shower, my muscles felt slightly better. I still couldn't run, but at least I was walking. I spent a minute standing in front of the mirror, searching myself for signs of transition, but found none, thankfully. The potion was still working.

I found a duffle bag on the bed. My duffle bag. I frowned at the familiar sight, then hurried to it and unzipped it.

Inside were my favorite T-shirts, jeans, leather jacket, pants, PJs, and even my underwear with polar bears on them. My lucky pair. There was a note on the top. I pulled it out and unfolded it.

I sent someone to pick up your stuff. Your friend Claire packed it. -Roarke

Awesome. I pulled out my favorite penguin PJs and lucky underwear, then tugged them all on. Once I was fully swaddled in Arctic-themed flannel, I felt a heck of a lot better. There was just something about wearing your own clothes after being attacked by a murderous Ubilaz demon that felt great.

A glance at the clock showed that it was now 7:00 p.m. Good. I needed another full night's sleep.

My stomach growled.

"Shut up, you," I muttered.

I followed the sound of music out of the room and down the hallway. The house wasn't huge—just four bedrooms on the top floor—but everything was top-notch. Nosiness was a major failing of mine, and now that I had a chance to snoop around the house that belonged to the Warden of the Underworld, I wasn't going to miss it.

Each bedroom was decorated beautifully, complete with its own fireplace and bathroom. A balcony overlooked the river and another interior one overlooked the living room where the ceiling soared high overhead, punctuated by skylights. The room below was one of the most beautiful I'd ever seen, a comfortable space that screamed *Expensive Ski Lodge*, just like my bedroom had. The fireplace was huge and the TV bigger.

The Warden might not have a huge place, but it was *nice*. Then again, he also owned a castle in the Underworld, so maybe he wanted to feel like a normal dude on Earth.

I made my way down the wide wooden staircase and easily found the kitchen by following the sound of the Allman Brothers. So he liked good music. I didn't want to like that about him, but I did. Of course. Because I was an idiot easily swayed by my hormones.

The kitchen was a large space with sleek wooden cabinets, black granite, and top-of-the-line appliances. I didn't actually know how to identify top-of-the-line appliances, but they looked big and expensive, which I figured qualified. There was a breakfast nook on the other side of the kitchen. Windows surrounded it, and I'd have bet big money that they overlooked the river.

Roarke was just pulling something out of the oven as I entered. He'd changed into a clean T-shirt, and it looked like his wounds had stopped bleeding.

"I thought you didn't like frozen pizza," I said.

"I was occupied."

Occupied sitting at my bedside. Right. "Looks great."

"I think it has potential." He pointed to the counter. "Help yourself. There's no boxed wine, but I do have a bottle of red."

"Hey, no need for snark. I happen to like boxed wine. It's both convenient and portable. No breakage. Three bottles for the price of one."

"I noticed you liked it. You looked pretty happy about it when you had it at your place."

"I was." I went to the counter and found two coffee mugs sitting by the bottle of expensive wine. I held them up. "You like drinking wine out of coffee mugs too?"

"Sure."

"No, you don't."

"Honestly, I don't care how I drink it. But you like coffee mugs."

"Maybe I don't have any wine glasses."

"You do."

"Snoop!"

"Guilty." He grinned and my heart flopped around in my chest.

I couldn't exactly yell at him, though. He'd snooped while cooking me dinner. Probably because he needed cooking tools or whatever. As long as he stayed out of my bedroom, I didn't care. And I had just snooped around his place, so it looked like we were both nosy.

"Well, thanks for the wine." I poured myself a mug and made my way to the table, unable to stand for much longer.

Roarke set a plate on the table in front of me. It held half a pizza. His plate held the other half.

"That looks awesome." I took a big bite. While I chewed, memories of the fight back at Glastonbury flashed in my mind. What had that dragon been? And where had it taken the Ubilaz demon?

I reached out with my dragon sense to find the demon. But I couldn't find anything. No tug, no sense of its location.

What the hell?

A cold sweat broke out on my skin. "The Ubilaz demon might be dead."

Oh, fates. What did that mean for me if I couldn't get its blood for the antidote?

Roarke's brow creased. "It's not dead. I'd know if it had returned to the Underworld."

Hope flared. "What do you mean?"

"When demons reappear in their Underworld, my staff knows. I asked, but they said he hasn't arrived."

I set the slice of pizza down. "So he's definitely still on Earth?"

"Yeah. But you can't find him?"

I shook my head. "No. That's weird. He's blocked from my sight."

"What can do something like that?"

"Um… A concealment charm, for one." For years, I'd worn one to protect myself from the Monster who lurked in my past. Ever since we'd escaped from him at fifteen, he'd hunted me and my *deirfiúr*. He was gone now, killed by Cass, but the charms had hidden us from his seer's vision for years. Concealment charms were rare and hard to come by, though.

The memory of the demon yanking the golden pendant off the neck of the skeleton flashed in my mind.

"You didn't see a golden charm or necklace in that pit at Glastonbury, did you?" I asked.

"No. There was nothing there other than the sarcophagus."

"Then that's what the demon was after. Before he was taken away, he grabbed a necklace off the skeleton."

"But you can't sense him."

"Doesn't mean I can't find him other ways." I picked up my pizza, which was now cold, and chowed down as my mind raced. I replayed the scene in the crypt. Finally, something stood out. "Who do you think Gwenhwyfar was?"

"Was that the name on the sarcophagus?"

"Yeah."

Roarke pulled a sleek cell phone out of his pocket, fiddled with it for a moment, then looked up. "Nothing on Google."

A man after my own heart. "We can go ask Dr. Garriso tomorrow. He's a historian at the Museum for Magical History. He knows just about everything, and if he doesn't, he's got a book that will have the answer."

I might have some of this info in the books in my trove, but I didn't even know how to start searching for the name Gwenhwyfar. I needed a card catalogue in my library, or something. Between the demon hunting and all the rest, my life was too busy to properly curate my collection. I knew where some things were, like demon books, but obscure history was more difficult to find.

"So we're changing tactics," Roarke said. "Using books to find the demon."

I shrugged. "Technically, I've been using books since the beginning. Most historical mysteries like this can be solved with books."

Roarke nodded. "Fair enough. It's the best we've got."

CHAPTER TEN

I finished eating as quickly as I could, then stood. Just that little motion made my muscles ache and my head spin.

"You okay?" Roarke asked.

I nodded slowly. "Yeah, just recovering. A good night's sleep will do it. Thanks for getting the healer, by the way."

"Not a problem."

"Well, I'm lucky."

Those wounds could have killed me. Lofta's magic was the only thing that had stood between me and a quick return to the Underworld. What would have happened at that point was anyone's guess. And frankly, I didn't want to know.

"I'm going to call Dr. Garriso and set up a meeting for tomorrow morning. Once we know what Gwenhwyfar is, we'll find the demon." *I hoped.*

Roarke nodded.

I stood there awkwardly for a moment before grabbing my plate and putting it in the sink, then hurried from the room. It didn't take me long to reach my bedroom, though I wanted to poke around his place more. I resisted and felt like a saint for doing so.

A quick scan of the bedroom revealed my phone plugged into the wall near the bed. Roarke's thoughtfulness made me grin. I hurried to it and called Dr. Garriso, arranging to meet him at eight. I hung up and put the phone back on the bedside table, then looked at the bed.

I was exhausted and achy, but restlessness stole through my muscles. The sound of rushing water outside the windows caught my ears. There'd been a balcony off the hallway, I recalled. I wanted to see the river. And maybe I could even see the portal from here. It was fixed, right?

Before I could second-guess myself, I grabbed my jacket from the duffle bag and headed out. By the time I made it outside to the balcony, the moon had risen high in the sky. I made my way across the wide expanse of wooden deck and leaned on the railing.

The river rushed below, glittering in the light of the full moon. Something rustled in the bushes across the water, and I stiffened. When a deer poked its head out from behind a bush, my muscles relaxed. Normally I could hold my own in a fight, but my injuries were slowing me down. I didn't like being in this weakened state.

But nothing was going to get me while I was at the house belonging to the Warden of the Underworld. Not only was his title scary as hell—pun intended—I'd seen him in a fight. No one would mess with him on his own territory.

When the door opened behind me, I almost jumped out of my skin.

"Can't sleep?" Roarke asked from behind me.

I turned. He was wearing the same clothes he had been, but this time, he held my sword in his hand. My palm itched to yank it from him.

"What are you doing with that?" I asked.

"I thought you should have it back." His gaze was grave. "I'm sorry I took it from you. If you'd had your own weapon, you might have stood a better chance against the Ubilaz demon."

An image of the relief and happiness on his face when I'd woken from my wound-induced slumber flashed in front of my vision.

"Thanks." I reached out for it, and he handed it over. My hand brushed against his and sent my heart rocketing through my chest.

His gaze lingered on mine—briefly—before he looked away.

I tried to focus on the smooth, familiar grip of my sword instead of on the memory of his touch. In truth, the feel of my sword made my heart swell.

Roarke joined me at the railing, leaning his elbows against it and looking down into the water below.

"That's the blade you use when you hunt demons, then?" he asked.

"Yeah."

"Why that job?"

"Why do you care?"

He shrugged, tilting his head until his dark gaze met mine. "I'm interested."

In me? Whew. I didn't know what to do with that information, so I packed it away. I didn't necessarily want him to be interested, but there was no harm in sharing the basics.

I shrugged. "I'm good at it. And it pays well."

"Did you train with the sword for long? You're talented with it."

I leaned against the railing, needing to take some weight off my aching muscles. "That's the weird thing. I didn't have to train a lot. At least, not that I remember."

"What do you mean?"

I glanced up at the stars, my mind drifting back to the first time I'd seen them. "When I was fifteen, I woke in a field with no memory. I was with Cass and Nix. We didn't even remember our names. I can't remember the first fifteen years of my life. But I'm a natural with a sword. Maybe because I practiced when I was a child. I don't know."

Why was I telling him all this? Maybe because it felt good to confide in someone other than my *deirfiúr*. I'd always found it unsettling that I was so good with a sword. What kind of childhood had I had that I didn't remember training with weapons?

And maybe if he knew me better, he'd feel guilty about taking me back to the Underworld.

"What the hell happened to you that you woke as a child alone in a field?" Anger rang clear in his voice.

"Um, we'd been held prisoner by a sociopath. I don't have any memories of it, but Cass does."

"Why? And where is he?" Roarke growled.

"Dead." I grinned. "Cass killed the bastard."

As for why he'd held us prisoner, that was info I wouldn't be sharing. The Monster from our past had wanted us because we were FireSouls. He'd planned to use our talents for his own benefit. But there was no way I'd reveal that side of my nature to Roarke. A rule follower like him would have a hard time not turning me in to the Order of the Magica.

I shivered at the thought. Roarke was part demon. He'd turned his brother over to the law. I had to keep these things in mind. Constant vigilance through my life had kept me safe. Forgetting what Roarke really was—what he was really like—would do me no favors.

"Do you know anything about me other than my last name?" I asked. "And is my first name really Delphine?"

"Yes. It's Delphine. But you said you didn't know your own name."

"I didn't. But maybe that's what made me choose the constellation Delphinus for my name. Deep down, I recognized it." The thought made my heart ache for something I couldn't even recognize. "But what about my last name? Do you know any more?"

"No. I knew only your name and how to find you."

"I thought you tracked me by the blood I left behind."

"I did."

Was he lying? Before I could ask, he said, "What did you do after you woke in the field?"

"Stayed on the run. Eventually we raised enough money for concealment charms to hide us from the Monster's seers who sought our location. Then we opened Ancient Magic." With our skills for finding treasure, it was the only way we'd known to make a living. "The demon hunting for the Order was just a gig on the side to make more money. But with Ancient Magic doing better, I can now do more treasure hunting."

"You lead an interesting life, Del Bellator."

"You're not too shabby yourself."

He shrugged. "It's a job."

I laughed. "Some job."

"It keeps things in line."

"Which you do like." And that was what I was afraid of. Staying in line probably meant taking me back to the Underworld.

After leaving Roarke on the porch, I slept like a log. By the time I woke at seven the next morning, all my aches and pains were gone. If I hadn't woken in Roarke's spare bedroom, there'd have been no way to tell I'd almost been killed by the Ubilaz demon.

"There's coffee in the kitchen!" Roarke yelled through the door. "We'll leave in ten."

"All right!" I showered quickly, regretting not waking early enough to spend more time in his enchanted forest shower, then pulled on my black leathers.

When I took my sword off the dresser, I couldn't help but grin. Having it again felt so danged good. I sheathed it at my back and then headed down the stairs. The kitchen was lit by the warm glow of the rising sun, and I got a fairly big stab of kitchen envy.

Coffee was sitting on the counter, along with a travel mug, so I grabbed a quick cup and headed out to the driveway. The morning was brisk and chilly as fall leaves tumbled off the trees.

Roarke, dressed in a dark blue sweater, leaned against his car, holding his own cup and looking like he fit into this rustic-chic mountain life so easily. No one would guess that the Warden of the Underworld owned a matching pair of travel coffee mugs or looked so good in a sweater. Mostly they'd just imagine his Were-demon side.

"Ready?" he asked.

"Yep." We climbed into the car, and I almost groaned at how cozy the pre-warmed interior was. "You're not a big fan of being late, are you?"

"Nope." He backed the car out of the drive.

"You know where the Museum of Magical History is located?" I asked.

"Yeah. Big building near the old library, right?"

"Exactly." But it was weird he'd know so well. "How often are you in Magic's Bend? I never see you around." And I'd have noticed a guy like him

"Not often, honestly. A housekeeper does my shopping in town, and I know where the museum is but only because I looked it up on my phone. I keep to myself mostly. And my colleagues are demons, so… I'm not around other supernaturals much."

"Do you like that?"

"It's all right. Not all demons are evil."

I glanced at him, remembering how he'd saved me. "No. Maybe not."

We arrived at the museum thirty minutes later, and I led the way to Dr. Garriso's office in the back. I'd never actually been here before, but I'd gotten to know Dr. Garriso over the last few months. He'd helped Cass with a few problems, and I was hopeful he'd help me, too.

"Come in, come in." He opened the back door to the museum. Dr. Garriso was a small man, about seventy, and always sported the tweed coats that made him look like he should be hanging out in the drawing room of some country house in England.

We followed him down the sterile, cold hallway to his office, which immediately transported me to another world. An English country house, in fact. The narrow space was done up like the library in one of those fancy old houses. Bookshelves lined every wall and were stuffed full of leather-bound books that were far older than anyone in the room. It smelled of paper and leather, which was just about the best scent I could imagine.

Colorful Tiffany lamps cast a warm glow on the leather chairs and small wooden tables crowded into the space.

Dr. Garriso's office was a wonderland.

"Have a seat." Dr. Garriso gestured to the far end of the room where two plush chairs sat under the window. A smaller wooden chair was pulled up beside the two. "I've just put the kettle on."

I followed Roarke to the chairs. He took the small one, leaving the nicer ones for me and Dr. Garriso, who followed us with a tea tray. He set it on the little table between the chairs, then handed out the cups.

I grinned at Roarke, who delicately cradled the china in his massive hands. He looked like a bull in a china shop, determined not to break anything.

"How can I be of assistance?" Dr. Garriso asked.

I set the tea aside, hoping Dr. Garriso didn't notice that I hadn't drunk any. It really wasn't my thing. I'd try to force down a couple sips in a minute to not be rude.

I dug into my pocket where I'd written Gwenhwyfar's name on a piece of paper, then handed it to him. "We found a sarcophagus with that name carved on it."

He squinted down, his spectacles reflecting the low glow of the lamps. He made a tutting sound, then said, "This name looks very familiar. One moment."

He stood and hurried to the far wall, then climbed a narrow ladder and pulled down a few small books. As he walked back, he'd already started reading them.

"Ah, yes," he said. "As I thought. Gwenhwyfar is the old Welsh spelling of Guinevere." His bright gaze lifted and met my own. "You've found the grave of Queen Guinevere."

"As in, King Arthur and Merlin?" I asked. And *oh*, that was no coincidence at all. First we find the demon at Merlin's Cave, now at Guinevere's grave?

I met Roarke's gaze. He knew exactly what I was thinking.

"Exactly," Dr. Garriso said.

"I guess the names do sound almost the same," I said.

"Yes. Many cultures in Britain have myths and stories about Guinevere, Arthur, and Merlin. They are popular figures."

"Were they real?"

Dr. Garriso shrugged. "In some form, yes, I think. However, there are so many stories and myths that no one knows the truth of them."

"So, is Arthur buried there as well? Or Lancelot?"

"I do not know," Dr. Garriso said. "No one knows. There are several places they are purported to be buried. There are so many stories about those figures that it's as if they lived a dozen lives."

"Do you know anything about a magical charm that Guinevere might have owned?" I asked. "A pendant she wore around her neck that may have been a concealment charm?"

Dr. Garriso's eyes brightened, and a grin stretched across his face. I'd never seen him look so excited. "Oh! Did you find one at her grave?"

"Yes. There was one draped around her skeleton's neck." Guilt streaked through me, though I hadn't been the one to push off the lid of her sarcophagus. It'd been the demon. But still, I hated the damage caused to her grave.

"Well, I'll be." Dr. Garriso's eyes took on a distant cast, as if he were reliving a memory. Or a story.

"What do you know?" Roarke asked.

His gaze met ours, pleased as punch. "There are many stories about Queen Guinevere. According to who you ask, be it the Britons or the Picts or the nineteenth century Romanticists, in almost all cases, she is a pawn. She has agency, yes, but not as much as she deserved. As anyone deserves. More often than not, she was used as a plot device to further the stories of the male characters, like Arthur or Mordred or Lancelot. In many cases, she meets a dire end. I never liked those stories. She was in an impossible situation most of the time, given too little credit and too little agency."

"But there's another story, isn't there?" I could see it in his eyes. There was a story he treasured above the others.

"Yes." Dr. Garriso nodded. "In one story, written by an unknown author many centuries ago, Guinevere took her fate into her own hands. She saw how those around her tried to use her, so she commissioned Merlin to create the strongest concealment charm ever known. She took the charm and ran, becoming master of her own fate. She appeared occasionally thereafter, but only on her terms. The rest of the time, she lived the life she pleased, hidden from those who would use her."

Oh, I liked this Queen Guinevere. I liked her a lot. And first chance I had, I'd be visiting her grave to repair the damage. Maybe I could even get her to come to life and have a chat.

That probably qualified as abusing my powers, right?

"You said the author was unknown?" I asked.

"Yes. But I suspect that Gwenhwyfar wrote it before she died. If I were her, I wouldn't be able to resist sharing my cunning plan with the world."

"Neither would I," I said. "So she finished out her days at Glastonbury Abbey."

"If that is where you found her grave, then it appears so. There was a legend that she might have ended up there."

"She did."

"Splendid that you found it," Dr. Garriso said.

"Except for the fact that we lost the concealment charm," Roarke said.

Dr. Garriso's face fell. "That is not good."

"No." Not only did we lose something that should be in its proper resting place with Guinevere, but it was now concealing a dangerous demon. "We're hoping to learn more so that we can track down the demon who stole it. He's using the concealment charm to hide from my…seeker sense."

I was so excited about Guinevere, and so stressed about the demon, that I almost tripped up and said *dragon sense*. That would be baaaad.

"Hmmm." Dr. Garriso frowned.

"We have some clues," Roarke added. "The demon first visited Merlin's Cave at Tintagel, then Guinevere's grave."

"That's a trend," Dr. Garriso said.

I nodded. "Yes."

"But I'm afraid I know no more." He stood.

Disappointment surged through me.

"There are many myths and stories about Guinevere and Merlin and all the rest. Read these. You may find something helpful." Dr. Garriso handed me the books, and I took them, my chest loosening as hope pushed away disappointment.

Some of my problems I solved with my sword. But many others, I solved with books. They might look unassuming, but there were worlds within these pages.

And, I hoped, the answers that we would need.

CHAPTER ELEVEN

As Roarke and I hurried out to the car, I called my *deirfiúr* on my comms charm.

"Nix? Cass? Are you in Magic's Bend? Can we meet at the shop? I've got some books we need to look through." Normally I'd ask to meet at P & P, but this was during working hours so Nix couldn't leave the shop.

Roarke glanced at me, surprised. I hadn't told him I was going to call them.

"Trust me," I said to him.

"We're back. Nothing panned out in New York. I can meet you at the shop," Nix said.

"I'll be there," Cass added.

"See you in fifteen." I cut the connection and turned to Roarke. "We're going to need to read these books fast. To do that, we need help."

"Books are really our best bet?" he asked.

"Quit doubting. Right now, they're our only bet. We're working with a trend here—first Merlin's Cave, then Guinevere's grave. Maybe we'll get lucky and find something else connected. You have any other ideas?"

"No."

"Then we've got a plan. Anyway, I'm a fast reader. It won't take long if we all work together."

"All right." He climbed into the car.

I could tell from his expression that this wasn't usually how he did things, but until we had something else to go on, it was our best bet.

It didn't take long to reach Ancient Magic, but there was no parking when we arrived.

"Drop me off, will you?" I asked.

"Sure." He pulled over to the side.

I hopped out, then hurried into Ancient Magic while he parked the car. Entering the cluttered, magic-ridden shop always felt like coming home. Nix stood up from where she'd been seated behind the counter, a book in one hand and an apple in the other. She set them down on the counter and hurried around it to me.

"Hey! How's it—" Her jaw dropped, and her eyes widened.

Startled, I glanced behind me to see if we were being robbed. No one was behind me. But then, a robbery wouldn't surprise Nix. She'd just beat them up and call the cops.

I turned back to her, but before I could ask what her issue was, I caught sight of the familiar blue glow extending out from where I stood. It crawled across the floor, almost reaching our counter.

No. No, no, no. It couldn't be happening again.

"What the hell is happening?" Nix's voice was high-pitched.

The room filled with people. They started out blue, but turned corporeal. They were clothed in long dresses and suit coats from another era. Nineteenth century. Behind the counter, an old man with a bushy mustache appeared. An ancient brass register appeared on the counter, squashing Del's apple.

No, no, no. My hearth thundered in my ears, and my skin chilled to ice.

This was *my* fault.

I spun, ran out of the shop and across the street to the park on the other side. My mind whirled like a Ferris wheel as I turned and gazed through the shop window.

Everything had disappeared. Nix stood alone amongst our usual clutter of artifacts, her face shocked.

The breath whooshed out of me in relief, and I nearly swayed.

It was gone.

But I'd done that. *I'd* done that.

Sweat broke out along my skin, my relief short-lived. Holy magic, this was a problem. I was bringing the past back. Bringing the *dead* back.

"Del!" Roarke's voice sounded from the other side of the street.

Startled, I glanced up to see him hurrying across the pavement toward me.

"What are you doing over here?"

I glanced around, mind scrambling. "Uh, I thought I saw my neighbor's dog. He shouldn't be out."

Roarke's gaze searched the street and park behind me. "You find him?"

"No. I must have been mistaken." I looked at him hopefully.

His brows lowered. "No, you're up to something."

"Am not."

"No, something is off about you. But don't worry, I'll figure it out."

That was *exactly* what I was worried about. "Come on. Let's head in."

As we crossed the street, I prayed to magic and every god I wished I believed in that the crazy magic wouldn't happen again. When we entered the shop, the first thing I noticed was Nix's squashed apple on the counter. There were a couple of artifacts tumbled to the ground, as well.

"Hey, guys," Nix's voice was slightly strained, but she looked mostly normal. "Cass is in the back. I'll go get her."

"Will you hang out here?" I asked Roarke. "I'm going to use the ladies' room."

He nodded, his gaze already traveling over the assortment of crazy artifacts cluttered onto the shelves lining the walls. I followed Nix into the tiny back room where I found Cass changing into a new T-shirt.

"I freaking spilled on myself again," Cass muttered as she tugged the thing over her head.

"That's not going to seem like a very big problem in a sec," Nix said as she turned to me. "What the hell was that?"

"What was what?" Cass asked.

"Keep your voices down," I hissed. "Roarke is out there. He thinks I'm peeing. And you missed it, Cass. I think I'm manifesting new powers. I'm bringing old places back to life. Bringing *people* back."

"What?" Cass's shocked gaze met mine.

"Yeah," Nix said. "Our shop used to be the general store that served the factory workers above. Del just strolled in and brought with her this weird blue glow, and out popped a whole bunch of people in old-timey attire. She brought the dead back. She brought the *past* back."

"Not good," Cass said.

No. Bringing the dead back to life was strictly forbidden. That was a *very* bad power to have, even if they did disappear when I left. With the way my weird deathling powers were changing, maybe next time, they wouldn't stay gone.

"Why's it happening?" Nix asked. "Can you control it?"

"You're going to have to control it," Cass said.

"I know." I dragged my hands through my hair. "But I don't know how. And I don't know why it's happening. I mean, I turned into a Phantom when those other Phantoms embraced me. Aethelred said it was a trigger. Maybe something triggered this."

"Going to the Underworld might do it. That's a solid trigger, I'd bet."

"Yeah." I nodded, feeling the slightest fraction better. At least I had a why. Kinda. "But that still doesn't explain what the hell I am if I can bring folks back from the dead."

"A secret," Cass said. "That's what you are."

She was right. And I'd have to learn to control it. What if it happened in a grocery store? Not to mention, sometimes the people I brought back didn't want me on their turf. Tintagel Castle had been proof of that.

"Yeah," I said. "Yeah, I'll practice. But first we have to figure out this demon thing and get Roarke off my tail."

"We'll help." Nix glanced at the books that I just now realized were still clutched in my hands. "Those the books you mentioned?"

"Yep."

"'Kay, let's head out there," Cass said. "Aidan is coming over on his lunch break and bringing pizza."

My stomach grumbled. I'd nearly forgotten I hadn't eaten. I followed my *deirfiúr* out into shop. Roarke was admiring a pair of wicked looking daggers on the shelf.

"Let's get started," I said. "I don't know what kind of clue we're looking for, but I hope it's in one of these books."

Aidan walked through the door carrying two pizza boxes and a six-pack of soda. He grinned and held them up. "Lunch."

He set the food on a little table against the wall, then approached Roarke, who held out his hand to Aidan.

"Roarke."

Aidan shook his hand. "Aidan Merrick."

Roarke inclined his head. "Origin."

"Warden," Aidan said, using Roarke's title in return.

"Let's eat while Del gives us a run-down," Nix said. "I need to know what direction I should be looking in."

"Good plan," Roarke said.

We scavenged chairs from around the shop and in the back. Nix and I ended up sitting on the counter after having surreptitiously tossed the apple in the trash.

"So here's the deal." I told the story of Merlin's Cave and Guinevere's grave while trying to inhale a slice of cheese pizza.

"So he stole a concealment charm created by Merlin," Aidan said when I finished.

"Yes," Roarke said.

Aidan shrugged. "That could be your clue right there."

"What do you mean?" Cass asked.

"For the last two months, Origin Enterprises has been conducting research on the fallibility of concealment charms." Origin Enterprises was Aidan's security company.

"Smart," I said. "Trying to find ways to further protect your stuff."

His gaze traveled to Cass. "In a sense, though we've never worked much with concealment charms. We protect property, primarily."'

"Three months ago was just about when you met us," Nix said, her gaze thoughtful.

Aidan nodded. "Once I learned that you three used concealment charms to protect yourselves from the Monster who hunted you, I wanted to make sure that those charms couldn't be cracked. If they could, he could find you."

Cass's face pretty much melted—that was the only way I could describe her expression. To be fair, my heart did the same.

"You were trying to protect us?" she asked.

He reached for her hand. "I hardly think that should come as a surprise."

"You didn't tell us, though," Cass said.

"Let a man have a few secrets." His gaze turned thoughtful. "But it appears this information might help you."

"What'd you learn?" Roarke asked.

"Research and Development determined that if you can figure out how the charm was made—either through potions, conjuring, blood magic, or whatever—you might be able to break them. You'd need to know the origin of the magic and what type it was. There are a lot of different ways to make charms. But that information is almost impossible to come by. Mage's don't usually advertise how they make their goods, or they'd lose their business. Keeping that in mind, it's almost impossible to get the information needed to break the charm."

"If you get the info you need, how do you break the charm?" Cass asked.

"Blood magic," Aidan said. "Aerdeca and Mordaca were our consultants on this. It's not an easy spell, nor technically a legal one. But since the creator of the charm is dead, it walks a gray line."

Roarke scowled, as if he didn't like the sound of breaking the law.

I hurried to clarify, saying, "Mordaca and Aerdeca are our friends who live and work in Darklane. They're blood sorceresses, but they're not evil." They lived just three doors down from Aethelred, in fact, and I'd seen them while visiting. They worked on either side of the law, but most of the time they were on our side. I'd never seen them do anything outright evil. "I don't suppose you could find Merlin in the Underworld and ask how he made the charm?"

Roarke shook his head. "No. Eventually, perhaps. But it could take years. I don't like the sound of blood magic, but if it's the only way to stop the Ubilaz demon, then it's worth it."

"So Del just needs to use her seeker sense to try to find information about the magic used to create Guinevere's concealment charm," Nix said.

"It's worth a try," Cass said.

"It's an off chance." But I saw no harm in it. I really wanted that info, so my dragon sense might give me something. Even better, both of my *deirfiúr* could look for it, too. If one of us got a lead on it, we could pursue it.

I closed my eyes and called upon my magic, working to keep my signature repressed so that Roarke didn't get a sense of my distinct FireSoul signature. I envisioned the locket and Merlin and Guinevere, guessing at what they'd looked like, but giving it my all. Anything would help.

When the magic tugged about my middle, I grinned.

"I've got something." I opened my eyes. "Near Edinburgh."

"Scotland?" Nix asked.

Cass nodded. She'd must have gotten that sense as well.

Roarke looked back and forth between us, his gaze assessing. *Shit.* We hadn't been very careful.

I turned toward him. "Do you have an Underpath exit in Edinburgh?"

The Ubilaz demon was strong. Roarke would need to be as close to full strength as possible when we found him, so tearing a hole through the ether wouldn't be smart.

"I do. I'll have a demon drop a car off outside."

"A demon? Are they, like, your minion network?"

"Essentially."

"Handy." I stood and passed some of the books I'd been holding to my *deirfiúr*, keeping one for myself. "Will you guys look through these while we're gone? See if you find anything interesting?"

"Sure." Nix stood. "And call us if you need anything, okay?"

"Ugh, I hate that." I stumbled out of the Underpath into a small, dimly-lit pub.

Copper mugs hung from the ceiling, and a crackling fire warmed the wooden-walled space. Once again, patrons didn't seem to notice us as we stepped out of the wall.

Roarke's hand cupped my elbow to steady me, which snapped me out of my funk pretty dang quickly. I shivered, unable to help liking his proximity even though he might be the architect of my final demise.

Which would *not* happen.

"This way," he murmured and led me from the pub.

Snow sparkled in the glow of the ancient-looking lamps as we stepped outside onto the cobblestone street. A quick glance behind showed that we'd arrived via a pub called the White Hart Inn.

When I turned back to the street, a black SUV had pulled up to the sidewalk, and a brown demon with small horns climbed out of the driver's seat.

"I didn't think Edinburgh was a supernatural city," I said.

"It's not." Roarke took the keys with a quick thank you, then climbed into the driver's side. I followed. "But the Grassmarket is. This neighborhood has been a supernatural haven for half a millennia. Humans avoid it because of a spell similar to the one on Magic's Bend."

I buckled the seatbelt and peered out the window, taking in the row of brightly lit pubs and the winding stone staircases that led up toward another street. If I ducked my head down really far, I could just catch a glimpse of the romantically lit castle on the hill above. Edinburgh Castle.

"If you have a network of demons waiting at your beck and call to deliver cars, why didn't you just use one of them back in Cornwall? Why let Melly drive us?"

He frowned. "I thought it would make you more comfortable to have an outside person."

"Uh." Didn't know what to say to that.

"I'm really only in the business of intimidating the Kings of Hell."

I glanced at him, surprised. Though I really shouldn't have been. He could tear off heads with a flick of his wrist and punch his way through the ether. He clearly didn't feel the need to exert his power in stupid ways, like controlling everything around him. Only weak men did that. Roarke was comfortable with the idea that he could handle his environment, and if he wanted to drag me back to the Underworld when this was all over, he was confident he could do that, too.

"Thanks."

He shrugged. "You still have to go back to the Underworld when this is all over, but I don't have to be a total jerk about it."

To say that I had mixed feelings about this whole situation was an understatement. His courtesy with Melly gave me the weirdest warm fuzzies. But the idea that he'd drag me back to hell made my blood heat while my skin chilled.

Might as well get this show on the road. I pointed toward the castle. "We can go that way."

I kept my head buried in the book about Guinevere and Arthur as Roarke navigated through Edinburgh and the countryside beyond. Occasionally, I poked my head up to direct him and caught sight of rolling mountains or running sheep.

At one point, my scalp itched. I reached up to scratch and found one of the tiny bumps that indicated horns were starting to form on my head.

A chill went through me as I reached into my pocket to retrieve one of Connor's potions. I found only one.

Damn. That was the last of it. I was transitioning too quickly. We had to find this demon, or I was in trouble like I'd never known.

With trembling hands, I drank the potion as subtly as I could, jumping when I heard Roarke's voice.

"Do you know what form this information is going to take?" Roarke navigated the lonely mountain road. Snow sparkled in the grass on either side. We'd turned onto a mountain path that led us into the lowland mountains outside of Edinburgh.

"No idea. I just asked my seeker sense to find information about the charm Merlin made for Guinevere. It could be anything. But I'll know it when I see it."

A few moments later, my dragon sense tugged hard.

I gasped. "Stop!"

Roarke pulled over on the side of the tiny road. We were in a valley between two rolling hills speckled with the first snowfall of the season. The sun was setting behind the hills, casting a golden glow over the frost-crusted grass.

"We're near," I said.

"There's nothing here."

To confirm his statement, a sheep bleated in the distance.

I grinned. "Sure there is. There's history everywhere."

We climbed out of the car. The frosty grass crunched underfoot, and the chill air froze my nose. I shivered and zipped my jacket, then adjusted my sheathed sword at my back.

"This way." I set off away from the car, following the tug of my dragon sense toward the setting sun.

The rolling mountains around us were desolate and beautiful. When we came to a wide, rambling river crusted at the edges with ice, I stopped on the bank and analyzed my options. A path of wide, flat stones looked like they had potential.

I pointed to them. "We can cross there."

"I could just give you a ride."

My gaze snapped to his, and I swallowed hard. A ride? Like, in his arms. Yeah, my peace of mind could not handle that level of closeness.

"Ah, I'll take the rocks," I said.

He grinned wickedly, as if he knew my thoughts. "Suit yourself."

I smiled weakly, then hurried to the rocks and hopped over, wobbling occasionally. Roarke followed behind, graceful as usual. When we reached the other side, my dragon sense went off like an alarm in my chest.

"We're super close." I squinted into the distance, doing my best to see through the semi-darkness. Dusk had fallen fully, and the moon was only partially full.

A small copse of trees sat alone in the valley. I hurried toward the little forest, shivering at the sickly sensation that welled over me as I neared the trees.

"Del, there's something wrong with that forest."

Roarke's voice snapped me out of my focus on the trees. He was right. There was a charm of some kind trying to repel us.

"We should turn back," Roarke said. "This place is evil. Dark."

"No." But suddenly, I couldn't agree more. This place was terrible. I shivered and turned, ready to race back to the car.

Roarke had already turned around and was heading back to the river. The sight of him walking away from a challenge shocked some sense back into me.

"Roarke! It's an enchantment." A strong one. My feet were still moving toward the river even though my mind knew that I wanted to get into that forest.

I hurried toward Roarke and grabbed his arm, pulling him to a halt. He turned to me, his dark gaze cloudy.

"We must go." His rough voice sounded a bit drunk.

Hell, my head felt a bit drunk. I shook it, trying to clear my mind. It worked a little. I bit my tongue hard enough to send a streak of pain through my mouth. It kept me in the present, at least.

"It's an enchantment, Roarke. It's protecting the grove." Which meant the clue was definitely in there. "Come on."

He resisted my tug on his arm, so I reached up and slapped him. The crack of my hand against his cheek echoed through the valley. The fog in his gaze cleared and he stiffened, then shook his head hard.

"Strong enchantment," he muttered.

"Try biting your tongue." I tugged on his arm. "Come on, let's run for it. Try to be quick. Once we're inside, it might fade."

He nodded and held out his hand. "If one of us falters, the other can lead."

I nodded and gripped his hand, no longer surprised at the shiver that ran up my arm. I liked holding his hand, and I always would because I was an idiot with a poor sense of self-preservation. But he was right—we'd do better as a team.

We set off, racing hand-in-hand across the grass toward the forest. As we neared the oaks, the sense of foreboding grew.

We had to turn back. We shouldn't enter.

This place was haunted.

Which made it perfect for me.

I bit my tongue harder and pushed forward, fighting the compulsion to retreat. When Roarke slowed, I glanced over. His gaze had turned cloudy once again. My own head was foggy, the desire to turn back welling even stronger.

Fight it.

I embraced whatever haunted force lurked in the woods and clung to my dragon sense like a lifeline. It pulled me forward into the forest, so I squeezed Roarke's hand as hard as I could and tugged him. He shook his head, and his gaze cleared. We set off again.

By the time we crossed into the forest, the horrible sense of foreboding was nearly enough to send me to my knees. But I kept going, winding through the stunted, twisted oaks that had no doubt stood here for hundreds of years. Clinging to my dragon sense was the only thing that kept me going. As long as I could focus on that tug, I could just barely ignore the repelling charm that tried to evict me from the forest.

Once we were deep into the trees, the sense of foreboding fell away. My shoulders relaxed.

"Feel that?" I said.

"Yeah." Roarke's voice finally sounded normal. "That was an excellent repelling charm."

"No kidding. I doubt anyone has been in these woods since it was enchanted." Only my dragon sense had kept me going. And we were close now. Really close.

A clearing ahead held a group of stones that protruded from the ground.

I pointed to them. "There!"

"I see them."

We hurried across the grass. When we neared the stones, I raised my hand to ignite the magic in my borrowed lightstone ring. The glow illuminated the three large, flat stones that stuck up out of the ground. Almost like gravestones, but not quite. They were nearly as tall as I was, each carved with beautiful, ornate scenes. They were stele, not gravestones, and their style was familiar.

"They're Pictish stones," I said. "The Picts lived in this part of Scotland in the late Iron Age, early Medieval period. They made stones like this between the sixth and ninth centuries AD."

Roarke leaned close to study them. "They tell a story."

"Yeah."

In between the ornately carved swirls were figures. The detail was extraordinary. Many Pictish stones were decorated with beautifully ornate designs. Yet, stories of this detail were unusual.

My gaze raced over the three stones, trying to figure out where the story started. On the left, I thought. At the top was a man. Concentric circles appeared around him, like they represented magic. In the next scene, he was standing over a large cauldron, his hand hovering over the top.

So he'd used potions to create the charms.

"It's Merlin," Roarke said. "Creating the charm with potion magic."

I gasped. "No, two charms."

In the scene below the one with the cauldron, Merlin stood with a charm dangling from a chain clutched in each hand.

"Guinevere was only wearing one." My gaze raced down the stone. Where did that other charm go?

Roarke pointed to an image at the bottom of the first stone. "There he is, giving the first charm to Guinevere."

I crouched down and peered at the carvings. Below, on a separate scene, Merlin gave a charm to a mounted knight. A large crown adorned the brow of the knight.

"Arthur," I said. "One for Guinevere, one for Arthur."

"Why would Arthur want a concealment charm?" Roarke asked.

"Maybe he didn't." My gaze raced down the stone, taking in the various scenes. "Maybe he needed something else."

The bottom of the first stone showed Arthur and Guinevere parting ways, though it was impossible to tell how they felt about the separation. Happy? Sad? My heart thundered as I moved to the second stone.

The second stone showed Guinevere at a cathedral. She sat outside in a garden. Though the details of her face had been worn away by hundreds of years of wind and rain, her posture made her look content. There were other scenes of her life—her meeting with other people, her dancing, singing, and finally dying and being laid to rest in a crypt. I recognized the distinctive tower that had adorned Glastonbury Abbey. This stone finished her story.

I moved to the third and final stone. At the top was a scene of Arthur riding his horse toward a massive castle. I expected a battle in the next scene, but instead, he was welcomed to the castle. The pendant that Merlin had given him was clearly displayed around his neck. But rather than witnessing his life as I had Guinevere's, I saw Arthur go down into a crypt beneath the castle walls. Several knights followed him as well. His knights of the round table?

"He's going to his death," Roarke said.

"How can you tell?"

"He climbs into a sarcophagus in the next scene. And look at the mourners."

Roarke was right. Arthur was shown kneeling in a great stone box, unmistakable as a sarcophagus. And the people around him had their heads bowed. My gaze skipped to the next scene where Arthur was shown drinking a potion. The next carving showed him resting peacefully, his sword laid upon his chest just below the charm pendant.

"Why?" I asked. "Why would Arthur poison himself?"

"He doesn't." Understanding laced Roarke's voice. "This is the only myth about Arthur that I ever really knew, because it explained why he never ended up in the Underworld."

"You would know." He'd sure noticed when I'd gotten out. "What happens?"

Roarke nodded. "Arthur puts himself into eternal slumber beneath one of his strongholds where he waits to rise again, should England need him."

"Oooh." That was good. Very romantic and self-sacrificing. My favorite type of myth. "But you said he never goes to the Underworld."

"Exactly. Because if he did, he couldn't come back and defend England in its hour of need." Roarke turned to me, catching my gaze with his own, which pinned me to the spot. "It's impossible to escape the Underworld and rise again."

I swallowed hard. The undercurrent in his words was clear. *You, Delphine Bellator, have done the impossible.* Something even King Arthur knew he could not do.

"So what's the deal with Arthur? How will he rise again?" I asked, hoping he'd follow my lead away from talking about me.

He gave me a sharp look, but continued. "No one knows. He wasn't born immortal. No one is." Roarke pointed to the final scenes.

Arthur, rising from the crypt while a horde of warriors attacked his castle. The pendant around his neck was surrounded by concentric circles that made it look like it was vibrating.

"The pendant," I said. "Merlin's charm. It must have kept Arthur from crossing over to the Underworld."

"That's why he never ended up in my domain. His soul has been waiting here on Earth, ready to rise when it is needed. Merlin's magic made it possible."

"Whoa." I stepped back, my mind spinning. "So Merlin's other charm can keep the wearer out of hell."

"Yes. I'd heard rumors of such a thing amongst some of hell's darker denizens, but thought they were ridiculous. But those rumors came from Merlin himself, bragging of his old magic." Worry entered his dark gaze.

"What is it?"

He shook his head. "There's something worse about this kind of charm. That if you wore it once, you were imbued with its magic."

"Wait, so if the Ubilaz demon even puts it on, it doesn't matter if we take it from him? He's immortal forever?"

"Precisely."

CHAPTER TWELVE

"No question, then," Roarke said. "That's what the Ubilaz demon is after."

"Yeah, he could have learned about it in the Underworld. Ubilaz demons are ancient. He may have even spoken to Merlin in the Underworld and learned what the charm can do."

Roarke nodded. "He's smart, and those are the most dangerous adversaries. It's the perfect plan if you're going to try to escape. He'd know I wouldn't rest until I found him. But with Merlin's charm, he *can't* be forced to return to the Underworld."

A nuclear explosion of an idea formed in my head, so powerful that I might have stumbled. I glanced at Roarke, hoping he hadn't noticed my temporary insanity.

But this charm. Oh, my fated magic, Merlin's charm. If I couldn't convince Roarke to let me stay out of the Underworld, maybe I could force him to leave me be. If I had the charm, he couldn't make me return.

I tried to shut the thought down, hard. If I had the charm, I'd be immortal. I didn't want to be immortal.

Focus. I had to focus on finding the Ubilaz demon and winning my way free. It was the best way. The only way.

I met Roarke's dark gaze. "If we can't break the concealment charm, maybe we can find the demon at Arthur's grave. That Pictish stone told us that Merlin used potion magic, but that may not be enough information."

"That's what I was thinking," he said.

"But it will be hard." The many myths in the book I'd just read swam in my head. "There are about a dozen places that claim to be the resting place of King Arthur. There are so many different stories. All the cultures who have stories about him—the Picts, the Britons, the Romanticists—they're *different* stories. Like, as if the guy had lived a dozen different lives. Just like Dr. Garriso said."

Roarke knelt near the stone. "Maybe there's a clue here."

I joined him, my gaze devouring the details on the carvings. I kept returning to the top scene, to the castle that Arthur rode toward on his noble steed. The ramparts on top of the tower were so distinct. Lower in the middle, higher at the corners with graduated stairs leading up. How many castles could look like that?

Something tugged at my memory. "I might have seen this castle before."

"Where?"

"The book I was reading. I'm almost sure of it." I pulled my cell phone out of my pocket and breathed a sigh of relief to see that it still had some battery. Quickly, I snapped some pictures of the stones, then turned to Roarke. "Let's go. I've got a good feeling about this."

As it turned out, the castle was in my book. It was even referred to as "the defensive stronghold from which Arthur will defend England should the need arise." Given what we already knew, that was pretty clear.

I showed the image to Roarke, holding up my cell phone at the same time. "Richmond Castle in Yorkshire. It looks identical to the castle on the carving."

"Good enough for me."

"We're about five hours away by car," I said.

"Taking the nearest Underpath entrances puts travel time at about two hours. It could be too long. He may already be there."

"You could tear a hole in the ether, but then you'd be tapped out, right?"

"Close to it." He dragged a hand through his hair. "If we rush off now and use the Underpath, I'd have a hard time defending you against so many demons with my powers diminished like that. I'd need at least a couple hours to regenerate."

"I can defend myself pretty well, thanks." Despite the fact that the Ubilaz demon had almost torn me apart, my pride didn't like the idea of Roarke thinking he was all that stood between me and doom.

His gaze turned admiring. "I know you can."

Okay, *that* my pride liked.

"I've got an idea," I said. "Cass is a transporter. Since this is an emergency, it's probably worth having her transport us to Richmond Castle."

Roarke nodded. "Excellent."

"Let me call." I stepped aside and pressed my fingertips to my comms charm. "Cass? Nix?"

"Hey!" Cass said. "Gimme a minute."

"She's busy," Nix said.

"No kidding."

"Okay, I'm here," Cass said.

"We think we found the demon. We want to go after him, but in the meantime, could you give Aidan some info about how the concealment charm was made? Maybe Aerdeca and Mordaca can get started with trying to break it, just in case I'm wrong about the demon's next move."

"Sure," Cass said.

I explained what I'd seen on the Pictish stone, describing the cauldron and the rest of the image.

"Got it. I'll pass it on."

"And one more thing, Cass," I said. "Think you could come pick us up and transport us to him?"

"Anytime, pal. Seriously, for you, I'm a taxi."

I grinned, nostalgic for my lost power. I missed it, but losing it had been inevitable. And Cass would always have my back. I gave her directions, then cut the connection and turned to Roarke.

He was standing closer than I expected him to be with a wistful look on his face.

"They'll be here in a few minutes," I said.

"You're lucky. To have family like that."

"We're not blood family in that sense."

"Doesn't matter. You're family." His jaw was as square as ever, his expression just as stoic as if we were going up against the Ubilaz demon. But there was something in his eyes. Some kind of pain or damage.

I moved closer, drawn by sympathy or curiosity, I wasn't sure. Probably both. Because I couldn't possibly be seeing this right. The Warden of the Underworld was hard as a rock. He was iron. Steel.

But there was a strange expression in his eyes. I was so close now that I could see it clearly.

"You lost someone," I said. "Someone close."

His expression turned hard. "I don't know what you're talking about."

Oh, but he did. He'd lost someone, and the story wasn't pretty. Because there was guilt there, too. Was it his brother?

"Does this have anything to do with why you always follow the rules?" I asked. "Because back at your place, you said you broke them once. But you never would again. Never, ever again."

Something flashed on his face, but I couldn't identify it. Something dark and sad.

"You can tell me, Roarke."

His hands flashed up to grip my arms, tight but not painful. My heart leapt in my chest, thundering to the beat of the thousand drummers in my mind.

"Don't pry." Roarke's voice was hoarse. "You may not like what you find."

I shook my head. "You're a good guy."

"Not all of me. Not all of my decisions." He pulled me closer, clearly desperate to shut me up.

But the pain in his gaze made me want to keep talking, keep poking, keep learning.

He tugged me toward him until our bodies almost touched, but I could feel the heat of him across the inches that separated us. I shivered despite the warmth. How could there be so much fear and confusion and desire in so little space?

Unable to help myself, I stood up on my tiptoes, tilting my head up to his. My gaze was riveted on his mouth. It was the most beautiful mouth I'd ever seen, and suddenly, more than anything, I wanted it pressed against my own.

Roarke's dark gaze raced over my face, hot and fierce. He wanted me back. I knew he did. He had to.

The air vibrated around us.

I stiffened, stepping back from Roarke just as Cass appeared about twenty yards down the road.

She caught sight of us and yelled, "Hey!"

I didn't meet Roarke's eyes as I turned and hurried toward her. I could feel his gaze on my back as I walked, but I did my best to ignore it.

"Thanks for coming," I said when I reached Cass. She was dressed in her usual battle wear. Brown leather jacket, jeans, and her two favorite obsidian daggers strapped to her thighs. Her hair glinted dark red in the dim moonlight.

"No problem. You said we were headed to Richmond Castle in Yorkshire?"

"Yep. I think we may have found our demon."

"Excellent. Aidan has Aerdeca and Mordaca on the concealment charm. It helps to know it was created with potion magic, but he's not confident it's enough."

"It's a start."

"Yep." Cass held out her hands. "Ready?"

Roarke and I reached for one of her hands. A moment later, the ether sucked us through space and spit us out at the edge of a river.

I stepped back from Cass, feeling so much better than I did when I traveled through Roarke's Underpath. Transporting was infinitely easier.

"Thanks," I said.

"About time you got here." Nix's voice sounded from behind.

I turned to see her standing on a big rock by the river, a compact bow and arrow strapped over her back. Like me, she normally fought with weapons instead of magic.

"Hey! What are you doing here?" I peered behind Nix to see Aidan approaching from a ways down the river.

"Did you really think we'd let you do this without us?" Nix said. "Now that you know where the demon is, we didn't want to miss the party."

"Though he did pick quite the location," Roarke said from behind me. "There's a lot of magic here."

I stepped back from the river and examined our surroundings. We stood on the bank of a wide river. Behind me, a rocky hill rose up to support a massive castle wall. On both sides, the wall terminated at round towers, presumably turning away from the river at that point. Magic swelled from the castle, but not the kind I'd felt at Tintagel. This was something different.

"There's a town surrounding the castle on the other side of the wall," Roarke said.

"Why here, exactly?" Cass asked.

"The Ubilaz demon may be after a second charm that will keep him out of the Underworld. King Arthur wears the charm, and he's been asleep for a thousand years under this castle, waiting to rise and defend England in their hour of need."

"Cool." Nix looked back at the castle wall. "That is seriously bad ass."

I couldn't help but agree. I didn't want this fight to get all the way to Arthur's tomb—but freaking King Arthur! I wouldn't mind seeing him.

"Okay, we need to get into the castle," I said.

"I don't think we should go through the village," Cass said. "Too many places for unknown threats to hide."

Memories of the last time we'd tried to cut through a village to reach our destination flashed in my mind. I'd been changed into a Phantom. Or been triggered. Whatever.

"Yeah." I looked up at the craggy castle wall. "Let's climb the wall. There are enough handholds."

"I could give you a lift," Roarke said.

I glanced at him, my mind temporarily blanking out. Let Roarke carry me to the top of the wall, which meant holding me in those stupidly hot arms of his? It hadn't been a great idea at the river in Scotland; it wasn't a great idea here. Though he did seem pretty keen on it.

"Uh, no thanks," I said. "I feel like a good climb."

We'd scaled plenty of walls in our time in the treasure-hunting business. This little castle wall was nothing.

"Me too," Nix said in solidarity.

"Well, I'm taking my ride," Cass said.

Beside her, silver light swirled around Aidan. A moment later, a massive golden griffin stood in his place. His wings were as big as Roarke's, but he was a lion/eagle/magic combo instead of a demon half blood. Scary as hell, though, with his massive claws and a beak that could crush a Buick.

Cass climbed onto his back, and he launched himself into the air.

"Better get started," Nix said.

I didn't hang around to watch Roarke shift. Nix and I scrambled to the top of the craggy hill. Dim moonlight lit the way, giving us just enough light to see. When we reached the base of the castle wall, I was relieved to see that the stone and mortar were a bit eroded by wind and rain. Enough so that I could easily get a handhold and start climbing.

Side by side, Nix and I made quick work of climbing up the wall. But I couldn't help but worry about my magic triggering the history here and bringing back the dead. As soon as the thought crossed my mind, the magic in the castle started to vibrate. Like I'd jinxed it.

No!

Magic vibrated in the air, as if the castle were coming alive. We were only halfway to the top. Too far to fall. I glanced around frantically, but didn't see the familiar blue glow extending out from me.

Maybe it wasn't coming alive.

I looked up, heart pounding.

A face stared down at me, confusion in his gaze. He was clad in one of the historic Norman helmets favored by eleventh century warriors. The ones with the weird nose pieces.

"Shit!" I hissed. "Climb faster!"

The man shouted an alert. At least, that's what I assumed he shouted. He didn't speak English as I knew it.

There was a scuffling at the top of the wall, and a second later, a shout.

I looked up to see a black, shining liquid being poured from above. Steam rose off of it. My skin chilled in an instant.

Boiling oil.

And there was nowhere to go.

The burning black substance was almost upon me when a strong arm grabbed me around the middle and pulled me off the castle wall. My stomach plummeted as my grip was torn away, but a second later, my brain processed what had happened.

Roarke.

Oh, thank fates.

Below me, Aidan grabbed Nix in his claws, pulling her away from the wall before a second vat of oil could be poured on her.

I clung to Roarke as he carried me to the top of the castle wall and set me down. Six helmeted guards turned toward us and shouted. I drew my blade and charged them, plunging my sword deep into the chest of one who had only half the teeth he'd been born with.

At my side, Cass hurled a fireball at another guard. Its orange glow lit up the night. Roarke and Aidan each tore into one—Aidan with his beak, Roarke with his clawed hands. Blood sprayed in all directions. Nix sent an arrow into the eye of the fifth attacker while I sliced into the jugular of the final one.

When the bodies lay still around us, Nix leaned close to me and whispered, "Was that your weird magic?"

"No, I don't think so." Thank magic. I hadn't seen the blue glow, at least.

One by one, the bodies faded to nothing. They hadn't been real. Not truly.

"There are strong enchantments protecting Arthur's resting place from intruders," Nix said.

I had a feeling she'd have said that anyway, just to cover for me, but I thought she was right.

"Yeah," Cass said. "Keep a wary eye out. There's still a lot of magic here."

She was right. In the quiet night, I could feel it humming in the air, shrouding the ancient castle like a protective cloak. Who knew what would trigger the protective spells, but I had a feeling we would run into a few more.

The top of the tower wall was wide—at least twenty feet across. I walked to the interior edge and inspected the castle grounds. A labyrinth of ruins surrounded a grassy courtyard—buildings and rooms built up against the exterior castle wall. It would have once been filled with people and smaller wooden buildings. No way was I going in there. Who knew what I could bring to life in an area that had once been so rich with activity. I'd stick near the wall.

On the far side of the courtyard was the main keep, the massive, tower-like building that had been so distinct on the Pictish stone. That looked promising. Perhaps it was under there.

Cass and Nix joined me as Roarke and Aidan spread out in either direction, no doubt looking for threats.

"Can you feel where Arthur is resting?" I asked.

After a moment, Cass said, "No."

"Dead as a doornail," Nix said.

My dragon sense was dormant too. No matter how hard I tried, I got nothing. "I think the magic here is blocking me. Making it harder to find what it protects."

"But he's definitely here," Nix said. "Right?"

"Yeah." I studied the ruins below us. "Or something equally valuable, given all these protections."

"If we can get closer, maybe we'll sense him," Cass said.

"Until then, we'll search the old-fashioned way," I said.

Roarke approached, his dark, silvery gray skin lending him some amazing camouflage in the night. His black gaze met mine. "Which way?"

I looked left and right, which both looked about the same. So I just picked, pointing right. "That way."

We set off as a group, Roarke and me in the lead. He stuck close by my side, something I tried and failed to ignore. Though Aidan had changed back to his human form, Roarke remained a demon. It was damned hard to ignore a seven-foot-tall shirtless man with giant wings.

We kept our footsteps silent on the stone beneath us, a group moving in the shadows. The night was nearly moonless now that the clouds had crept over the sky. Rushing water sounded from below, and occasionally I thought I could hear distant shouts from within the castle.

The Ubilaz demon and his minions?

Maybe. Probably.

I picked up the pace, my gaze on the corner tower. There should be stairs within that would lead us down. From there, we could explore the ruins.

We entered the tower silently, Roarke leading the way. Fortunately, there were no guards within. I raised my borrowed lightstone ring to light the way, and we started down the stone, spiral staircase with Roarke in the lead. The treads were worn down at least half an inch, a testament to the thousands of people who had walked these steps over the last thousand years.

We were halfway down when a little hole in the wall caught my eye. It was right at the level of Roarke's head.

A murder hole.

Shit!

I yanked one of his wings backward just as an arrow flew out of the hole and slammed into the wall on the other side. It narrowly missed piercing Roarke's skull. My heart pounded, and my hand tingled where I had touched him.

"Thanks," Roarke said.

"Murder hole," I said. "Common castle defense."

Arrows continued to fly from the hole, too fast to be shot by anything other than magic. They left little chips in the stone with every blow. I shuddered at the thought of one piercing Roarke's skull.

He bent, passing under the stream of arrows that continued to thud into the wall. We followed him, finding only one more murder hole on our way down.

"Medieval folks were crafty," Nix muttered as we ducked immediately and avoided any chance at getting shot.

As soon as we reached the bottom of the tower, the sound of a shuffling footstep caught my ear.

"Watch out!" As soon as the words escaped my mouth, a fireball hurtled at us from the dark corner of the tower.

We were trapped in the stairway, fish in a barrel.

Quick as a flash, Roarke spun and flared his wings, creating a barrier between us and the fireball. The fireball exploded against his back, and he winced.

From the stair above me, Nix nocked at arrow and said, "Duck!"

We did, and she fired into the corner of the room. A shout sounded, then a thump. Roarke turned and surged from the stairwell. I followed, my ring illuminating the room at the bottom of the stars and revealing another demon in the corner. His skin had a pale, icy tinge.

He threw a bolt of ice, but Cass shot a fireball at it before it could strike Roarke. The ice evaporated immediately, and Roarke threw himself at the demon, breaking its neck before it could conjure another jet of ice.

With his back to me, I could see the extent of the damage to his wings and back. His back was raw, and his feathers were singed where his wings grew.

I hurried to him. "Are you all right?"

He turned, his gaze startled. "Fine."

"But your back." I reached out as if to make him turn around so that I could see it again, but he stepped away.

"It will heal." His gaze searched the rest of the tower. "But it's safe to say the Ubilaz demon is here. And that he's brought his minions."

CHAPTER THIRTEEN

We crept out of the tower, keeping our footsteps silent. Surrounded by the castle walls, the open, grassy courtyard stretched out in front of us. Rooms and buildings were built up against the castle walls, some in ruins, others more complete. Across the courtyard was the massive tower keep.

I pointed to it. "Let's make our way over there, following the castle wall. On the way, we can peek in these buildings and see if we find anything."

And Cass, Nix, and I would just hope our dragon sense picked something up. We set off across the grass, hugging the wall and splitting off to check out various doorways. The first room that I peered inside was entirely empty. My dragon sense didn't get a whiff of Arthur's tomb, either. But the second room, a long, rectangular one, had a trapdoor in the floor.

I poked my head back out of the room to tell my friends I was headed inside. They'd already moved on to the next building, so I ducked in to check it out.

My dragon sense didn't get a lead on anything inside the room, so I was not surprised to open the old, wooden trap door and find nothing but an old storage space inside. It was unlikely a wooden trapdoor would remain useable for a thousand years, so it was likely a more modern addition. When I shut the door and straightened, an eerie tingle of magic raced across my skin.

Oh no. The castle was coming alive to defend itself again. I stiffened, searching for the coming threat, but all I saw was the telltale blue glow spreading out from where I stood.

No!

It was me. The blue glow raced across the floor. Rushes appeared on top of the stone, the traditional floor covering of medieval castles. I had to try to control this. I had no idea how, but I couldn't keep doing this!

My limbs trembled as I sucked in a deep breath and tried to call the magic back to me.

Nothing happened.

I tried to suppress the magic within myself, shoving it deep down inside so that it couldn't do whatever weird thing it always did.

Briefly, the blue glow on the floor flickered. Hope flared in my chest, and I tried harder. But the blue glow returned, continuing to spread, climbing up the walls. Shelves appeared in its place, each holding hundreds of small glass vials of all colors.

An apothecary's shop.

A noise from the corner made me jerk my head around. An old woman had appeared with a child at her side. Both were dressed in medieval style clothing. Her startled gaze met mine, and she opened her mouth to scream.

Shit! I couldn't kill her, even though she probably wasn't a real person.

I shoved my hand into my pocket, scrabbling for the last of Connor's potion bombs. When I pulled out the familiar golden vial of a freeze bomb, relief surged in my chest. I hurled it at the old woman and little girl, and they froze solid.

Thank magic.

I didn't spare another glance at the room as I hurried out. As soon as I exited, I slammed into a warm, solid wall. My grip tightened on my sword as I stumbled backward, but strong hands grabbed my upper arms and steadied me.

"It's me." Roarke's black gaze met my own. "What's wrong?"

"Uh, nothing." I straightened my spine to try to catch his gaze again before it could travel behind me to the enchanted room. "You just startled me. Come on."

He nodded, then turned to catch up with my friends who were disappearing into the doorway of a building about twenty yards ahead. I followed, hurrying along in the shadows of the castle wall.

We entered the room, finding my friends inspecting the contents. This had clearly once been a barracks, probably sometime in the castle's more recent history, given that the heavy wooden beds were still intact against the walls. On one of the beds lay a fine sword made of yellow metal.

"A demon blade," Roarke said.

"Yeah." I eyed it, noting the distinct features. "But where's the demon?"

"Not here," Cass said as she approached me from the other side of the room. "But why the hell would it leave its—"

The ground fell out from beneath Cass's feet. She plummeted, disappearing into the ground.

"Cass!" Aidan, Nix, and I yelled at the same time.

I rushed forward, but there was no hole in the ground. When I reached the spot where Cass had fallen, a tingle of magic flowed through the floor and up my legs. Immediately, the ground fell out from beneath my feet. I clawed at the air, trying to grab anything I could reach, but found nothing. When I crashed to the stone floor beneath, pain sang up my legs. I scrambled up, a bit achy but with no broken bones.

"Del!" Cass cried.

Relief surged through me. She stood nearby. I looked up at the ceiling. There was no trapdoor.

The floor had closed as soon as it had sucked us both down. A spell.

A moment later, Nix fell through the ceiling and landed hard on her butt.

"Didn't you see us disappear?" Cass said.

"We're a team," Nix said as she stood. "Of course I jumped in the mysterious hole after you."

Aidan fell through the ceiling, followed by Roarke, whose gaze sought me out immediately. Aidan hurried to Cass.

"You've got to be careful!" His Scots brogue was thick with worry.

"I didn't know the room was enchanted!" Cass said. She looked around the dark, underground space.

So did the rest of us. It was dank and cold, with low vaulted ceilings. Several doors led off from the room.

"Are we in the dungeon?" Nix asked.

"Looks like it," Roarke said.

"Handy enchantment," Aidan said. "It takes the intruders straight to the prison."

"That's where the demon went," I said. "He fell through. But what happened to—"

My gaze landed on a black lump in the corner as a familiar smell hit my nose. Burned flesh. Fresh burned flesh.

A shadow in the back of the room moved, surging forward. I caught one glimpse of massive fangs and acid green eyes set into a face covered entirely in black scales before a burst of flame bellowed into the room. My skin blazed with heat, and my eyes smarted.

"Run!" I yelled.

My friend's gazes landed on the monster, which looked like some kind of giant lizard had bred with a wolf the size of a school bus. We ran for it, sprinting down the only hallway we could find.

We were fighters, sure. But we were also survivors. And sometimes, surviving meant running.

"Faster!" Nix yelled from the back. "It's coming!"

The beast's footsteps pounded as it chased after us. Were we going to have to fight it? We could, but not without casualties, given how fast and far that thing could breathe fire. My heart thundered in my ears as I sprinted down the dark corridor, threatening to explode.

I glanced behind to see it charging after us, its fangs glinting in a head the size of a VW Bug. It was gaining, fast enough to make me consider turning and fighting. But a moment later, I spotted the doorway at the end of the hall.

It was narrow enough that the monster wouldn't fit.

We raced toward the door, hurtling up the stairs. A roar sounded from below. I glanced back to see the monster howling its rage to the ceiling before disappearing in a poof of dust.

Whew.

Enchantment broken. Gratefully, I hurried out of the stairway behind my friends.

And straight into a crowd of more than fifty demons.

"Shit!" Cass said.

We were in the great hall of the main building. It was so big, and so high-ceilinged, that it was the only place this could be. Within, the demons caroused, no doubt killing time while their master sought Arthur's charm.

I caught sight of the Ubilaz demon leaving the room.

"There he is!" I said, just as the rest of the demons noticed us.

"Fight time," Cass said. "We'll hold them off. You follow the Ubilaz."

"On it." I clutched my sword and raced into the room with my friends.

The demons roared and ran toward us. It was close to the worst odds we'd ever faced, but with Roarke and Aidan on our side, we had a chance.

As he ran, Aidan shifted into a griffin. Roarke, already in his alternate form, took off into the air, charging the nearest demon. He broke the neck of one without ever setting foot on the ground, then headed for the next. In his griffin form, Aidan dodged a massive fireball, then bit the head off the demon that had thrown it.

Cass's magic swelled on the air as she hurled a lightning bolt at a pair of demons. Thunder cracked as the jet of white light slammed into them and fried them to a crisp. Nix fired her arrows in quick succession, taking out three demons straight through their eyes.

My friends could handle this. I just had to get to the other side of the hall. To do that, I had to make it through the demon in my way. It was a massive beast with huge horns sweeping back from his head and clawed hands that wouldn't have looked out of place on a dinosaur.

I raced toward him, sword at the ready. When I neared, he swiped out with a massive claw. I went low, expecting his attack, and sliced at his legs with my sword. He roared and stumbled. Before he could right himself, I hopped up and stabbed him in the back.

"Go!" Cass called.

I yanked the blade free and ran for the exit, leaving the sounds of battle behind. The night was cold and silent as I sprinted out of the great hall. I skidded to a halt, straining my eyes and ears as I searched for the Ubilaz demon.

But I saw nothing except the quiet, grassy courtyard. No demons, no people.

Damn it!

I tried to calm my racing breath enough to focus on my dragon sense. *Come on, come on. Let me find Arthur's resting place.*

But the magic protecting this place stayed strong, blocking my ability.

When I opened my eyes, a faint silver glow appeared in the distance. My gaze raced around. Was I doing that thing again?

But no. Nothing else was changing.

The glow coalesced slightly, forming a person.

A ghost!

I hurried toward it, determined to make use of my weird gift and ask a ghost for directions. It was a long shot, but that was the only kind of shot I had.

The ghost wore a dirty apron over pants and shirt that didn't look medieval. At best, they were eighteenth or nineteenth century. My heart sank. He wasn't old enough to know where the tomb was.

"Can I help ye, lass?" he asked.

This close, I could tell that the substance on his apron was dried clay. A potter, perhaps.

"Um, I'm looking for Arthur's tomb," I said.

His eyes brightened. "Ah, I've been there once. I'm Potter Thompson, lass. I'll lead ye right to it."

My heart leapt at this crazy bout of good fortune. "Really?"

"Of course." He set off along the wall, headed toward the east side of the castle compound at a quick pace.

I hurried alongside.

"I found it once while I was living, you know. But I ran for it—too afraid was I that I would wake the king. I could never find it again in life, but I kept looking. Perhaps it's why I didn't pass on. Finally found it as a ghost. But then, only one of our kind *could* find it."

"Uh huh." I nodded, though I didn't entirely understand what he'd said, and picked up my pace, trying to encourage him to move more quickly.

Fortunately, he took the hint and quickened his stride. "It's just so lovely to see another person," he prattled on. "Not those nasty demons."

Maybe that was why he was helping me. Whatever the reason, I'd take it.

When we reached the ruins of what looked to be an old church, he pointed to the door. "There's a tunnel entrance in the East Abbey. It will take you straight to the tomb."

"Thank you so much."

"Hurry now. I didn't like the look of the demon that came this way. The entrance is in the far left corner. Behind the tapestry. There is no door. You must use your Phantom form to enter."

My head whipped toward him, my jaw almost dropping. "What?"

"Your Phantom form, lass. Don't think I didn't recognize you. It's why I've helped you."

"Okay." This was new. I wanted to ask more questions, but there wasn't time. Perhaps I could come back and find him later.

"Hurry now, the demon has gone. Though I don't know how he'll get through the wall to the passage, if that's what he's looking for. But you can. Use your Phantom form."

"Okay. Okay. Thank you!" I raced through the door, cutting through the empty abbey that was missing its roof.

In the far left corner, there was no tapestry, just a few hanging scraps of one that might have once hung there. And there was no door, just like Potter Thompson had said.

But there was a big hole in the wall. I hurried toward it. I was finally alone, no longer watched by Roarke, so I raised my sword, letting my Phantom power flow through my arm and light up the blade with a blue glow that allowed me to see.

The rubble around the hole looked fresh—there were no weeds growing amongst it.

The demon had torn through the wall.

Damn, he was strong. And fast.

I jumped through the hole, almost losing my footing on the stairs below, and sprinted down. Once I reached the bottom, my dragon sense finally flared to life.

I was close! Close enough that the castle's protective magic could no longer block my dragon sense. I hurtled down the stone passageway, sprinting full out after the demon.

So close. I was so close!

I had to catch him. I couldn't spend eternity as a demon.

Ahead, I could just make out the back of the demon. He was bigger than I remembered, and fast.

But not as fast as me.

I pushed myself harder, wishing that I had one of Connor's potion bombs or some of Cass's fireball or lightning magic. She'd had to kill to get those powers, something I didn't want to do, but they'd come in handy about now.

But my Phantom form was faster and stronger.

Roarke wasn't here to witness it, and what did it matter at this point? The demon had almost won. I couldn't let him.

As I ran, I called upon my magic, letting it flow through me with a shivery tingle. My pumping arms turned fully blue and transparent. The weight of my body fell away. My speed increased. I pushed myself harder.

When I spilled out into a massive cavern tomb, the sight made me catch my breath. The demon had almost reached the platform in the middle where a body lay, but a knight with a massive sword fought him off. The knight was neither human nor ghost, but some strange enchantment.

Another protection for Arthur, who slept on the table in the middle of the ornately carved tomb.

Around the edges of the room, statues of knights stood, their hands resting on the hilts of their upright swords. The enormity of it hit me.

The knights of the Round Table.

And they were coming to life.

With motions as smooth as water, they raised their swords and stepped forward. Though they no longer looked like stone, they were not human either. Just like the one who fought the Ubilaz demon.

Some converged upon me, others upon my enemy.

"I'm here to help!" I cried.

But they stalked forward, unable to tell friend from foe. I would have to fight them off. But I could only hope they killed the Ubilaz demon before he got to Arthur. I could just make out the glint of gold around his neck, right above Excalibur, which rested on his stomach.

My dragon covetousness pinged, wanting those two treasures even though I would never take them.

I forced my gaze away and met the oncoming knight with my sword raised high. His blade whistled through my Phantom form, leaving no damage behind. While he recovered his blow, I turned corporeal long enough to land a blow with my sword.

The trick to my Phantom form was that my sword became a Phantom too. While it made me impervious to blows, I had to become human again for my sword to turn back to steel. My strike severed his arm, but there was no blood. Just as he swiped with his blade, I became Phantom again, changing back to human in time to remove his head.

Though he toppled to the ground, another knight replaced him. They circled me, ready to pounce. I panted and strained as I fought. It took all my skill and strength to hold them off. But there were too many. Twice, their blows landed, leaving deep cuts on my back and stomach. What I wouldn't give for that Phantom dragon to show up and save the day.

But it didn't show. So I forced the pain away as I fought, trying to keep my eye on the Ubilaz demon. He'd felled all but one of his own knights using only his massive strength and speed.

Pain flared at my shoulder as a knight's blade sliced me, drawing me back to my own fight.

Instinctually, I turned into a Phantom and spun to face him. One well-placed blow sent him to his knees. There was only one knight left who sought my blood, but I was weakening.

I charged, stabbing the knight in the middle with my blade before tearing it away. The knight fell to his side.

Almost there!

I whirled to find my prey, only to see all his knights on the ground and the Ubilaz demon climbing onto Arthur's platform.

"No!" I raced toward them in my Phantom form, but I was too late.

The Ubilaz demon grabbed the charm and threw the chain over his neck. My heart plummeted, but I hurled myself at the demon, catching him around the waist and throwing him to the ground.

He shrieked in pain, no doubt because of my Phantom ability to make those I touched live out their worst fears. While he thrashed beneath me, I turned corporeal and grabbed both of the charm necklaces, yanking as hard as I could. They tore away, and I flung them across the room.

The demon threw me off him. I skidded on the floor, then clambered to my feet. My injuries were slowing me down, so I took on my Phantom form. I charged the Ubilaz demon, who lashed out at me with his massive claws. They sailed right through my Phantom shoulder.

I turned corporeal and landed a blow to the demon's neck. Blood spurted, spraying me in the face as he stumbled and fell. I leapt for him, delivering a killing blow into his back.

He shuddered as I pulled my blade out, but he did not fall.

Though he bled, he didn't move like he was wounded. He spun as fast as a snake and swiped out with his claws. I returned to my Phantom form just in time. His claws sailed through my belly. Before he could swipe again, I turned corporeal and landed another blow to his chest, deep enough that it should've killed him.

Still, he stood.

He wouldn't die. He *couldn't* die.

But I couldn't stop. If I stopped, he would run. So I turned corporeal to stab him again. This time, I was too weak and too slow. He slashed me on the arm, sending pain radiating through me, then plowed a massive fist into to my stomach.

I stumbled backward as the breath whooshed out of me, adopting my Phantom form once more. The demon lurched toward me. I danced away.

There had to be something I could do! I had unknown death powers. According to seers, I *was* death. That had to be good for something. My head spun. I was so weak from blood loss that I was about to go to my knees.

I willed the demon to die, knowing it was hopeless.

A shriek sounded from behind me. Familiar.

A half-second later, the Phantom dragon swept into the room on gossamer wings. A sense of recognition slammed into me. What had before been a slight sense of knowing was now overwhelming. As if repeated contact had forged a bond between us.

Or reminded me of a bond.

I didn't know who or what the dragon was, but it was important to me.

The blue dragon whirled, its transparent blue wings carrying it toward the demon and myself. When the dragon's claws sank into the demon's back, instinct propelled me forward, a driving force I couldn't ignore.

While in my Phantom form, I grabbed the demon's shirt and yanked him toward me. At the same time, the dragon pulled backward, heaving its massive wings.

The demon's body went with the dragon, but its soul stayed with me.

It was a wispy, pale thing that sent electric ice shooting up my arms. I threw it aside as hard as I could. It flew through the air as mist before disappearing entirely.

I stumbled back, horror carving a hole in my chest, then fell to my knees, no longer strong enough to stand.

What the hell had just happened?

On the other side of the cavern, the dragon dropped the demon's body. When it crashed to the ground, it lay still.

Dead.

My gaze glued to the dragon as a thousand questions pinwheeled inside my head. The graceful beast whirled on the air, approaching me as a formless cloud.

When it stopped in front of me, it coalesced into the shape of a woman wearing a long, simple dress. She knelt in front of me as I struggled to stay upright on my knees.

She was a Phantom like me, though she looked ageless and strange. Her magic felt ancient, though she didn't look it. And though her face was familiar, I couldn't place it. I wanted to say she was my mother, but I was certain she was not. She was like nothing I'd ever seen before.

"Who are you?" I asked.

"I am Draka." Her voice sounded like the dull roar of waves. Her words were stilted, as if language—any language other than shrieks and roars—was unfamiliar to her. "I followed you from the Underworld."

"What—?" I asked.

I started to ask *what* she was when she spoke.

"They call you the Demise," she said. "But they are wrong. You must make them wrong. You are the Guardian."

No way. "Of what?"

"Life and Death. That"—she gestured to the body of the demon behind her—"was no coincidence. It has begun. When you entered the Underworld, it all began. The demon was your first task."

"Task?" I had a hundred questions, but shock made them come out one word at a time. I swayed.

Draka appeared to search for words, as if they were just out of reach. Finally, her mouth opened. "Protecting. Guarding. You must use your gifts. When they come, learn them. Use them. It is your inheritance. Your legacy."

"What legacy? Tell me more!"

"You have a role to play. Some want you to play it, others do not. But you must all the same." Her form wavered, turning blurry at the edges. As if she couldn't hold her human form. "I must go."

"No!" Frustration roared within me. "You can't."

But she shimmered and turned to blue smoke, then into a dragon once more. With a swoosh of air, she took off, gracefully swooping for the exit. Woozy from blood loss, I fell to my butt, turning to watch her fly out of the cavern.

Through darkened vision, I caught sight of Roarke, staring at me while I was in my Phantom form. My head spun and I collapsed. Maybe from blood loss, maybe from the shock of seeing him. I tilted my head so I could see him clearly.

Blood flowed from wounds dotting his chest and arms. His wings hung a little lower.

Behind him, Cass and Nix staggered in, supporting each other. Aidan prowled in as a griffin, playing guard at the rear.

Roarke said something to Cass and Nix, but my hearing was fuzzy. He pointed to the fallen Ubilaz demon, and Nix and Cass hurried over. To get its blood?

Roarke approached me quickly, his gaze indecipherable in his demon form. What happened now? Did he drag me back to the Underworld?

The Ubilaz demon was gone, and that fight was over.

But I'd bet the next one was about to begin.

CHAPTER FOURTEEN

Guinevere's tomb was quieter without the demons.

All I remembered from the end of the battle at Richmond Castle was Roarke picking me up and carrying me out of there. I'd woken in my own bed, Cass and Nix at my side. They'd gotten the blood to Connor, who'd made the antidote.

So, yay! I wasn't going to turn into a demon. In all seriousness, though, I was pretty thrilled about that.

Nix had handed me a letter from Roarke that had said only, "When you're better, come to me. Or I *will* come to you."

Well, that had been pretty clear.

At least he was giving me a chance to recover, which was good. I was going over to his place soon, but I had something to do before I faced the music. I didn't know what Roarke thought about what he'd seen, but he seemed to be on slow burn mode and that made me nervous. I hoped helping him catch the Ubilaz demon was enough to get me off the hook, but I wasn't sure.

So I'd come to Guinevere's tomb to clean it up since I wasn't sure if I'd have another chance. I didn't like the idea of it being disturbed. Of any archaeological site being disturbed.

"What do you say we get started?" Cass asked from where she stood beside me.

I stared down into the pit that held Guinevere's sarcophagus. The top was still shoved off, and her skeleton lay in its big stone box.

"Yeah." As much as I'd wanted to talk to her before, I really didn't want her to come back to life right now. I needed a break from the whole death-magic thing. Fortunately, the cathedral above hadn't come to life, but it still might.

I set my backpack on the ground, then jumped down into the pit beside Nix and Cass. I pulled Guinevere's charm out of my pocket and put it around her skeletal neck.

"Too bad the magic isn't more decayed," Cass said.

"Yeah." I nodded. It would've been a nice addition to our shop. But it wasn't decayed enough yet. Magic was like milk—it expired eventually. Once it went bad, it went *bad*. But instead of a foul smell, you got explosions and the like. So that was the magic that we took for our shop.

But Guinevere's charm contained such strong magic that it still had a lot of life left in it. That meant we had to return it to her sarcophagus.

I took one last look at her, then turned to Cass and Nix. "Want to do this thing?"

Nix cracked her knuckles. "Can't wait."

It took some huffing and puffing, but we got the lid of the sarcophagus back onto the base.

"Now for the last bit." I climbed out of the pit, followed by Cass and Nix.

We grabbed the shovels we'd brought and heaved the dirt back into the pit.

"Weird that she's been buried down in the crypt. All the other sarcophagi are just sitting out," Nix said.

"Extra protection, maybe," I said. "And there might be more bodies down below."

We sweated in silence as we filled the pit, then stomped the dirt down tight.

"Well, it's not perfect," Cass said. "But it's pretty good."

"Yep." I put down my shovel and grabbed my backpack, then pulled out the mini box of wine and three coffee mugs. "Now time for a toast."

"For real?" Cass asked.

"Hey, I didn't see you bring any of that swill you drink," I said. Cass preferred Pabst Blue Ribbon, the beer of hipsters and hillbillies, as she called it. "And anyway, red wine doesn't need refrigeration. And the box is portable."

I sat on the ground and pinched the little spout, pouring some into each coffee mug. Cass and Nix joined me, and I handed them each a half-full mug.

In unison, we raised our glasses and glanced at each other, then said, "To Guinevere."

"The woman who changed her fate," I added.

We drank, staring at the place where Guinevere's body lay.

"Do you think we can change our fate?" I asked.

Cass looked at me. "Do we want to?"

"I don't know." I frowned. "It's been quite a year though."

"Yeah," Nix said. "Defeating the Monster who kept us prisoner as kids, then you coming back from the dead. And I don't think it's over yet."

"No, it's not. Draka said more is coming." Earlier, I'd told them about the Phantom dragon and what it had said. "But I don't know if I'm ready."

"You will be," Cass said.

"You think?" Even as I asked, my chest felt empty and helpless. Draka had said someone called me *the Demise*. Wasn't I just as likely to be that as to be *the Guardian*? "How could I be called something as important as the Guardian?"

"Of life and death," Nix repeated Draka's words, which I'd told her. They just made the task ahead of me seem more impossible.

"Exactly!" I cried. "How can I live up to that?"

I wasn't half as good a FireSoul as Cass or Nix. I was just a book loving, boxed wine drinking mercenary, prophecy or no prophecy. I wasn't ready for this. Maybe I never would be.

"You can do it," Cass said.

"Seconded," Nix added. "You've got some crazy powers that'll help. I mean, you tore the soul out of that demon. Pretty scary."

"Yeah." It made me vaguely sick just to remember. I could always count on Nix for the truth, though. Between bringing back the dead, if only for a short time, and tearing souls from demons—I had some scary freaking powers. Someone with powers like that *would* be called the Demise.

"You're going to have to learn to control your powers," Cass said. "This newest power, the soul-snatching one—it's important. You're going to need it, I think. But no way you can let the Order discover that you have it."

"I know." She sounded like a broken record, repeating it all the time, but she was *right*. So right. My new power was the scariest one I'd ever heard of. No way the Order would let me live if they knew I could do that. "If Roarke lets me stay out of the Underworld and keeps my secret."

"We'll take care of him if he doesn't," Nix said.

Could we? Probably, between the three of us and Aidan. But I didn't want to risk Cass or Nix getting hurt. And I didn't want to hurt Roarke.

"You're important," Nix said. "The Guardian, whatever that means. Roarke will understand that we need your gifts. I don't know for what—but for something."

"But I don't understand my gifts! I don't know why I sometimes trigger historical sites, and why I don't. I have no control!" There was no way I could handle this responsibility.

"You will," Cass said. "You can handle this."

It was like she read my mind. "As long as it doesn't handle me. I mean, I could be evil. I liked the Phantoms when they turned me. It felt great. And I tear out souls.

That's scary shit. I'm scary. And what if I can't harness my power?" *That* felt impossible.

"I have faith in you," Nix said. "Even if you're scary."

"Me too," Cass added. "And I think you can handle this. You're strong enough. Whatever is coming at you— you're strong enough."

Warmth filled my chest, though doubt still tugged. "Thanks, guys."

We clinked our plastic coffee mugs together. I hoped this wouldn't be the last time I hung out with them. But I couldn't say it wouldn't be, not for sure. Because break time was over, and the reckoning with Roarke was about to begin.

I pulled Scooter onto the narrow road that led to Roarke's house, my heart lodged somewhere in my throat.

He must have heard the roar of Scooter's engine, because when I pulled up to the house, he was waiting for me on the porch. He looked better, though it was impossible to really tell without being able to see beneath the dark green sweater he wore. Some of his wounds had been deep, and his wings and back had been a mess.

I got off and removed my helmet, then climbed the steps, trying to subtly knock on my head. For good measure, I touched the lucky pendant I wore around my neck.

"How are your wings?" I asked as I approached.

"Fine." His gaze was indecipherable. "How are you? All symptoms gone?"

"Yeah." I held out my arms. "Human again." *Mostly.* "I guess you have some questions."

"Some." He gestured to a porch swing to the right of the door. "Sit?"

"Yeah."

The autumn air was crisp and orange leaves tumbled off branches as we sat on the gently rocking swing, exactly like two old people would after a life of fifty years together. Somehow, I didn't see that in our future.

"You going to take me back to the Underworld?" I asked.

"I haven't decided yet."

"Yeah, those questions. Right." My fingers drummed uncontrollably on my leg. I was an absolute wreck about this. If he insisted on taking me back, I didn't know what I'd do.

"It's no coincidence that those places came alive," he said. "That the dead came back, even for a short time. You're a Phantom, but that is impossible."

"Apparently not."

He grinned, as if unable to help himself, and my heart sped up.

I hurried to explain what I knew about the prophecy and what Aethelred had told me, putting emphasis on how I was necessary. "And believe me, I wouldn't make this up. I don't exactly *like* having some big prophecy sitting on my shoulders. I'm not even qualified to be the Guardian, whatever that is. Honestly, I've got some serious doubts I can even do whatever I'm supposed to do."

I was pouring out my guts to him, but I couldn't help it. Maybe I could tell him that I was a FireSoul as well. Get it all out on the table. But it wasn't only my secret. It was Cass and Nix's. I couldn't put them at risk.

"I believe you." He turned so that his gaze met mine. "Though I do think you're qualified."

That made one of us, at least.

"But you've put me in a tough situation." He scrubbed his hand through his hair. "The rules are clear. Your magic is dangerous. Forbidden."

"So how is this a tough situation for you? Mr. Rule Follower should know what he needs to do." Even though I hated it.

"Because I like you, Del. A lot."

"Yeah?"

"Worse, I think you're special."

"Special?"

"Yeah. I *know* you're special. I've known it from the beginning. I didn't track you by your blood when you escaped. Or by that bracelet I put on you." He gestured to the metal band around my wrist. "I could sense that you were special as soon as you arrived in the Underworld and I could track you. I can't do that with anyone else, but I could do it with you."

I had no idea what to say, so I kept my mouth shut, staring out at the brilliant fall foliage of the forest around his house and occasionally peeking at him. The rushing river roared in my ears, or maybe it was my heartbeat.

"I didn't know what to expect when I tracked you to Ancient Magic, but it wasn't someone like *you*. I like you." He looked away, as if this was more emotion that he was used to feeling, and he needed a breath of air to keep going. "Especially after getting to know you. I couldn't take you back to the Underworld or turn you in to the Order. Not for anything in the world."

"And that's a bad thing?"

"I don't know. I know that you make me willing to break the rules." His gaze met mine, fierce, and he pulled me toward him.

He hesitated for a second, just long enough to let me pull away. His intentions were clear. My escape would be easy. But no way in magic was I doing that. It might be a bad idea, but at this point, I didn't care.

His dark gaze burned into me as he lowered his head. When his firm lips pressed to mine, I swear my heart jumped out of my chest. He smelled like sandalwood and tasted like wine, but also like himself. Something that wasn't his magic. It made goosebumps prickle over my skin.

A weird little noise escaped my throat as his lips moved skillfully on mine. I kissed him back with everything I had, reaching up to grip his sweater in my hands. I was growing so lightheaded that I had to hold on for balance. I couldn't get enough of this.

He pulled away abruptly. "I'm sorry. Now isn't the time."

"Um." My heart fluttered in my chest, a frantic beat of wings as I tried to recover. "So, you ah, like *like* me?"

"How could I not like the woman who saves the day with her books and her sword?"

My heart just about exploded at his words. *He got me.* My books were a crutch because my dragon sense wasn't super strong, but they were still me. And my sword was definitely me.

I struggled to find something to say. "You've kept it pretty much on the down-low. I wasn't exactly expecting that kiss."

"Really? I felt the tension in the woods in Scotland. You did, too."

"Yeah. Why didn't you kiss me then?"

"At that point, I was still threatening to take you back to the Underworld. I didn't want to ask for a date at the same time. And a kiss was out of the question. I'm not interested in compelling a woman's affections."

Oh, so he was super honorable. I'd been told to expect it, but just knowing that he hadn't used his position of power to get in my pants was pretty awesome. I'd really been wrong to doubt him because he was half demon. "So, no trading dates for time out of the Underworld, then?"

"No. I'm not making you return there. You're special, Del. You have a role to play in whatever is coming, and I'm going to help you accomplish it. I don't know what makes you so special, but you are."

"I don't know either." Just the idea of what might be within me scared the crap out of me. And the idea of fulfilling the role of Guardian? Yeah right. How was I going to do that?

"We'll figure it out together." He reached for my hand and squeezed, then met my gaze. Sincere, determined.

We could figure it out together. With Roarke and my *deirfiúr*, I wasn't alone in this. But wherever this was leading, it was becoming clear that it was something only I could handle. Which meant I had to try. Even if I failed, that was all I could do. Keep trying, until I succeeded. Or it killed me.

I knew which outcome I was hoping for.

THANK YOU FOR READING!

Want to find out how Del died? Dragon's Gift: The Huntress, which stars Cass, is the series to read. There is an excerpt of book one, Ancient Magic, on the next page.

Reviews are so helpful to authors. I really appreciate all reviews, both positive and negative. If you want to leave one, you can do so at Amazon or GoodReads.

Turn the page for an excerpt of Ancient Magic.

PROLOGUE

Blood. I rubbed my tongue against the top of my mouth. Definitely blood. Fear shivered through me. The ground scratched my bare arms and the back of my neck. Prickly grass? My eyelids were gritty as I lifted them and blinked into the darkness. Stars twinkled down.

Night? Where was I?

Panic closed my throat. I gasped for air.

I pushed myself up and looked down. A ragged dress covered my skinny form, but didn't protect me from the chill night. I shivered as cold embraced me. A battered golden locket lay on my chest. It looked old, but I didn't recognize it.

A field stretched out around me, illuminated by starlight and a moon that hung low over the earth. The hair on my arms stood up at the sound of night creatures in the distance. A cold breeze rustled the grass, but fear chilled me more than the wind. Why was I out here?

Please don't let me be alone.

My heart thundered in my ears as I glanced around.

Two girls who looked to be about fourteen or fifteen lay sprawled on the ground beside me. They wore ragged dresses like mine.

Why was I here with two other girls my age?

Wait—were they my age? When I thought about it, I couldn't remember how old I was exactly. Just trying to think of it sent an icepick of pain through my skull.

With a trembling hand, I reached out and shook the girl closest to me.

"Wake up," I said. Panic sunk its claws into my chest. Why were we here?

When she didn't wake, I shouted, "Wake up!"

The girl gasped and shot upright, her black hair stuck with grass. Her terrified blue eyes met mine.

"Run," she gasped.

She spoke Irish, like I did, and the word shot straight through me.

"Hide," I said. "We have to hide."

I wasn't sure why, but I knew it more strongly than I knew anything else in the world. Her word—*run*—had triggered my own. *Hide.*

"Get up!" I scrambled to my feet. "We have to hide. Now. Now, now, now."

She clambered up, and we frantically tugged at the arms of the girl who still lay on her back. She was so pale she looked dead.

But I couldn't leave her. "Get up!"

She shrieked and jerked out of our hold, then crouched like a terrified animal. Her dark hair hung in her face.

What had happened to her, to us, that we were like this?

"FireSoul," she whispered, also in Irish. Her wide green gaze met mine through the curtain of hair.

The fear in her eyes must have mirrored my own. Her word pricked at my consciousness, but fear overrode it.

My heart pounded in my chest, trying to break my ribs. "Come on. We have to hide!"

She nodded and her head whipped around, searching for shelter like a cornered animal. I looked too. A small patch of woods about a hundred yards behind me caught my eye.

"This way." I spun and set off running across the field. They followed.

My lungs burned and my legs ached as we raced. I clearly wasn't used to being outside, nor to exercise.

But why? When I tried to think of the reason, nothing came but pain. My head ached when I tried to remember myself or my past. A sob burst from my chest. I couldn't remember anything.

Fear and the desperate need to hide drove me on when I wanted to stop and collapse to the ground, weeping. The trees loomed ahead—leafless, claw-like branches reaching for the sky. They were terrifying, but far better than the open field.

There was nowhere to hide in an open field.

Hide.

We dove into the woods, plowing through the underbrush until we were deep in the forest. Night creatures continued to rustle around us.

When we came to a large pile of collapsed trees, I plunged into them. Bark and branches scratched my arms as I found a nook created by the collapsed wood. The other girls crowded in behind me.

They were warm. Familiar, though I didn't recognize them. Safe.

We huddled together, panting. It wasn't quite as dark when they were near me, though it was more a feeling than reality.

Cold pinched my cheeks. I reached up and touched wetness.

Tears.

One of the other girls sniffled.

"What's your name?" I asked.

"It's—" The green-eyed girl started panting. Moonlight illuminated her panic-filled eyes. "I don't know!"

"I don't either!" the other girl cried. "I don't know my name!"

I tried to think of my own, poking for memories.

Pain.

I didn't know how old I was. Or where I was from. It hadn't been a fluke before. I really couldn't remember. "I don't know anything either!"

We gasped and cried, huddling closer. Their warmth felt familiar, like we'd done this a hundred times before. Slowly, it soothed me. I tried reaching into my mind to draw out some memories.

"Ouch." I cringed.

"What's wrong?" asked the dark-haired girl.

"Every time I try to remember something, my head hurts."

"Me too," said the green-eyed girl.

"And me," sniffled the other.

"Then what do we remember?"

"Run," said the dark-haired girl. "We're running, but I don't know from what."

"Is that how we got into the field?" I asked.

"Maybe." Her voice shook. "*Run* was all I remembered. When I woke, it was the only thing in my mind."

"*Hide,*" I said, thinking back. "That's what I remembered. We must hide. From a bad man." I rubbed my temple. "Or woman? From someone very bad."

Just the shadowy memory made tears pour down my face. My shoulders shook. The trembling traveled down my arms and legs until my entire body quaked.

I couldn't remember who we were hiding from, but my body remembered. Hiding from evil. Bad. *Bad, bad, bad.*

The green-eyed girl threw her arms around me. "Hey, hey, calm down. It'll be okay."

I gasped through my sobs and realized I'd been saying *bad* out loud. I didn't believe that it'd be okay—not really—but her words made me feel a little better.

"What do you remember?" I asked.

"FireSoul," she whispered. "We are FireSouls."

I gasped and jerked out of her arms. "No, we're not. We can't be."

I might not have remembered my own past, but some knowledge of the world still seemed to be intact.

FireSouls were bad. Even the word sent a shiver of panic through me.

Run, *hide*, and *FireSoul* were my only memories? That couldn't be. In my mind, I poked for the biggest, most important pieces of information. I wanted to know something.

What came was that I lived in a world full of magic. Thoughts burst in my mind. "I'm one of the Magica— you two feel like Magica as well."

I could feel their power now that I tried. Could smell it and taste it. The green-eyed girl's power felt like water on my skin and smelled like flowers. Tasted like vanilla. The dark-haired girl was just as powerful. Her magic felt like soft grass beneath my feet and smelled like fresh laundry. It tasted sweet, but I couldn't place it.

"Magica?" the dark-haired girl asked.

"Magica can create magic!" the green-eyed girl said, excitement in her voice. "I remember now. But I don't remember what kind I am. Witch, or sorcerer, or… mage."

"Or shifter, demon, or fairy," I added as the memories flowed back. "But they aren't Magica. They are supernaturals like us, but they don't use magic the same way we do. But they know about us. Unlike humans. The Great Peace keeps us hidden." It came back to me in pieces. Though we lived alongside humans, the Great Peace—the most powerful bit of magic ever created— hid us from human eyes. It took the powerful spells of hundreds of Magica and shifters to create the Great Peace. "Humans can see us but not our magic, which we shouldn't use around them anyway."

"Right, I remember now," the dark-haired girl said.

"I feel your power too. But you don't feel evil," I said. "Not like a FireSoul would feel."

"We're not evil," the green-eyed girl said. "We haven't killed…I don't think. But I do remember that we're FireSouls. I know it."

"Everyone hates FireSouls," I whispered. They were the bogeyman because they stole the magical gifts of others by killing the original owner. Was *I* the bogeyman? Me and these two girls? Had I killed another Magica to steal his gift? Wouldn't I remember something as terrible as that?

"Is that why we're hiding?" the dark-haired girl asked. "Are we hiding from the Order of the Magica and the Alpha Council?"

"No," I said, though the two supernatural governing organizations would be after us if they knew we were FireSouls. "We're hiding from someone worse. But if we really are FireSouls, we can't tell anyone. They'll throw us in prison."

"We are FireSouls," she said. "When I woke, I knew it. It was my memory. As strong as yours."

I swallowed hard, remembering how strong that urge to hide had been. I'd woken confused, but when the dark-haired girl had said *run*, it had burst back into my consciousness.

"Are we really FireSouls?" the dark-haired girl asked. "I don't feel like a FireSoul. I don't feel evil."

I didn't either. I felt hungry and cold. My stomach growled and I shivered. If only I had something to eat. If only I was warm. I wanted it so badly.

A strange feeling tugged at my middle. As if there were a string tied around my waist that pulled me to the left. A sense of food and warmth flowed from the invisible string.

"There's food and shelter nearby," I said. "I feel it."

"Treasure," whispered the green-eyed girl. "You can sense treasure."

Treasure. Of course I could sense food and shelter. I coveted them. They were treasure to me right now.

I was a FireSoul. That was proof.

FireSouls were given that name because they shared a piece of a dragon's soul, though no one knew how it had happened. If dragons still existed, they were hiding. But legend said that all magic descended from dragons. FireSouls somehow shared a part of their soul.

That's why we could steal powers and find treasure. Dragons were covetous. They coveted treasure of all varieties—including the powers of others. The greatest treasure of all could only be obtained through death.

"We can find what we need with our dragon-sense," said the green-eyed girl. "If we want it badly enough, it becomes treasure. Then we follow our sense to it."

Was that how we were supposed to survive? Become hungry enough to find food and then steal it?

I looked down at my ragged dress and skinny body. The only thing I had of value was the necklace, and even that was probably almost worthless. It didn't look like I had a lot of choice right now. If I had parents, I had no idea who they were or how to find them.

My throat tightened. Did I have a mom and dad? Where were they? I pushed through the pain in my mind, trying to remember. But nothing came. Just blinding agony. I slumped against the other girls.

"Are you okay?" one asked.

"Yes." I pushed thoughts of parents away and focused on surviving. "If we use our dragon sense, we have to be careful."

If we were caught, we would be thrown in the Prison for Magical Miscreants. It was a cold, dark, terrible place, I remembered that. A shiver ran over me. My own personal bogeyman. In the corner of my mind, it felt like someone had once threatened me with that prison, but when I poked at the memory, the blinding pain came again. Why didn't I learn? I needed to quit poking at my personal past.

"We need names," I said.

"Yes. I hate not having one," said the dark-haired girl.

The green-eyed girl looked up at the sky. "I will be Phoenix. After the constellation. Call me Nix."

I liked that. Naming ourselves for something bigger gave me hope. I looked up too. A cluster of bright stars caught my eye. I didn't know what in my past had taught me the constellations, but I was grateful for it. "I'll be Cassiopeia. Call me Cass."

The green-eyed girl looked up and sighed. "You took the best ones."

I giggled, the sound surprising me.

"I'll take Delphinus," she said finally. "But it'll be Delphine. And you can call me Del."

"Okay. Del and Nix." They both looked so different. Panic gripped my throat as I realized that I didn't know what I looked like. I pulled my hair around. Red. "We look nothing alike. I don't think we're related by blood, even though we're all FireSouls."

They were rare from what I remembered, but I didn't recall the gift being genetic.

"We're sisters now," Nix said. "Because we're all we've got. I don't remember my parents."

"Me neither." Del sniffed back tears.

"We'll find them." I closed my eyes and focused on the idea of parents. I wanted them more than anything, so I should be able to find them.

But the magical string didn't tie itself around my middle. I thought harder, reaching into my mind, pretending it was a book I could flip through.

Agony pierced my skull.

I retreated, gasping.

"I tried to find them," I said. My parents were lost to me. My throat tightened and tears burned. "I don't think I know enough about them. I could imagine food and find that. But people are harder, I think."

"We'll find them somehow," Del said.

I nodded, trying to hope but finding it hard.

"We can only use our dragon sense to find food and other things we need," I said. "No killing for other powers." I didn't want to be a murderer, no matter how much power it got me.

Nix nodded. "I don't want to be a monster."

"Me neither," said Del.

"If another supernatural asks how we can find things, we say we are Seekers," I said.

The green-eyed girl smiled. "That's a good idea. Camouflage ourselves."

"Exactly." Seekers were a type of supernatural who could find things. As long as we didn't kill and steal powers, we could use our ability to find treasure and just say that we were Seekers.

"Do we have other powers we can use?" Del asked.

"I don't know," I said. If it was about me directly, I couldn't seem to remember. "FireSouls can be other types of supernaturals as well. You both feel magical to me."

Nix closed her eyes. I felt her power surge against me like water lapping at my skin. The taste of vanilla burst on my tongue, and her flower scent filled my nose. Her hands began to glow. She cupped them in front of her.

Eventually, a small match appeared in her palms.

"You're a conjurer," I said as my power swelled within me.

"Not a very good one," Nix said. "I wanted to conjure a fire for warmth."

I listened with half an ear as the power in my chest grew. It felt like it was in response to hers, spurred on by what she had. I embraced it, though I didn't understand it, and held my arms out. The magic pulsed within me, roaring to be released. I raised my palms to the sky and let it go.

An enormous fireball shot from my palms, throwing me back onto the ground as it roared into the sky. It burned away the tops of the trees and exploded into the night. Orange flames surged through the air, burning my skin.

Panic rose in my chest as I scrambled to my feet. We were trapped. Del and Nix looked at me with horrified eyes.

"I don't know what happened!" I said. The sky above me continued to burn, though the forest around us was untouched. "People will see the flame! We have to hide!"

Del lunged for me. She enveloped me in her arms and grabbed Nix, pulling her into the hug. A second later, the ground fell out from under me.

We collapsed to the ground a moment later. It was colder here, the wind stronger. I climbed to my feet. We were on a mountain looking down on the field below. Fire roiled in the air above it, a beacon of magic. But at least it wasn't lower. The animals and the people would be safe.

"We were in a valley," I said as I turned to Del. "And you can transport."

Del's wide eyes met mine. "Apparently. It was instinct. I followed it. And thank magic for it. What did you do down there?"

I looked down at the field that was lighting up the night. It would draw people. We were fine on the mountain for a little while because we were so far away, but we needed to get out of here soon.

"I didn't mean to light it all on fire," I said. "When Nix conjured the match, I felt like I could create a match too. So I let my power out."

"You're a Mirror Mage," Nix said. "You borrowed my conjuring power."

"A strong one," Del said.

"Too strong. I couldn't control it."

Mirror Mages weren't rare or very dangerous, from what I recalled. They could reflect back the magic of any supernatural that they were with. But it was just temporary, and the other supernatural got to keep their powers the whole time. From what I remembered, if Mirror Mages didn't use the borrowed gift right away, they could use it later. But it was a one shot deal. I could have held on to the conjuring gift I'd borrowed from Nix, but I'd only have been able to use it once.

In a way, Mirror Mages were a tiny bit like FireSouls because they used the powers of others. But they weren't very dangerous because they couldn't keep the magic or replicate it more than once.

I turned toward the valley. The fire was starting to dissipate, but it was still an unnatural spectacle, the sky alight with flame.

"I could have killed us if I hadn't pointed my hands to the sky," I whispered. "I'm dangerous."

"I think you need to practice," Del said.

"Or not use my power at all." Tears pricked at my eyes. Why was I like this?

"Let's not worry about that now," Nix said. "We should get out of here. Let's find food and shelter."

I nodded and blinked the tears away. "Okay. Let's go."

We set off along the mountain ridge, following the magical string tied around our waists. I was tired and scared, but at least I had my *deirfiúr*. My sisters.

But as I walked, the most horrible thought occurred to me. Had I been born a Mirror Mage, or had I killed someone for this gift?

CHAPTER ONE

Ten Years Later
Temple of Murreagh
Deep Beneath Western Ireland

"Cass! Answer me, damn it. Are you hurt?" Nix's voice echoed quietly from the pendant around my neck.

"Gimme a sec," I wheezed as I shoved the huge rock off my leg and scrambled behind a big boulder. Pain radiated from my shin, but nothing felt broken, thank magic. I didn't have time to deal with it anyway. A nasty looking shadow demon was currently trying to blow my head off. As long as my limbs were mostly functional, I was good to go.

A blast of magic blew apart the stone over my head.

I ducked and rubble bounced off my shoulders.

Damn demon!

When it stopped, I peered over the boulder at the demon who guarded the altar in the middle of the underground temple. It'd taken me nearly six hours to get through the enchantments that led to the temple. Fire charms, moving rocks, an awful riddle—the whole lot. Real Indiana Jones stuff, but I didn't have the cool hat.

After all that, it seemed like it should be smooth sailing. But no, this treasure was protected by a shadow demon. Who was apparently very displeased with my presence.

His skin was dark gray, his powerful body clad in simple pants and a shirt. He was basically human-shaped, except for the exceptionally bulky arms and the narrow black horns that came out near his temples and ran back along his skull. Dark eyes glinted maniacally through the dust in the air.

Though big, he was dwarfed by the subterranean temple that housed the Chalice of Youth, my current assignment. The chalice sat on an altar behind the demon, gleaming gold. Graceful columns supported the soaring stone ceiling, each carved in the shape of a different long-forgotten goddess. The only light came from eerie torches that lined the walls. The air was stagnant, permeated by the scent of smoke that wafted from the shadow demon.

"Do I send backup?" Nix asked through static.

"No. I've got this." I didn't usually need my friends to step in and save my butt on a job, but it gave me the warm fuzzies to know they were willing. "You're breaking up, Nix. Too much magic from the demon. I'm turning you off now."

Strong magic, like the kind the demon was throwing, usually interfered with the comms charm that hung around my neck. Something about the magical signature overpowering the puny charm that fueled my necklace.

I usually worked alone, but sometimes—okay, always—a riddle enchantment stumped me. At that point, Nix was there to back me up via a quick call through my comms charm. But now that she'd gotten me through the riddle that had opened the main door to this temple—Why does a dragon cross the road?—I no longer needed her help.

"Fine, don't—" More static broke up Nix's voice.

"If I'm not out in an hour, remember that I hate lilies," I said. "Worst funeral flower."

"But—"

I touched the silver charm around my throat, and its magic went dormant. Only the sound of the shadow demon's breathing echoed in the chamber.

It was time to get this over with. I was starving, and this was my last gig before the long weekend. My leg screamed as I pushed myself to my feet. *Breathe through the pain. It's just bruising.*

I drew my obsidian blades from the sheaths strapped to my thighs and stepped out from behind the boulder. Torchlight reflected wickedly off the black volcanic glass. Lefty and Righty, I called them—not nearly regal enough names for their power—but I'd never been good at clever names.

"Time to go back to hell, fella," my voice echoed in the stone chamber. "The devil says he's missin' ya."

The shadow demon laughed, his dark gray skin absorbing the light. Fine, it was a little corny, but I was tired.

The demon raised his hand to throw another blast of magic at me. I flung Righty at him, dodging the whoosh of magic that he managed to get off before my blade sunk into his arm.

Perfect hit. Ten points.

He roared in pain as heat seared my shoulder through my leather jacket.

Oh, so he wanted to play that way? With heat as well as wind? I thought wistfully of blasting him back with a reflection of his own power. His magic manifested as burning smoke. I'd give him a flaming tornado.

Except that was the problem. My magic was too powerful for me to control. I just blew shit up if I tried. I didn't want to draw attention to myself, so I didn't use my power. But I didn't hide that I was a Mirror Mage—strong supernaturals could tell I had magic. If I didn't use it often, my magical signature appeared weak to those strong enough to sense others' powers.

So I'd gotten really good with weapons.

I pricked the back of my hand with Lefty before immediately throwing the blade at the demon's heart. My blood ignited a spell that would call its twin back to me.

As Lefty hurtled toward the demon, Righty pulled itself out of the demon's arm and flew through the air toward me. As long as I was quick—which I usually was—I always had a dagger at hand.

I reached up and snagged Righty as I kept an eye on the dagger that zoomed toward the demon. He used magic to blast it away.

"That's all you've got?" he roared.

I dove behind the nearest column, a stone warrior woman in a flowing cloak, both of her hands gripping swords.

A guardian. Of me, I decided.

I swiped my dagger over the small amount of blood welling on the back of my hand so that my other blade returned to me.

The demon roared again, his muscles bulging beneath his thin shirt as he drew his arms back to throw twin blasts of magic at me. All supernaturals had different gifts and his seemed to be throwing blazing blasts of smoke that blew things apart like a grenade.

The smoke blast hit my guardian column. Her bottom half blew apart, rock and debris flying across the temple. With an enormous cracking sound, the guardian crashed to the ground. The stone floor vibrated beneath my feet. Dust filled the air until I could hardly see.

Guilt ate at me over the damage done to such an ancient place. Don't worry about that now. Fix it later. I jumped onto the guardian, who was now lying on the ground in several large pieces, all lined up in a row. I raced across her skirt, jumping from piece to piece until I was right above the shadow demon.

I leapt for him.

He looked up at the last moment, his eyes widening. He twisted and Lefty sank into his meaty shoulder. With a roar, he threw me off him. I skidded across the floor, then groped my way behind the top of the fallen column. He was strong, both in magic and form, and his magic smelled ancient. Like dust. I'd bet he was an old demon.

"Blades?" he yelled. "You come at me with blades? Use your magic and give me a real fight!"

"What? You bored? Been guarding this tomb a long time, eh?" I said as I flung Righty at him.

It sank into his chest, nearly a perfect shot at his heart. Or at least, where I figured a shadow demon's heart might be.

He yanked it out and said, "You have no idea."

I swallowed hard.

Missed his heart, I guess.

Quickly, before he could fling the dagger, I called it back to me. Righty pulled itself out of the demon's hand and flew home.

The demon didn't startle, nor did he look weakened by the dark blood leaking from the wound in his chest. Old and strong, like I'd thought. Even if I hadn't hit his heart, he should at least be incapacitated. But this one was different. He wasn't even winded from the blade that had sunk six inches into his chest.

"Well? Won't you give me a real fight? You are one of the three. Strong enough to fight, but you don't."

My heart tried to climb into my throat. "What does that mean?"

The three? Did he mean me and my *deirfiúr*? How could he know about Del and Nix?

"What do you mean?" I screamed when he didn't answer quickly enough.

"You don't use your powers." He threw another blast of magic at me. Blazing smoke blasted away my column barricade, and I scrambled back.

He wouldn't use his powers either if it meant getting locked up in the Prison for Magical Miscreants. As long as I didn't use them, I could pretend that I was nothing but a low-strength Mirror Mage and have a lovely life where no one tossed me in prison.

The shadow demon threw another blast of fiery smoke. It plowed into the ground in front of me. The stone floor exploded. The blast threw me backwards. Pain streaked through me. My entire front felt singed, pierced by small pieces of shattered stone. A cough tore through my lungs and I blinked blindly, my throat and eyes burning.

I could barely see, and he kept throwing those damned blasts of smoke at me, driving me ever backward. I just had to get him to lay off for a sec. Then I could question him.

Through the dust, I could make out his hulking form approaching. It was risky, but I threw each of my blades in quick succession, hoping to incapacitate but not kill.

The thud of a body collapsing sounded. The blasts of power stopped coming.

I climbed to my feet and limped toward the form sprawled on the ground. The stone bit into my knees when I dropped beside him. My blades protruded from his chest, one embedded in each pectoral. His breath strangled in and out of his lungs, but he wasn't dead. I grasped his rough shirt and shook him.

"What do you know about me?" I said.

"What"—he coughed—"you are."

"But—"

His lips parted, and I snapped my mouth shut, frantic to hear what he had to say.

"FireSoul."

I stumbled back, my stomach twisting. Chills raced over me. How could he know that? No one knew that but my *deirfiúr*.

"I'm a Mirror Mage." My voice came out hardly louder than a whisper. I tried again, louder, fear choking my throat. "I'm a Mirror Mage!"

Panic welled in me, and I crawled back to him, reaching for his shirt again, desperate to shake answers from him.

His eyes were dimming, their gleaming black light turning a dark gray. A great breath shuddered out of his lungs, followed by stillness.

The light faded from his eyes, and his body disappeared. My blades, no longer embedded in a chest, clattered to the floor.

"No!"

My heart threatened to break my ribs. I hit the ground, frustration and fear beating in my chest.

The demon was gone. Not dead—you couldn't really kill a demon—just send them back to whatever hell they'd originally come from. Normally very neat and tidy. Except this one had information about me, and my blades had been too accurate. The demon had seemed so strong when my first blade had found its mark. I'd wanted to question him more. This was what happened when I freaked out. Like a bull in a china shop. And it was the main reason I could never use my magic.

My breath echoed too loudly in my ears. Think, think. How could the demon have known that I was a FireSoul? Was it because this job was in Ireland, my homeland? At least, what I assumed was my homeland, given that I could speak Irish and had red hair.

One option was so terrifying I couldn't even poke it with my mind. It was the bogeyman that lurked at the corner of my memories. Whenever I pressed too hard, it leapt up, bringing with it a splitting headache and adrenaline like nobody would believe.

I had to get out of there. Talk to Nix.

Quickly, I grabbed my blades, shoved them into their sheaths, then climbed to my feet. I limped to the altar, pain singing up my leg, and grabbed the golden chalice. It's magic sang beneath my palm, an unsteady beat that indicated this was old magic. The perfect age for selling. There were other priceless objects too, no doubt tributes to the gods carved onto the columns.

My fingers itched to pocket a couple, namely a golden dagger encrusted with rubies and a strange hexagonal blade that looked wickedly sharp on all sides. Despite my terror, covetousness surged within me. My hand trembled as I reached toward the golden dagger. Just one touch. I wouldn't take it.

No.

I sucked in a deep breath and clenched my fist. Not mine. Not mine. Like an addict resisting a fix, I dragged my gaze away from the glitter.

With a shaking hand, I pulled a small black rock out of an inner jacket pocket. My last transport charm. Like all magic that wasn't my own, they were expensive and hard to come by. Del could make them because she could transport, but her power was limited and they commanded a lot of it, so she couldn't make them often.

I should use the charm only in emergencies.

But this sure felt like a heck of an emergency.

I threw the stone to the ground. It shattered and a glittering silver cloud rose in front of me. I stepped into the sparkling stuff and envisioned my home. Magic grabbed me around the waist and threw me through the ether.

AUTHOR'S NOTE

Hey, there! I hope you enjoyed reading *Magic Undying* as much as I enjoyed writing it. In addition to being a writer, I'm also an archaeologist. This influences my books enormously and is why so many of them have scenes set at historic sites. I try to stay as true to history as I can, but sometimes I have to fiddle with things to make a more entertaining story. If you're interested in reading about what I borrowed from history and what I modified, read on. At the end, I'll talk a bit about why Del and her *deirfiúr* are treasure hunters and how I try to make that fit with archaeology's ethics (which don't condone treasure hunting, as I'm sure you might have guessed).

Magic Undying is particularly full of history and myth, even for one of my books. I chose to go with a Guinevere, Merlin, and King Arthur theme after talking to my friend Melly about Tintagel Castle. I visited a few years ago and loved it, but I missed Merlin's Cave, which Melly highly recommended. When it came time to send

Del to a cool location, Tintagel Castle and Merlin's Cave popped right to mind. Which, of course, led me down the path to the myths surrounding King Arthur.

As I mentioned in the book, there are many stories surrounding King Arthur and his compatriots. According to British folklore, he was a hero who may have defended Britain against Saxon invasion in the late fifth and early sixth centuries AD, though historians still aren't sure if he was real.

For *Magic Undying*, I created a Frankenstein of Arthurian legend, taking the different stories and sticking them together to create a mystery for Del and Roarke to solve. Tintagel Castle, Glastonbury Abbey, and Richmond Castle were not from the same stories or even the same cultures. Arthur is associated with Tintagel Castle through Geoffrey of Monmouth's twelfth century book, *Historia Regum Britanniae*. According to Geoffrey, Arthur was conceived at Tintagel. Merlin's Cave is a real place beneath Tintagel, but it wasn't made famous until the nineteenth century, when Alfred Tennyson wrote the twelve narrative poems *Idylls of the King*. In this version of events, Arthur was washed ashore at Merlin's Cave as a baby and carried to safety by Merlin.

Glastonbury Abbey became associated with the story of Arthur and Guinevere in the twelfth century, likely as a publicity stunt to draw more pilgrims to the abbey, which had burned in 1184. According to historian Gerald of Wales (b. 1146 — d. 1223 AD), the abbot of Glastonbury Abbey, Henry de Sully, commissioned a search beneath the abbey in the 1190s. The search discovered two skeletons lying beneath a cross that was inscribed with *Hic jacet sepultus inclitus rex Arthurus in insula Avalonia*, which translate to "Here lies interred the famous King Arthur on the Isle of Avalon." Modern historians have determined that this was a hoax meant to draw pilgrims to the abbey, which I think is fascinating in itself.

Richmond Castle, the location of the final quest, is an eleventh century Norman castle. According to legend, Arthur lies asleep beneath the castle, along with his knights, waiting to rise and defend England in its hour of need. Unfortunately, the only sources that I can find for this legend are several sites on the internet. I believe this is because these are primarily oral traditions that have moved to the internet, as is natural, but it's not nearly as impressive as being able to say that Geoffrey of Monmouth wrote the legend down in the twelfth century.

Some of my research comes from primary sources like Geoffrey of Monmouth, some comes from travel, and the rest comes from Googling things while sitting on my couch. There can always be an element of error, particularly with Google, but that's not going to stop me from using something if it will improve the story. At least I'll 'fess up if I do it, though.

I chose to use Richmond Castle for a few reasons. One, it's an impressive structure that makes a great final setting. Castles have all kinds of excellent things for an epic fight scene—dungeons, murder holes (that's really what they're called!), giants walls, and secret passages. I had to add a few extra rooms and buildings, but the massive wall, courtyard, and great keep are accurate.

Cadbury Castle in Somerset is also said to be a resting place for Arthur, from which he will rise to defend England, and the location is actually a bit better because it is closer to Tintagel. However, Cadbury Castle is an Iron Age hillfort. While hillforts are impressive (and actually more contemporaneous with Arthur than the Norman Richmond Castle), they lack the massive stone castle-like structure that I was looking for as a final setting. So I ditched Cadbury Castle and went with Richmond Castle, even though it was built a few hundred years after Arthur's death.

I chose Richmond Castle for a couple other reasons as well. According to local legend (according to the internet), there is supposed to be a secret tunnel between Easby Abbey and Arthur's tomb. Easby Abbey is actually located outside of the castle walls. I wanted to send Del down that tunnel (because how cool is that?), but I couldn't make her leave the castle and hike a few miles downriver just to get to the tunnel entrance. So I moved the tunnel entrance into the castle and called the abbey "the east abbey."

Potter Thompson, the ghost who directed Del to the tunnel entrance, is a figure from legend as well. It is said that he found a tunnel entrance into King Arthur's tomb while out walking. He made it all the way to the tomb where he found the sleeping king and his knights in full armor. On a table, he spied Excalibur and a horn. To prove that he had found the tomb, he decided to take Excalibur (bad idea, right?). Upon touching the sword, the king and the knights began to move. Frightened,

Potter Thompson ditched the sword and ran for it. Upon exiting the tunnel, he heard a voice say:

"Potter Thompson, Potter Thompson
If Thou hadst either drawn
The sword, or blown the horn,
Thou wouldst have been the luckiest man
That ever yet was born"

Potter Thompson tried to relocate the tunnel, but could never find it. So I brought him back to life as a ghost and had him assist Del.

It was particularly egregious of me to combine two Arthurian legends. Pictish stones would not have contained a carving of a Norman castle (Richmond Castle). Pictish stones were created between the sixth and ninth centuries AD by the Picts who lived in eastern and northern Scotland. Richmond Castle was built in the eleventh century and is located over 200 miles away in England. So why did I include Pictish stones?

When I first started researching Arthurian legend, I would not have expected to find anything Pictish. However, there is a Pictish standing stone called Meigle 2, which once stood at the entrance to the Meigle Churchyard in central Scotland, just outside of Perth. Carved into it is a figure surrounded by four beasts. It could be a picture of Daniel surrounded by lions (which is honestly the most likely case), but some interpretations say that it shows the execution of Vanora. Vanora is another name for Guinevere. It's actually a really vile story in which Guinevere is torn apart by wild dogs, so I won't share it here, but it is the reason that I chose to use Pictish stones as the clue that led Del to the Norman castle.

As for Guinevere taking her fate into her own hands, I made that up entirely. You could probably tell because it involved a concealment charm, which are not real as far as I know. I did it for the reasons that Dr. Garriso stated in the books. I didn't like how she was treated in the older stories (particularly the Pictish one with the dogs—yikes). Women, particularly noble women, were often pawns in history, and Guinevere was no exception. Sure, she shouldn't have cheated on Arthur (if you're going to go with that version of events), but this wasn't exactly a time when a woman could say, "Hey, husband. We've grown apart. We should consider a separation." And that's the least of what Guinevere had to deal with. I'm not very familiar with modern stories, which may be better, but the old ones made me want to put Guinevere in control of her own fate. It was one of my favorite parts of the book. In fact, the final scene, with Del, Nix, and Cass sitting by her grave, was my absolutely favorite scene in the book.

That's it for the historical influences in *Magic Undying*. However, one of the most important things about this book is how Del and her *deirfiúr* treat artifacts and their business, Ancient Magic.

As I'm sure you know, archaeology isn't quite like Indiana Jones (for which I'm both grateful and bitterly disappointed). Sure, it's exciting and full of travel. However, booby-traps are not as common as I expected.

Total number of booby-traps I have encountered in my career: zero. Still hoping, though.

When I chose to write a series about archaeology and treasure hunting, I knew I had a careful line to tread. There is a big difference between these two activities. As much as I value artifacts, they are not treasure. Not even the gold artifacts. They are pieces of our history that contain valuable information, and as such, they belong to all of us. Every artifact that is excavated should be properly conserved and stored in a museum so that everyone can have access to our history. No one single person can own history, and I believe very strongly that individuals should not own artifacts. Treasure hunting is the pursuit of artifacts for personal gain.

So why did I make Del and her *deirfiúr* treasure hunters? I'd have loved to call them archaeologists, but nothing about Cass's work is like archaeology. Archaeology is a very laborious, painstaking process— and it certainly doesn't involve selling artifacts. That wouldn't work for the fast-paced, adventurous series that I had planned for *Dragon's Gift*. Not to mention the fact that dragons are famous for coveting treasure. Considering where the *deirfiúr* got their skills from, it just made sense to call them treasure hunters.

Even though I write urban fantasy, I strive for accuracy. The *deirfiúr* don't engage in archaeological practices—therefore, I cannot call them archaeologists. I also have a duty as an archaeologist to properly represent my field and our goals—namely, to protect and share history. Treasure hunting doesn't do this. One of the biggest battles that archaeology faces today is protecting cultural heritage from thieves.

I debated long and hard about not only what to call the heroines of this series, but also about how they would do their jobs. I wanted it to involve all the cool things we think about when we think about archaeology—namely, the Indiana Jones stuff, whether it's real or not. But I didn't know quite how to do that while still staying within the bounds of my own ethics. I can cut myself and other writers some slack because this is fiction, but I couldn't go too far into smash and grab treasure hunting.

I consulted some of my archaeology colleagues to get their take, which was immensely helpful. Wayne Lusardi, the State Maritime Archaeologist for Michigan, and Douglas Inglis and Veronica Morris, both archaeologists for Interactive Heritage, were immensely helpful with ideas. My biggest problem was figuring out how to have the heroines steal artifacts from tombs and then sell them and still sleep at night. Everything I've just said is pretty counter to this, right?

That's where the magic comes in. The heroines aren't after the artifacts themselves (they puts them back where they found them, if you recall)—they're after the magic that the artifacts contain. They're more like magic hunters than treasure hunters. That solved a big part of my problem. At least they were putting the artifacts back. Though that's not proper archaeology, I could let it pass. At least it's clear that they believe they shouldn't keep the artifact or harm the site. But the SuperNerd in me said, "Well, that magic is part of the artifact's context. It's important to the artifact and shouldn't be removed and sold."

Now *that* was a problem. I couldn't escape my SuperNerd self, so I was in a real conundrum. Fortunately, that's where the immensely intelligent Wayne Lusardi came in. He suggested that the magic could have an expiration date. If the magic wasn't used before it decayed, it could cause huge problems. Think explosions and tornado spells run amok. It could ruin the entire site, not to mention possibly cause injury and death. That would be very bad.

So now you see why Del and her *deirfiúr* don't just steal artifacts to sell them. Not only is selling the magic cooler, it's also better from an ethical standpoint, especially if the magic was going to cause problems in the long run. These aren't perfect solutions—the perfect solution would be sending in a team of archaeologists to carefully record the site and remove the dangerous magic—but that wouldn't be a very fun book.

Thanks again for reading (especially if you got this far in my ramblings). I hope you enjoyed the story and will stick with Del on the rest of her adventure!

ACKNOWLEDGMENTS

Thank you, Ben, for everything you've done to support me in this career. Thank you to Carol Thomas for sharing your thoughts on the book and being amazing inspiration. Thank you to Melanie Jayne Spencer Webster for inspiring me to write about Tintagel, and therefor Guinevere and her gang. This is a vastly better book thanks to you! Thank you to Susan, Steve, Holly, and Harvey for teaching me how to get off a moor. Del appreciated the tip, and the assistance of Holly and Harvey.

The Dragon's Gift series is a product of my two lives: one as an archaeologist and one as a novelist. Combining these two took a bit of work. I'd like to thank my friends, Wayne Lusardi, the State Maritime Archaeologist for Michigan, and Douglas Inglis and Veronica Morris, both archaeologists for Interactive Heritage, for their ideas about how to have a treasure hunter heroine that doesn't conflict too much with archaeology's ethics. The Author's Note contains a bit more about this if you are interested.

Thank you to Jena O'Connor and Lindsey Loucks for various forms of editing. The book is immensely better because of you! And thank you to Rebecca Frank for the beautiful cover. You really bring Del to life.

GLOSSARY

Alpha Council - There are two governments that enforce law for supernaturals—the Alpha Council and the Order of the Magica. The Alpha Council governs all shifters. They work cooperatively with Alpha Council when necessary - for example, when capturing FireSouls.

Blood Sorceress - A type of Magica who can create magic using blood.

Conjurer - A Magica who uses magic to create something from nothing. They cannot create magic, but if there is magic around them, they can put that magic into their conjuration.

Dark Magic - The kind that is meant to harm. It's not necessarily bad, but it often is.

Deirfiúr - Sisters in Irish.

Demons - Often employed to do evil. They live in various hells but can be released upon the earth if you know how to get to them and then get them out. If they are killed on Earth, they are sent back to their hell.

Dragon Sense - A FireSoul's ability to find treasure. It is an internal sense that pulls them toward what they seek. It is easiest to find gold, but they can find anything or anyone that is valued by someone.

Elemental Mage – A rare type of mage who can manipulate all of the elements.

Enchanted Artifacts – Artifacts can be imbued with magic that lasts after the death of the person who put the magic into the artifact (unlike a spell that has not been put into an artifact—these spells disappear after the Magica's death). But magic is not stable. After a period of time—hundreds or thousands of years depending on the circumstance—the magic will degrade. Eventually, it can go bad and cause many problems.

Fire Mage – A mage who can control fire.

FireSoul - A very rare type of Magica who shares a piece of the dragon's soul. They can locate treasure and steal the gifts (powers) of other supernaturals. With practice, they can manipulate the gifts they steal, becoming the strongest of that gift. They are despised and feared. If they are caught, they are thrown in the Prison of Magical Deviants.

The Great Peace - The most powerful piece of magic ever created. It hides magic from the eyes of humans.

Hearth Witch – A Magica who is versed in magic relating to hearth and home. They are often good at potions and protective spells and are also very perceptive when on their own turf.

Magica - Any supernatural who has the power to create magic—witches, sorcerers, mages. All are governed by the Order of the Magica.

Mirror Mage - A Magica who can temporarily borrow the powers of other supernaturals. They can mimic the powers as long as they are near the other supernatural. Or they can hold on to the power, but once they are away from the other supernatural, they can only use it once.

The Origin - The descendent of the original alpha shifter. They are the most powerful shifter and can turn into any species.

Order of the Magica - There are two governments that enforce law for supernaturals—the Alpha Council and the Order of the Magica. The Order of the Magica govern all Magica. They work cooperatively with the Alpha Council when necessary - for example, when capturing FireSouls.

Phantom - A type of supernatural that is similar to a ghost. They are incorporeal. They feed off the misery and pain of others, forcing them to relive their greatest nightmares and fears. They do not have a fully functioning mind like a human or supernatural. Rather, they are a shadow of their former selves. Half bloods are extraordinarily rare.

Seeker - A type of supernatural who can find things. FireSouls often pass off their dragon sense as Seeker power.

Shifter - A supernatural who can turn into an animal. All are governed by the Alpha Council.

Transporter - A type of supernatural who can travel anywhere. Their power is limited and must regenerate after each use.

Warden of the Underworld - A one of a kind position created by Roarke. He keeps order in the Underworld.

ABOUT LINSEY

Before becoming a writer, Linsey Hall was a nautical archaeologist who studied shipwrecks from Hawaii and the Yukon to the UK and the Mediterranean. She credits fantasy and historical romances with her love of history and her career as an archaeologist. After a decade of tromping around the globe in search of old bits of stuff that people left lying about, she settled down and started penning her own romance novels. Her Dragon's Gift series draws upon her love of history and the paranormal elements that she can't help but include.

Linsey@LinseyHall.com
www.LinseyHall.com
https://twitter.com/HiLinseyHall
https://www.facebook.com/LinseyHallAuthor

ISBN 978-1-942085-07-2